D0209665

FOR LOVE AND GLORY

Also by bill boyd

The Gentle Infantryman

Bolivar: Liberator of a Continent

Panama: An Historical Novel

FOR LOVE AND GLORY

A NOVEL OF WORLD WAR II

bill boyd

CAPITAL
BOOKS, INC.
Sterling, Virginia

Capital Books, Inc.
P.O. Box 605
Herndon, Virginia 20172-0605

ISBN 1-892123-17-7 (alk. paper)

Library of Congress Cataloging-in-Publication Data

Boyd, Bill (William Young)
    For love and glory : a novel of World War II / by Bill Boyd.
        p. cm.
    ISBN 1-892123-17-7
        1. World War, 1939–1945–Campaigns–France–Fiction. 2.
Americans–France–Fiction. 3. France–Fiction. I. Title.

PS3552.O884 F67 2000
813′.54–dc21   00-030349

Printed in the United States of America on acid-free paper that meets the
American National Standards Institute Z39-48 Standard.

First Edition

10 9 8 7 6 5 4 3 2 1

Bundled in a brown sweater and green wool scarf, Colonel William Talbot walked slowly down the deserted English beach early in 1944, keeping his hands deep in his pockets except when he'd bend now and then to pick up a flat stone to skip on the surface of the ocean, as he'd done when he was a boy in New England. Talbot was tall and athletic-looking, in his mid-forties. His West Point training was disguised by his casualness. His grey eyes held a hint of sorrow, even of pain.

In the distance, he saw a girl in a dark skirt and navy blue sweater sitting on some old wooden steps. She was looking out to sea.

Obviously she wasn't worried about being in a restricted military area any more than he was. As he came closer he realized she was so deep in thought that she was completely unaware of him. Her hat was off, and her light blonde hair blew loosely with the wind.

She was striking-looking without being beautiful. Her face was full of experience and strength, and something else that he recognized from experience—suffering. From afar she had looked like a young girl, but Talbot realized that she was a woman of about forty.

Talbot was standing right beside her before she looked up at him.

"What are you doing here?" Her clear cornflower blue eyes opened wide in surprise.

Talbot detected a note of authority in her voice, and it startled him. It was not what he had expected. She looked so vulnerable, yet her voice was strong.

"I'm walking on the beach," he replied easily. "I'm sorry if I startled you." Talbot took his army identification card out of his pocket. "I'm in the Supreme Headquarters, Allied Expeditionary Force, SHAEF for short. I got a few days leave so I came down here."

She looked at the sea and nodded silently.

Talbot stood there awkwardly. "Well, I'll leave you alone," he said, turning to go.

"Thank you," she said. "I hope I haven't been rude."

Talbot stopped and looked at her. He knew he should leave her in peace, but something held him. "Are you all right?" he asked.

She scooped up a handful of sand, letting it drift through her fingers into the winter wind. "Everything's fine," she said unconvincingly.

"It's wartime. How can everything be fine?" he asked.

She smiled slightly, then met his eyes and nodded. "You're right, of course," she said finally.

"I understand wars produce a lot of babies, though," he said.

She laughed then, lighting her face with such radiance that Talbot felt a wave of warmth pass over him. But then all was quiet, somber again, and the moment passed.

"I'm sorry," she said. "I'm just not accustomed to chatting with a strange American man on a Sussex beach."

"Maybe it's easier than you think," Bill said gently.

The woman took a deep breath. "I'm fine, really."

Talbot looked out at the grey waters, knowing he should leave but desperately wanting to stay.

"Does it break your heart?" she asked suddenly.

Talbot looked down at her, questioningly.

"The sea," she explained, her voice suddenly trembling.

Talbot cocked his head, hoping she would explain. She didn't.

She shook her head adamantly, regaining control. "I'm sorry. Please forgive me. I don't know what got into me. I don't even know you."

"Look, you'll probably never see me again, so it's all right, you can unburden yourself just as much as you like."

She sat silently for a full minute looking at him strangely. "You seem very nice. Thank you for saying hello."

Suddenly she scrambled to her feet. Talbot followed her stare and saw the line of landing craft coming in for a practice assault. They'd have to get out of there fast. The men on the boats could be armed with live ammunition and come out shooting, as they were supposed to in the actual landings in France.

He took her arm, and they ran up the old wooden steps. He raised the barbed wire so she could climb under it, then followed her out onto the coastal road. When they stopped, they were both out of breath.

"Goodbye," she said matter-of-factly, holding out her hand. Talbot shook it politely.

Before he could say anything else, she jumped on her bicycle and pedalled away, out of his life.

Six months earlier, on July 9, 1943, over the south coast of Sicily thousands of tracer bullets cut the night sky to pieces, and shock waves from exploding anti-aircraft shells knocked a lone U.S. Army transport plane around like a small boat in an Atlantic storm.

Standing in the open door of the transport, Major Bill Talbot held onto the sides with all his strength. Unless the plane flew a more level course, he would be thrown out before it ever reached the drop zone. There was solid land beneath the aircraft now, not the stormy Mediterranean that they had been flying over during most of the flight from North Africa. Talbot glanced around the sky. There didn't seem to be any other transports in the area.

"We're all alone," he said softly to the sergeant standing behind him. "That's not right. This is supposed to be an invasion. What's happened?"

They must have lost the others in the storm that had enveloped them even before they had reached the checkpoint over Malta. His heart sat in his throat for a minute before plummeting down into his boots, as the red light went on. It was almost time to jump, and there was no way of knowing how far off course they had flown.

"Okay, men. We're ten minutes from the drop zone. Make sure you're hooked up." As he spoke, Talbot checked to see that his line was attached to the static cord that would open his parachute when he left the aircraft. He could feel the repressed excitement of the other men as they stood up and readied themselves to leap into the black night sky and onto the enemy-held island of Sicily.

The plane was bouncing badly now. Talbot's knuckles were white from gripping the metal sides of the plane. Suddenly the transport flipped away from him hard, tearing his hands from the sides of the doorway and tossing him into the night like a rag doll. Tumbling towards the earth, he caught glimpses of the airplane. It had righted itself again, thank God. The second man in the stick was already standing in the door. But as Talbot's parachute opened, jerking him up short and billowing over his head, enemy fire made a direct hit, and the transport exploded.

Debris from the fiery ball sprayed in all directions. Talbot could only look on helplessly as the night sky filled with tiny flames. If just one spark hit his canopy, it would turn into a torch, and he would plummet to earth like a rock. But the sparks were already falling beneath him onto the ground below. Those poor men. It was cold comfort to know that the whole thing was over so quickly that they never knew what happened to them.

He couldn't think about it now. The ground was rushing up to meet him so fast that his boots crunched into the dirt of a rocky field at almost the same instant he had prepared himself for the shock of landing. He hit the ground hard, rolling his body to cushion the impact. Quickly he struggled out of his parachute harness. Talbot had no idea where he was—except that this was Sicily, and he could be shot and killed before he even had a chance to fight.

The quarter moon was still out, and he was alone in a plowed field, in plain view of anybody who happened along. There was a stone wall about twenty yards away and, he guessed, a road on the other side of it. Beyond was a small forest of cypress trees. He would have to get into those woods as fast as he could. There was no time to bury his parachute.

Crouched low, Talbot ran across the field and bounded over the wall onto the dirt road, which he had guessed would be there. With three long strides, he was in the woods, where he threw himself onto his stomach. Now concealed, he felt more secure. He lay still catching his breath. At least if there were any enemy soldiers in the area they hadn't seen him yet.

Still gasping for air, his heart pounding, Talbot realized all the beautiful plans he'd helped prepare, all the briefings, all the practice, had been for nothing. The airborne invasion of Sicily had come apart like a watch hit by a sledgehammer, and Major Bill Talbot, a forty-three-year-old American, was now huddled alone on an island held by the enemy. At any moment, they would find him and, in the blink of an eye, snuff him out.

☙

Talbot should never have been leading paratroopers in a combat jump. If he hadn't been so foolhardy, he would still be sitting behind his comfortable desk in a safe divisional headquarters along with the other non-combat members of the staff of the 82nd Airborne Division. But he'd talked Colonel Jim Gavin into allowing him to go along on this mission as an observer. He felt useless sitting around in the North African desert while brave men fought. This wasn't why he had joined up. Talbot desperately wanted to see some action, and to have a chance to do something heroic, if it came to that. Now he was getting what he had asked for, and more.

On the flight from Africa, the lieutenant in command of the troops Talbot was travelling with had doubled over with acute appendicitis. He'd been trying to ignore the stomach pains for the last few days because he didn't want to miss the jump. As the only remaining officer on board, Major Talbot had taken command.

Bill Talbot had arrived in North Africa two months ago. Commissioned a major only the year before, he had been given a non-combat position as the officer in charge of planning and training for the 82nd Airborne. After the Allied victory in Tunisia cleared North Africa of Axis forces in May, Sicily had become the next logical objective. If the Allies could take the island, it would be easy for them to invade the Italian mainland, which lay just ten miles across the water.

Taking Sicily would not be easy. Its terrain favored the defending forces. Except for the beach areas around Catania in the east and Gela in the south, the entire island was covered by hills and mountains, and a good road network crisscrossed it, making possible the rapid movement of centralized reserves to any point that might be threatened. And, as Talbot had discovered during the planning stage of the operation, the Germans and Italians were sending some of their best troops to defend the island against the attack they knew was coming. Against them, under General Eisenhower, Field Marshal Bernard Montgomery would command the British Eighth Army and General George S. Patton, the American Seventh Army.

Talbot had been occupied solely with the American plan to drop paratroopers from the 505th Regimental Combat Team of the 82nd Airborne Division onto the island the night before the dawn beach landings of the First, Third, and 45th Infantry Divisions.

The 505th was beautifully trained and in excellent condition but was as yet untried in combat. Led by Colonel Gavin, their job would be to prevent the enemy from reinforcing the invasion beaches. Then they were to link up with the First Infantry Division, at Gela. Bill Talbot had told the Troop Carrier Command officers that the route to be flown by the transport planes that night was far too intricate for even the most experienced professional navigators, to say nothing of boys with a minimum of training and almost no practical experience. But the air corps officers had politely told Major Talbot to please confine his efforts to the actual landings.

Clearly, Talbot had been right. On the flight over the Mediterranean, the C-47 aircraft had hit terrible weather and they had strayed off course.

But that was ancient history now. Talbot knew he was nowhere near where he was supposed to be. Still, he couldn't just lie there in the woods and wait to find out who'd won. He had to do something.

Talbot raised his head and listened. Not a sound. He slowly stood up—then heard the faintest of rustles in the woods behind him.

He crouched down slowly, not knowing who was in the woods. Animals, perhaps? Fellow paratroopers? Enemy soldiers? He was aware that he had stopped breathing and was staying very still. The sound became more distinguishable. It was made by men making their way through the woods and attempting to do it as silently as possible. Suddenly the silence was shattered. One of the soldiers yelled something in German. Talbot tensed and gripped his Thompson submachine gun tighter. Not fifty yards away from him, he saw a German soldier crossing the road, pointing at Talbot's parachute as he ran towards it. Behind him came the rest of the enemy soldiers in single file. They gathered around the parachute as their comrades continued to arrive.

Now they know I'm here, thought Talbot. They're obviously a German patrol sent out to search for enemy paratroopers, and in another minute they'll start looking for me here in the woods. They'll find me and kill me, of course.

Bill Talbot had been born with a wail on the first of January, 1900, the first day of the Twentieth Century, as his father liked to say. Descended from the original Pilgrim settlers of New England on both sides of his family, he had been duly christened William Endicott Brewster Talbot. Young Bill Talbot grew up in Endicott, Massachusetts, which was really two towns separated by what everybody called "the brook." On one side of this rushing stream was Main Street with its shops and banks, churches, the town hall, and trees in profusion. Beyond the main street were rolling hills and large stately homes where the more prosperous residents lived behind protective shrubbery and winding driveways. The spacious country club with its manicured golf course was the only open area, green as an emerald. On the highest point of the town, the Talbot mansion overlooked Endicott, its suburbs and surrounding hamlets.

The other side of the brook was industrial Endicott, dominated by the Talbot Mills. Surrounding it were the smaller houses of families who worked in the mills. Many years before, these homes had been heralded throughout the country as examples of enlightened management, each with its own flower garden and sense of pride. But by the time Bill was fifteen years old, they had become dirty and run-down. Talbot's mother had made the decision to withdraw all financial support from the houses of the mill workers. "An unnecessary extravagance," she'd said. "The expense is draining us dry. Let them take care of their houses like we do. God knows they get paid enough."

At the time, Bill's father had argued that the houses belonged to Talbot Mills, just like their own home did, and the homes of all the Talbots before them. "A worker who's comfortably housed works better than one who lives in a hovel," he claimed. But he lost. With Bill's mother, he usually lost. Everyone did. To his credit Mr. Talbot stood up to her, and sometimes they fought like tigers. It was just that Mr. Talbot was a gentleman and vulnerable to his wife's wiles against which he had no defense. He could never insult or lie to a woman. She had no such scruples.

Six mornings a week at seven sharp, Edward Talbot left his house, walked down the hill, and arrived at work at precisely 7:10. His employees, who considered Talbot a fair and kind man, mirrored his commitment, devoting their lives to the company's success.

But young Bill grew up knowing he would never work at the mill. It was a long-standing family tradition that the elder son—in this case, Bill's brother, Harry—would take over and run the company.

Even at ten, Bill was relieved. He felt stifled in Endicott and longed to move away. He knew his father would get him started in whatever he decided to do. That was also a family tradition. He could go into law and become a distinguished judge, like his uncle Nathaniel. Or enter the ministry like great-uncle Jacob. Or go into the military, as countless other Talbot men had done.

∞

Ever since his earliest childhood, Bill Talbot wanted to get away from Endicott. Although he didn't realize it at the time, he wanted desperately to flee from his mother. When he was five, his father gave him an allowance of ten cents per month. As soon as his mother heard about it, she shrieked, "Ten cents! That's ridiculous! I used to get a penny when I was his age. Little Bill will throw it away, that's what he'll do. Now, you cut his allowance to a penny or suffer the consequences!"

Even in 1905, a penny couldn't buy very much, so both Bill and his brother, Harry, went without.

∞

In grade school Bill was at the top of his class and was so proud he could burst. But when he brought his report card home to show his mother he'd gotten straight As, she had berated him as a "greasy grind," castigated him for not obtaining a "Gentleman's C" in his subjects.

He never knew what to expect from his mother. She tongue-lashed him for everything he did. And then sometimes, when she was feeling good, she'd lavish such praise and affection on him he wasn't sure whether she was his mother or a fairy godmother who had crept into her body. It made him feel so good, he'd laugh and sing and hug her, and the world was a beautiful place. Then, the next time he saw her, he'd run to her and throw his little arms around her, expecting the same love and affection. Instead, she'd pry him loose, shrieking, "Get away from me, you little monster! Look what you've done to my lovely dress!"

After the episode with his report card, Bill went timidly into his father's study. Edward Talbot looked up from the book he was reading and smiled at his son. "Come on in, Bill. You act as if I might bite you."

Bill held out his report card without saying anything. To tell the truth, he now felt a little bit ashamed of having straight As.

His father studied the report carefully, smiled and said, "Well done, son! Well done!" Then he reached out and hugged young Bill to him. "I'm proud of you!"

After his father had hugged and kissed him, Bill said, "Mother doesn't want me to get good grades. She wants me to get a Gentleman's C. She told me so."

Mr. Talbot seemed to be thinking. "You know, son, sometimes your mother gets strange ideas. They don't always last long, but they're difficult to deal with. Anyway, Bill, you just go on getting As, and everything will be fine. Never hesitate to try to be the best you can be."

This time, it was Bill who threw his arms around his father and hugged him. It was a great comfort to talk to him. Bill always felt better afterwards.

When he was twelve, Bill Talbot was happy to leave home to attend Phillips Exeter Academy. There was nothing his mother could do to stop that. Talbots had been going to Exeter since the late 1700s.

At Exeter, where many boys were homesick, Bill felt happier than he ever had before. When he grew strong and broad-shouldered, he began to play football and hockey, and it was then he developed the talents that later won him fame on the gridiron.

He wrote his father a letter one day, telling him how much he loved to play football. Unfortunately, since she opened all of her husband's mail, Mrs. Talbot read Bill's comments. She immediately wrote the headmaster of Exeter informing him that William E.B. Talbot's parents forbade him to play football. She gave, as her reason, the fear that young Bill would get hurt. When the headmaster informed Talbot, Bill knew this was a lie. His mother just wanted to hurt him. If only he could stand up to her, tell her that he would do what he wanted.

That afternoon Bill went to the locker room to get his things and close his locker for the last time. The gym was empty except for one boy, a youngster from Oklahoma, who was practicing tricks with a lariat—twirling it, raising and lowering it as it spun around his torso, then jumping out of it. Bill watched, fascinated. And an idea formed.

That night, he went into the darkened gymnasium. In his hand he held the Oklahoma boy's lariat. It was a good, strong rope. Eyes accustomed to the dark, Bill tossed the rope up and over a beam, then placed a wooden chair underneath the rope. He climbed up on the chair and put the loop of the lariat around his neck. Breathing hard, he realized that he was afraid. He started to have second thoughts, but then he remembered his mother. This was the only way to defy her, the only way to show her how much she'd hurt him.

Suddenly the gym lights flashed on. Bill jumped, almost falling off the chair.

"Good God, Talbot! What are you doing?" It was his football coach, who had been told that Talbot was leaving the team. He'd been searching the campus for him and had decided to check the gym as a last resort.

"Oh, uh, nothing," Bill replied nervously. "I was going to try a new trick with the lariat. That's all."

"You get down here right this minute."

Talbot slipped the rope from around his neck and got down from the chair. His mouth was dry.

"Sit down, son. Talk to me."

For a moment, Bill Talbot didn't know what to say. His first inclination was to bluff it out and maintain that he was just doing rope tricks. Then, he decided to be honest and tell his coach exactly what the matter was and what he had intended to do about it. "Well," he said, resignedly, "my mother is not a pleasant person. I know that now because I've met other boys' mothers, and I've seen the difference. Anyway, mother wrote to the headmaster that she prohibited me from playing football—she knows that's the only thing I really love. So, I decided I'd show her. I'd hang myself right here in the gym. But, you know, coach, she wouldn't have cared."

"I think I understand how you feel, but it's you you'd be hurting, not your mother."

Talbot looked at his coach and nodded his head. "I figured that out. That's why I didn't go through with it. I wouldn't have, even if you hadn't showed up."

Bill talked to his coach for an hour, telling him all about his mother, how hopeless everything seemed, and how much he hated himself for his cowardice.

"One day you will learn to stand up to her, and to stand up for yourself. Bravery isn't something you are born with, Talbot, it is something you earn. Think of this as your first lesson. Remember: Never take the cowardly way out, Bill. You have to face your battles head on. Run towards them, not away from them."

Through the darkness of his mind, a tiny light flickered. Bill was not sure exactly what his coach meant, but at least he had hope—and a goal. One day he would stand up to her. That much he promised himself.

The coach agreed to talk to the headmaster about Mrs. Talbot's letter.

"He can handle it if he wants to," said the coach. "All he has to do is write back and tell her that athletics are compulsory here at Exeter, and that you have to play football. That's all there is to it."

It was done as suggested, and Mrs. Talbot never brought the subject up again. It was merely a whim she'd had in one of her nastier moods.

The German patrol leader was shouting orders, clearly planning a search through the woods of Sicily for the lone parachutist. Flattened on the ground, Talbot waited to die.

Well, he thought, they may get me but I might as well take a few of them with me.

Talbot leapt to his feet and began firing his tommy gun in short, accurate bursts at the bunched-up Germans, who went down like pins in a bowling alley. His clip empty, Talbot crouched down and threw two of his three hand grenades at the Germans. His accuracy was astounding. He threw with the skill of a first-string quarterback, which, in fact, is what he had been at West Point. With a full clip in his Thompson, Talbot rose once more and let off a burst. But the enemy had recovered from the shock of his first onslaught and had begun shooting back. Talbot went to ground again, this time flat on his stomach. But he realized that there were only a few men shooting at him now.

So, I was right and it's only a patrol, thought Talbot. And I caught them off guard. Now I have to get them all while they're still in the field, exposed. His instinct for self-preservation had taken over.

Talbot lay as flat as he could and reached into his pocket for his last grenade. He took it out, pulled the pin, flipped the lever, and waited. One second, two seconds, three seconds, four. He saw the Germans start to rise to come at him. He saw there were now only three of them. He pulled back his arm and threw the hand grenade forward, then pressed himself into the earth. The explosion came so quickly, it surprised even Talbot. If he'd held the grenade a second longer, he'd have been shredded by its fragments.

Breathing hard, holding onto his reloaded Thompson submachine gun, he rose to his knees. In the dark, he sensed that there was nothing alive beyond the road to challenge him.

He began to rise to his feet and felt his knees shaking. The fact he'd taken on and wiped out an entire German patrol single-handedly began to dawn on him and it scared him to death.

"Hoch hand!" The voice came from behind him and struck him with terror. It was not a friendly voice. And it was telling him in German to put his hands up, which he did promptly.

Another voice said, "Aw, let's shoot the Kraut-head."

Hope sprang into his breast. These are Americans! "I'm a trooper!" said Talbot as calmly as he could.

"I'll be damned!" said the soldier. "Then, them was Krauts you was shootin' out there? I'll be damned!"

"Did you get them all?" came a voice from the dark.

"I think so," said Talbot. His knees still shook and he hoped none of the other troopers would notice. "They're all in the field over there. Go take a look."

To his surprise, Talbot saw that the American troopers were already checking the bodies in the field.

"They're all dead," someone shouted.

"Who's in charge here?" asked Talbot, peering into the darkness.

"I am. Sergeant Rosenberg. Who are you?"

"I'm Major Talbot."

"Thank God," replied Rosenberg. "We need an officer to take us over."

"What outfit are you?" Talbot asked.

"505th. Captain Halperen's rifle company. Half the guys got shot out of the air before we hit the ground. We must have landed in the wrong place. I got me eight troopers here. How many you got, sir?"

"Just me."

There was a stunned silence. The men who had begun to gather around their sergeant stared at the unknown officer in disbelief.

"You took on them Jerries all by yourself, sir?" asked Rosenberg incredulously. "You was the only guy we seen, but, hell, we figured you must have a bunch of guys covering you. That's why we stayed out of it, sir. We figured if you was troopers, you might think we was Jerries. Uh, also, sir, we wasn't real sure who was who. For some reason, we figured you was a Kraut and the guys in the field was troopers. We just figured that's where the troopers'd be, and here's where the Krautheads would be."

In the moonlight, Talbot tried to size up Rosenberg. The sergeant was a big man with the ugly face of an ex-prizefighter. It was clear from the way he spoke that he had been in the regular army and had earned his stripes some time ago. This man was a professional soldier.

"Listen. I'm taking command. We've got to get the hell out of here."

"Where are we going, sir?" Rosenberg asked in a voice both respectful and skeptical.

Talbot listened to the sounds of firing coming from much farther east. He was fairly certain that he'd been dropped to the west of the invasion objective of Gela. Probably somewhere between Gela and Licata.

"We're going east. To the high ground behind the beaches at Gela."

∽

Talbot and his men moved forward towards the distant ridge as fast as they could walk. There was a road that seemed to be heading directly for it, but Talbot knew that it was unsafe to march openly on the road. This was likely to be a well-trod route for the German and Italian troops. Alongside the road ran a stone wall, just high enough to give them cover, but low enough to see over, and they stumbled through the pitted fields, keeping the wall to their right. Talbot motioned to his men to halt. Ahead of them was a sharp curve in the road. The perfect spot for an ambush. Moving silently,

Talbot rounded the bend alone and found himself looking directly into the muzzle of a machine gun. A machine gunner sat behind the gun with his finger on the trigger; his loader sat beside him ready to feed ammunition into the gun. Talbot breathed a sigh of relief. They were troopers. Nobody spoke. Behind the machine gun that was aimed at him, there were at least ten men sitting on the stone wall, their legs dangling over the sides like an audience waiting for the show to begin. Beside them were several large bundles which Talbot hoped were more guns.

"Who are you and what's in the bundles?" Talbot demanded, speaking to a man with a lieutenant's bar painted on his helmet.

The man slid off the wall.

"I'll ask the questions. I got you covered. Now, who in hell are you?"

He looked tough. Angry as he was at being challenged, Talbot knew he'd better answer. These men were trained paratroopers and, if they so much as suspected he was an enemy, they'd cut him down in a second. Talbot wasn't going to risk a confrontation with a jumpy trigger finger.

"I'm Major Talbot. 505th Regimental Combat Team."

"No, you ain't. There ain't no Major Talbot in the 505th. What'd you do? Kill our men and steal their uniforms, you friggin' Jerry!"

The lieutenant was turning to his machine gunner motioning to him to fire, when a voice from behind Talbot called out.

"Hey! Lieutenant Jones?"

The lieutenant spun around and tried to see into the dark.

"It's me. Rosenberg," said the voice. "I used to be in your platoon."

Talbot heard the rustling behind him as Rosenberg made his way to the front of the column.

"Okay, Rosie, who is this guy?"

Rosenberg spoke clearly. "He's a major, sir, and he ain't no Kraut. He knocked off over a hundred Jerries all by himself. I saw it. The men with me saw it, too." Lieutenant Jones swung to Talbot. "Okay. Give. Who are you?"

In spite of wanting to laugh in amazement at how fast the number of enemy soldiers he'd killed had grown from a dozen or so to over 100, Talbot kept his voice level. "I'm Major William Talbot. I belong to the headquarters staff of the 82nd Airborne Division. I report directly to Colonel Jim Gavin. I am assigned to the 505th Regimental Combat Team for the invasion of Sicily, and, as the ranking officer present, I expect you to take orders from me. Now, answer my question! Who the hell are you?"

The authority in Talbot's voice left no doubt in the lieutenant's mind that he was in the presence of a senior officer and had better change his attitude quickly.

"Sorry, sir, but we were told before take-off to challenge everybody after we landed. I'm Lieutenant Jones, sir. And this is a machine gun section of a weapons platoon. We got separated from our company. We thought it'd make it easier for them to find us if we stayed in one place instead of wandering all over the countryside. But nobody showed up."

"Well, we can use you. Fall in and follow me."

In a few minutes the machine gun crew had shouldered their bundles. Carrying such heavy loads, it would be impossible for the men to continue walking on rough ground. Talbot counted his men. There were now twenty-five in all, plus three machine guns and a lot of ammunition for them. They would have to risk marching on the road.

As the men moved forward, Talbot thought about his confrontation with Jones. Nobody had remembered to use that night's password, "George," or the countersign, "Marshall." It would have made things so much easier. He wondered if Jones would really have had him shot. Probably not; just a bluff to scare him into identifying himself better, to be sure of exactly who he was.

Talbot raised his arm, and the column stopped. In the dark bushes to their right he was sure he had heard a rustle. The moon was setting now. That was the reason this evening, July 9th, 1943 had been chosen for the invasion. There would be moonlight until 2:45 a.m. for the airborne landing; then at 3:00 a.m., after the moon had set, the first Allied troops were scheduled to come ashore—at high tide and concealed from the enemy by darkness.

Talbot motioned his men to spread out and get down, then he knelt beside the wall and waited, his tommy gun ready. He listened. Now, Talbot could hear the rustling more clearly. Minutes passed. Whoever they were, the group of men coming their way were in no hurry. Without warning, the bushes directly across from him parted and two men stepped out onto the road. They wore jump boots and G.I. helmets, and they seemed shocked to find themselves surrounded.

"It's okay," Talbot whispered. "We're the 505th. Who're you?"

The first man just stood still and gaped. The other had to open his mouth once or twice before any words came out, "We're mortars from Heavy Weapons," he said shakily. He was wearing sergeant's stripes.

"I'm Major Talbot. You'll come with us. We can use some mortars. We're going for the ridge."

"Yes, sir," replied the sergeant, clearly relieved to have someone of rank making his decisions for him. "Men, it's all right. You can come out." At the sergeant's call, eight more men stepped out of the bushes, looking slightly dazed.

Talbot was glad to have the mortars. They would be a big help when the fighting began. They couldn't fire as far as artillery, but their tubes could fire explosive rounds which would blow the enemy out of their holes and cut them down as they attacked, like small bore artillery.

As he picked up more men on his march, Talbot was thrilled when he discovered one, a Lieutenant Fernandez, was accompanied by a navy ensign who carried a radio whose purpose was to contact the American fleet anchored offshore in order to direct their fire against enemy targets. Talbot knew such parties were scheduled to land with the airborne troops, but he never dreamed he'd be fortunate enough to take command of one.

Talbot was elated. He now controlled the most powerful artillery in the entire Mediterranean, the guns of the U.S. fleet.

The feeling was peculiar to Talbot. He'd so rarely experienced elation in his life.

After four years at Exeter, Talbot had decided to attend West Point. His decision to pursue a military career had been influenced not only by a desire to escape his past but also by a need to take part in world events. The Great War had been raging in Europe throughout all of his high school years and many men he loved and admired had rushed into uniform. A cousin was killed leading a rifle company of the Rainbow Division. An uncle went to France as an artillery officer with the Yankee Division. Even his brother, Harry, left Harvard and volunteered. He flew with the famous "Hat in the Ring" Squadron and was decorated three times. He came home a captain, the hero of Endicott. There was a tremendous "Welcome Home" parade, but Mrs. Talbot sulked in her room with a headache during the entire celebration, claiming that the tribute was undeserved. "Besides," she said, "it will just go to his head and make him unbearably conceited." Too young to join up, Bill had followed the war intently, wishing that he could go with Harry into battle.

During the four years that Bill attended West Point, he had taken a math course with Captain Omar Bradley of the class of 1915, whom he liked, and he'd gotten to know Captain Matthew Ridgeway who'd been in the class of 1917 and was then manager of athletics. The young cadet and the not-much-older captain got along extremely well, especially in view of Talbot's prowess on the football field. The Superintendent of West Point after the war was the famous General Douglas MacArthur, whom Bill met only once or twice.

Bill's father and brother kept in contact with him while he was at West Point. They were proud of him and told him so. His mother almost never wrote. When she did, it was to berate him for "showing off" on the football field and to tell him she wished he'd have more consideration for his family and stop behaving like a rough-neck every Saturday afternoon. Nothing, it seemed, had changed. Harry was working at the mill with his father. Both still lived at home with his mother.

∞

At his graduation from West Point, Bill was handsome in his grey and white uniform. He had every right to be proud. He was graduating in the top 10 percent of his class. As he walked up onto the dais to receive his diploma, he saw his father and brother beaming at him. Next to them was the empty seat that had been reserved for his mother. The crowd cheered as he took the diploma. After all, he was the star football hero of the Academy. That his mother was absent did not surprise or upset Talbot. She never went anywhere except on her own terms, which were always ridiculous and impossible, and West Point had no intention of changing their procedure to accommodate Mrs. Endicott Talbot's demand that she be seated next to the Superintendent of the Military Academy for the graduation.

After the ceremonies, Mr. Talbot took Bill's arm as they walked away. Bill greeted friends and introduced them to his father and his brother, whom he called *Captain* Talbot, which, of course, was correct. Away from the crowd, Bill's father said, obviously embarrassed, "Sorry your mother couldn't make it. Harry and I were all packed to come up here when we found her in bed with a wet cloth over her eyes and forehead. Dreadful migraine, apparently. Anyway, Bill, we're all very proud of you."

Bill turned to his father and said, "Dad, mother didn't have a migraine. She simply didn't want to come."

Mr. Talbot didn't say anything. Harry spoke up. "I think you're right. She told us we shouldn't come, either. We should stay home and look after her. Dad told her he and I would do whatever we damned well pleased, and here we are." Harry sounded as proud as if he'd won a football game or shot down the Red Baron.

"Good for you, Dad," said Bill. "I wish you'd do that more often."

"You shouldn't talk like that about your mother," said Mr. Talbot.

"Yes, sir," said Bill. He wondered how many times his mother had pulled the "sick" act and gotten away with it. He felt deeply sorry for his father. His mother wasn't going to allow him to forget this act of defiance for a long time.

☙

As a second lieutenant after graduating from West Point, Talbot was assigned to the usual peacetime army posts. His branch of service was the infantry, and he tried to learn everything he could about it. His football career at the Point had made him well known, even among the highest-ranking officers. They were always there to smooth the way whenever needed. He was considered a "comer," destined for high rank and great accomplishments.

In 1925, Talbot was sent to Hawaii to serve in the 27th Infantry Regiment. This was considered a plum post, and Bill suspected that his old instructor and friend from the academy, Captain Omar Bradley, had pulled some strings on his behalf. Bradley had been in Hawaii for several months before Bill arrived and had introduced him to the other officers stationed there, including Major George Patton, the G-2 of the regiment. Bill played cards occasionally with Major Patton, but they never became friends. Patton had brought with him a houseful of servants, including maids, butlers, and three grooms for his polo ponies. He spent his time with the Dillinghams and other affluent island families. Bill Talbot's stern New England background didn't approve of George Patton's conspicuous flaunting of his wealth.

Talbot kept in touch with his father by letter. He described the islands to him, told him how different they were from the pine woods and freshwater lakes of New England. How he loved the warm breezes, the lush vegetation, the beautiful sunsets, the perfect climate. The sandy white beaches, the sea churning and crashing against the shoreline while the palm trees swayed in the wind like the local girls doing the hula dance. Edward Talbot wrote back telling his son to keep writing. He loved receiving letters from Hawaii. It was another world to him.

To Bill, it was the closest thing to heaven he'd ever known. He loved the military life but often wondered why he did. He supposed it was because army routine was well ordered, yet filled with challenges for a promising young officer. One day in Hawaii, the real reason occurred to him rather unexpectedly. He was exchanging pleasantries with an older lady, the wife of a colonel, when it dawned on him. The army was a man's world. Except for attending dinners, receptions, and cocktail parties, where he was always exclusively in the company of the wives of married officers and, therefore, not only able but expected to keep his distance, he was in no danger of being tempted by a female. It made him realize, in the dark recesses of his mind, that he was actually afraid of getting into any meaningful relationship with a woman. They actually frightened him, and the cause of his fear came to his intelligent mind at once—his mother. She had succeeded in making him dread all women. Possibly because of this new awareness, which stayed with him and about which he thought constantly, his situation was about to change.

Bill Talbot's lack of any significant love life at his age had now begun to worry him. He had to prove himself. It was soon thereafter that he had the good fortune to meet the sister of one of his fellow officers. She had come to visit her brother in Hawaii for a month. Her name was Barbara Sommerville, and she was from one of the country's most prominent military families. As soon as Bill met her, he began to flirt with her. After being her constant escort for two weeks, he made passionate love to her on an army blanket on the beach. After that, they made love every night, always on the beach. After all, they couldn't do it in the Bachelor Officers Quarters or in her brother and sister-in-law's house. So he always kept the blanket in the small trunk of his old Ford coupe. It had been bliss, and he had enjoyed it more than anything in his life. He convinced himself that he was in love with Barbara and she with him. But, after those two glorious weeks of love-making, she had to return to her father, General Sommerville, in the United States. They wrote each other long, ardent letters every day at first. Then, her letters became shorter and less frequent. Finally, there were no more. It was from her brother that Bill learned Barbara had gotten engaged to a captain in the artillery who was twenty years older than she was.

With control of the guns of the U.S. fleet, Talbot felt more secure, even powerful. Just before his small force arrived at the foot of the hill, he had collected more troopers including another sixteen riflemen and a lieutenant named Vischer.

The moon had set, and Talbot's troopers had walked the last few miles in darkness. Talbot had to assume that the ridge was defended. But if so, where was the enemy hiding? He whispered for somebody to send him Sergeant Rosenberg. While he waited, he formulated his plan of attack. First he took stock. Including himself, he had fifty-six men, three machine guns, two mortars, and a radio that could control fire from the fleet. Of his men, two were medics. He had three lieutenants, Jones, Vischer, and Fernandez, and one ensign—the navy equivalent to a lieutenant. He had two non-coms, Sergeant Rosenberg and the sergeant commanding the two mortars. The rest were all riflemen. It wasn't a bad mix, all things taken into consideration. But he knew damned well that his only hope was the radio team who could bring the navy's big guns to bear.

"Sir?" Sergeant Rosenberg had arrived.

The men gathered around Major Talbot. They were tense. Talbot spoke softly but clearly to the leaders.

"Spread everybody out. I believe that small ridge in front of us is called Santa Bianca. It's the only defendable high ground around, so when we planned the invasion we assumed it would be heavily fortified and occupied by German or Italian troops." He remembered something else about Santa Bianca. "Or, the enemy might decide we'd never be able even to get near Santa Bianca and they simply zeroed it in with their artillery to blast us off it in case we did take it."

Looking directly into Rosenberg's eyes, Talbot continued, "I shall go up alone. Keep your men ready. If the ridge is defended, I'll be killed, but the rest of you will be all right . . ."

Rosenberg cut in. "Sir, I can't let you do that."

"Get everybody spread out," continued Talbot calmly. "We can't see them, but I'm fairly sure that there is a large enemy force up there. If there is, then just get the hell out of here fast and go looking for communications lines to cut."

"Sir," began Rosenberg.

"You have your orders, Sergeant. If I don't hit resistance, I'll whistle three times. That will be your signal to bring the men up. All of them, especially the ensign with his radio. Understood?"

"Yes, sir."

Talbot climbed boldly onto the top of the ridge, making no attempt at concealment. In the event that the ridge was defended by the enemy, he hoped to draw fire to alert his men. There was only a slight chance he would be hit in the dark. But nobody shot at him or even challenged him. He surveyed the area. It wasn't large, probably no more than 100,000 square meters in all. Mentally, he was already positioning his men, as he gave three sharp whistles and almost immediately heard the movement of his men below him.

Rosenberg reported. "Everybody's here, sir."

Talbot nodded in the dark. "Very good, Sergeant," he said. "Now we'll start digging in. Listen to me. We're going to dig in on the south end of this ridge. I'll need a large deep rectangular hole big enough to hold me, the ensign, Fernandez, and the radio. The rest of you dig foxholes. We'll shift men and weapons to other spots if we're threatened from other directions, but I feel the main attacks will come from the Gela side. But this is where we belong. We're on Santa Bianca, a key high ground behind the beaches at Gela. We took it, and we're going to keep it. If we have to fight, we fight. Do you understand me?"

"Loud and clear!" came the reply from some dozen or so men.

"Good," replied Talbot. "Now, where's the ensign?"

"Here, sir."

Talbot took the young man aside. "What's your name, son?"

"Higginbottom, sir."

"Okay, Higginbottom, as you know we're on top of Santa Bianca. It's not a large ridge. But from here you can see the three roads that lead to Gela. Our paratroopers were supposed to block those roads so the enemy couldn't get additional units down to defend their beaches. Then, the troops from the sea invasion would link up with us, and away we'd go. Understand?"

"Yes, sir."

"You can see the airborne part of the invasion has come unstuck. There aren't any paratroopers holding the highways leading to the invasion beaches at Gela."

"So we're going to go down now and block the three roads?"

Talbot shook his head. "No. During our planning of the invasion, we figured Santa Bianca would be too heavily defended for us to take it. It's so strategically perfect, we thought the 505th's problem would be to defend the roads with the enemy in a position to blow us to pieces from up here. The air corps was going to try to neutralize Santa Bianca by bombing and strafing, because our troops will have to move on those roads as soon as they get off the beach. You can bet that just as soon as the enemy discovers we're here, they're going to be all over us. They can't afford to let us stay."

The dawn was coming up. They would have to act fast now. "What do you think of this place as a position for you to spot for the guns of the fleet? Though you can't actually see the beach or the ships from here, you can see everything that's going on below. And you can radio to the ships to fire on any spot that needs it."

"It's perfect, sir," said Higginbottom. "I couldn't ask for anything better."

"First thing you'll need to do is tell them to cancel the air attacks on the ridge."

"Yes, sir."

"We'll hold this ridge for you just as long as we can, so get set up to start operating the radio. The men are already digging us a big hole so you won't be under direct fire."

"You know, sir," Higginbottom broke in, "the guns out there are extremely accurate. Why couldn't they help us defend Santa Bianca as well? They could keep the enemy from getting anywhere near us. You'd be surprised what a wallop an 8-inch gun packs, sir. Even a near miss will send a normal person running for his life."

"It's a good idea. You'd better get cracking. The sun is coming up and it's going to be a long day."

Talbot stood for a minute listening to the sounds coming from the invasion beaches. He could see the flashes of artillery. He could see airplanes. But he wasn't able to get any sort of picture of what was going on. Sergeant Rosenberg was having the men dig their foxholes all around the southern perimeter.

Talbot watched as Lieutenant Jones directed his group of machine gunners. He wanted Jones to take charge of the mortars as well as the machine guns and position them himself.

"Jones!" Talbot waved him over. Since their confrontation on the road, Jones had carefully avoided any contact with his superior officer, walking away whenever he saw Talbot approaching. He was a loose cannon; it was time to deal with him.

The lieutenant came towards him, carrying his helmet under his arm like a Crusader bearing the head of a Saracen. Jones was well built, about five feet ten or so and broad shouldered. He had red hair and freckles which made him look sweet and mischievous; but the straight line of his mouth and the glint in his eyes made it clear that this was a man to handle carefully.

Jones put his helmet on and saluted, pointedly refusing to look at Talbot as he did so.

"You sent for me, sir?"

"What do they call you, Jones? Do you have a first name? A nickname?"

"Most people call me Lieutenant."

"You don't like me, do you, Jones?"

"I don't have to, sir."

Talbot nodded curtly. If that's the way Jones wanted it, then that's the way it would be. "Since you're in charge of the machine guns, I assume you are also trained in mortars. Am I correct, Lieutenant?"

"Yes, sir."

"Good. I want you to take command of the machine guns and mortars. You're in charge of positioning them. Four alternate positions to repel attacks from the four sides of this ridge. You'll have to move your weapons from one to the other as the enemy assaults develop. If they have to move out of their foxholes, the riflemen will spread out and lay flat on the ground to give you protection. Do you understand?"

"Perfectly, sir."

"I'm putting Vischer in charge of all the riflemen. You'll work together on that basis. Any questions?"

"Yes, sir. As senior lieutenant here I assume I take command if anything happens to you, right?" Jones said in a cocky voice.

Talbot hadn't considered the possibility, though he should have. He could die on this ridge, and one thing he did not want was for this Jones kid to take over. He was insubordinate and testy—the last thing his men would need under fire. He looked towards Gela. Smoke was rising. It had begun. When he turned back to Jones, his face was hard and determined.

"No, Lieutenant. You do not. I'm giving Sergeant Rosenberg a battlefield commission, and then I am promoting him to captain. If anything happens to me, he'll take over as ranking officer present. Understood?"

"Yes, sir," said Jones. There could be no other response. He was a lieutenant. Talbot was a major. But the expression on his face was one of clear loathing. I'll have to watch my back during the fighting, Talbot thought. "When you've positioned your weapons, report back to me, and I shall inspect them." Talbot gave a curt nod. The interview was over. Jones saluted and left.

After inspecting the foxholes with Sergeant Rosenberg, it was time to spot-check a couple of Jones's positions. He hoped there wouldn't be any problems. Talbot was pleasantly surprised. Jones might be a nasty piece of work, but he knew his business extremely well. The machine guns were beautifully placed to protect the entire slope. The mortars immediately behind them were just waiting to decimate any enemy troops that came in range. Fifteen feet back from the ridge, Jones was quietly directing his men as they dug foxholes.

Returning to find Rosenberg, Talbot was glad to see that the command post was well under way.

"Rosenberg."

"Sir."

"Your men have done quick work."

"They are good men, sir. They work hard."

"How long have you been in the army, sergeant?" asked Talbot.

"Six years, sir."

"Any combat experience?"

"Yes, sir. North Africa with the 509th."

"Good." Talbot nodded. "Rosenberg. I'm giving you a field commission. Effective right now, you're a lieutenant."

"Thank you, sir," Rosenberg stammered, clearly taken aback. "Are you sure you want to do this? You know I ain't real educated or nothing. I . . ."

"I'm sure, Sergeant," Talbot broke in. "In fact, I'm so sure, I'm promoting you to captain. Effective immediately. So, Captain Rosenberg, if anything happens to me, you are the senior officer present and you will take over. Is that understood?"

"Lieutenant Jones won't like that, sir."

"You'll be a captain. Jones is a lieutenant. If he doesn't like it, put him under guard. Shoot him if you have to. Understand? You now outrank Jones, and don't ever forget it!"

Rosenberg nodded slowly. "Yes, sir. As long as it's only for this Santa Bianca deal, I guess it's okay, sir, but—"

"No," Talbot interrupted. "You are a captain. It's a temporary rank, but a captain you are."

Streaks of light were beginning to illuminate the big sky above Gela. Far away but all around them, Talbot could make out the smoke and flares of combat. "Our troopers have probably been making it damn hard for the enemy to move units around. Cutting their communications wires, too, I imagine."

By the self-assured manner with which the major moved and issued his orders, Rosenberg was fairly certain he was a West Pointer. He always felt better with a Military Academy man in charge, no matter how large or small the unit.

"What was your class at the Point, sir?" he asked Talbot when the two men had finished examining the final defensive positions.

"1922." Talbot smiled. "Clever of you to guess. I don't wear the ring."

"You don't have to."

The two men were silent, watching the digging. Smoke was rising from Gela.

"I joined up in '37," Rosenberg said finally. "I was a real good prize fighter, best in my weight. But the purses were small and far between. So, what the hell? I was single and healthy. I enlisted." He didn't mention that he had volunteered for the paratroops to get the extra pay.

"So what about you, Major?" Rosenberg asked. "You must have seen some pretty heavy combat already."

Talbot shook his head. "No, I had to leave the service in '31 to take over the family business."

"So where'd you get your combat experience?" Rosenberg asked, confused.

Talbot was silent for a moment. He liked Rosenberg and had trusted him from the moment they'd met. But still he was worried.

"Actually," he said at last, "this is my first time."

"You certainly learned fast, then, sir."

"Thanks, Captain," Talbot said, relieved at Rosenberg's reaction. "I guess it's in the genes," he laughed. "There have been a lot of soldiers in my family."

"Not mine." Rosenberg smiled. "Mostly a lot of stone masons."

In 1926, Bill Talbot left Hawaii and was sent to Infantry School at Fort Benning, Georgia. There, he learned the new concept of the war of maneuver, or "open warfare," as opposed to the static trench warfare of the previous world war.

It had been four years since Talbot had spoken with anyone in his family except his father. Although he wrote to Harry occasionally, he and his father had kept up a steady correspondence. Bill always addressed his letters to the mill. Otherwise, he knew his mother would short-circuit them and his father wouldn't see a single one. Occasionally, when he was able, Bill telephoned his dad at the mill, and they'd chat. When Bill got leave, he usually arranged to meet his father in Boston or New York, and they'd go to dinner or, sometimes, to a play. The two men, father and son, became close in those years. Mr. Edward Talbot understood that his son couldn't bear to be near his mother and accepted the fact. They never mentioned Mrs. Talbot until one night in New York, after a few drinks and a very fine wine, Mr. Talbot said, "I understand how you feel about your mother, Bill. But I want you to know this. When we were first married, I loved her very much. I thought we'd make a wonderful team. You know it didn't work out that way."

Bill reached over and squeezed his father's hand. "Dad, I understand," he said simply.

"If you ever get into a situation where it becomes intolerable, please promise me you'll be firm."

Bill nodded. "I will, Dad," he said almost in a whisper. "But it's a sobering thought."

∞

In 1928, only six years after graduating from West Point, Bill was promoted to captain, which was quite an achievement in those days. His future was extremely bright. It seemed nothing could go wrong. He decided to call and tell his father the news of his promotion. He thought of it on a Sunday when his father would be home. He'd have to take the chance that his mother might answer, though he prayed she wouldn't. She did.

"Hello, Mother, it's Bill. How are you?"

"If I thought you cared in the slightest I might tell you."

Bill sighed and said, "I'd like to speak with Dad."

Silence. "Your father is dead," she told him simply. "The funeral was yesterday." Then, she dropped her cold tone of voice and screamed, "Tell me something . . . How could he do this to me? He died without even telling me he had a bad heart! I was completely unprepared for this! How could he do this to me?"

Disgusted, Bill hung up.

∞

Two days later, Bill was on the train to Endicott, gazing out the window as the pullman car rushed past fields and hills and forests and slums. It had been ten years since Bill had been home. Perhaps he had made a mistake staying away so long.

"Harry was supposed to call you," his mother had said on the phone, but Bill didn't believe it. She had schemed to keep him away. It was so obvious. But why had Harry gone along with it?

As the train pulled into the station, Bill could see Harry standing on the platform, staring blankly at the hills. He was thirty-four but looked at least ten years older. Now that their father was dead and Harry would be in charge of the mill, Bill suspected he was feeling a lot of unneeded and unwanted pressure.

Harry had never married and though the brothers never discussed it, their mother loved to hint that a "war wound" was responsible. Harry never dared to contradict his mother. Unlike Bill, Harry had not been able to get away from Endicott after he'd returned from the war. As the eldest brother, he had been groomed for most of his adult life to take over his father's responsibilities.

Harry was a hard worker. He had never tried to shirk off his family duty. But everyone knew that the only thing he really cared about was flying. During the Great War, he had more than earned the title of "Ace" by shooting down eight German aircraft and attaining the rank of captain at the age of twenty-five. He now owned two planes and kept them in perfect condition. The sky was the one place Harry could go to escape. Now that he was in charge, there would be little time for that.

❦

Bill stayed in Endicott for a week, always careful to steer clear of his mother. But Harry was not so fortunate. With the family business to run, it was impossible for him to stay out of the line of fire. Every decision he made met with her disapproval; any opinion he had on making changes in the mill met with vicious abuse. It made Bill sick to watch.

"You'll run the mill the way I see fit to run it," she screamed at him. "Your father was an idiot and practically ran us into the ground. I will not allow you to ruin us any further." Harry said nothing.

"If you know what's best, you'll let me run the business," Mrs. Talbot said, getting up to leave the house. "You have no head for business, Harry, and the whole town knows it." Harry bowed his head in shame.

When their mother had finally gone, Bill asked his brother, "Why do you let her speak to you that way?"

"She's probably right, Bill," Harry said sadly.

Deeply depressed, Bill took the next train to Boston, vowing that he would never return to Endicott.

❦

But the promise was broken three years later, in 1931, when Bill was still a captain and had just moved to his new post in Georgia. Unexpectedly, one morning he read in the business section of the newspaper that Talbot Mills was in financial difficulties and had been unable to pay the interest due on its loans from the banks.

Until then, Bill didn't even know they had any bank loans. He tried to place a long distance call to Harry as soon as he heard the news. The operator told him she couldn't complete the call until the next day, so they set a time. When Bill called the following day, Mildred, the maid at the Talbot home in Endicott, answered. The operator told her it was a person-to-person call to Mr. Harry Talbot. The maid started to cry, and even after several proddings from the operator, she remained incoherent.

Talbot asked to put the call through to the manager's office at Talbot Mills, and, after some delay, the call went through. Bill didn't know the manager, but he introduced himself, and the voice at the other end identified himself as John Wilkinson. Wilkinson then assured him that he certainly knew who Captain William Talbot was and was at his service.

"Where is my brother, Harry?" asked Talbot. His heart was thumping in anticipation of the answer.

"We've sent you telegrams, sir. We tried to telephone."

"I just changed posts," Talbot cut in. "My change of address is probably still in the mail."

"I'm afraid I have bad news, sir. I don't know how to tell you . . . Your brother is dead."

Even though he was prepared for bad news, Bill Talbot could only exclaim, "What?" Then, he asked, "How? I didn't know Harry was even sick."

"His airplane crashed, sir."

Talbot paused, then asked, "On purpose?" He didn't know

why he had asked that question. It just popped out. Maybe it was because he knew Harry was too good a pilot to make a mistake that would cause him to crack up unintentionally.

Wilkinson didn't answer right away. Finally, he replied, "It would seem so, sir. Awfully sorry, sir."

Even before he placed the call, Bill Talbot had a premonition. And the maid's bursting into tears left no doubt in his mind as to what had happened and almost how it happened. If Talbot Mills was in such bad shape that it couldn't meet its bank payments, poor Harry had nobody to turn to. He could only look forward to disgrace and ridicule, and he couldn't have stood that anymore than Bill could have. No. There was only one way out for Harry, and he took it. Bill Talbot understood only too well.

Talbot always wondered how Harry had put up with their mother. He was the oldest. He had to stay. And if he'd ever suggested otherwise, Mother would have jumped all over him with speeches about duty and responsibility and obligation. Bill knew that Talbot Mills had remained prosperous during his father's lifetime only because—after the debacle of not maintaining the workers' homes—his father made one rule: Under no circumstances was Mrs. Talbot allowed to meddle in the affairs of the company. Poor Harry never had a chance. He'd been under his mother's thumb ever since he was born and ran the company the way she ordered him to. His flying gave him his only happy release from a job he hated in a town he loathed, even detested, because his mother ran it just as she ran him. Well, thought Bill, his airplane gave him his final release, too. He went the way he wanted to. Talbot almost envied him that moment.

Bill took emergency leave and boarded the first train north. When he arrived in Endicott, the town was in mourning. The mill was closed. There was the funeral, the relatives, the professional grievers, the townspeople. But the ones Bill wanted to see fast were the bankers.

When he did meet with them, he found that things were much worse than he feared. The company was insolvent. The old-fashioned methods by which his father and older brother managed the company had not kept pace. After an all-day conference, Talbot told the bank presidents, "Gentlemen, suppose I take over. Suppose I'm able to salvage this mess? Then you'll get your money back and your interest. But I shall need time. What do you say? If you turn me down, that's fine with me. I'm an officer in the United States Army. I have a career. A career I'm willing to sacrifice to save the jobs of several hundred people here, and to save this town. You have nothing to lose by giving me a chance. I have everything to lose by leaving the army and attempting to save this company and this town. It's up to you."

The bankers agreed. They wouldn't call the loans. They'd give Talbot a chance to save the company. As Bill had pointed out, they had little to lose. If they called in the loans they'd get nothing.

Talbot had made his decision on the spur of the moment. In the cold light of day, he almost regretted it. He loved the army, his chosen profession, his future. But, he realized, the dice were cast. He couldn't turn back. He owed it to his father and brother, his ancestors, his workers, and his town to do everything possible to save Talbot Mills. He ordered the mill reopened immediately to get the employees back to work.

Before he departed to take care of the formal arrangements necessary for him to resign his army commission in good standing, he stood up to his mother for the first time in his life. It happened after dinner. As they entered the living room, Mrs. Talbot began to tell her son how to run Talbot Mills. "The only way to make money at Talbot Mills is to cut all expenses to the bone. You are fortunate, indeed, to have me here to help you. I can tell you exactly what you have to do. And I'll help you ferret out those crooks at the mill, too. They're stealing us out of house and home."

Bill Talbot pulled himself up and took a deep breath. It was now or never. "Mother," he said, and he tried to give the words an affection he did not feel. "Such as it is, Talbot Mills belongs to me now. I have sole responsibility for running it, and I'll run it as I think I should. From what I can see, so far, we need to spend a lot more money than we have been spending, not less."

His mother started to object, but Bill held up his hand and continued. "Just a moment, Mother. I must also tell you that, as the head of Talbot Mills, I intend to move into this house. The house belongs to the company. It goes with the job."

His mother smiled ingratiatingly. "That'll be fine, dear. I'll be so happy to have you here."

"No, Mother. You're moving out before I arrive. I won't put up with your vicious tongue lashings anymore."

"How dare you! My own house! My . . ."

"My house," cut in Bill. "You have relatives all over this state. Go live with one of them. You are not staying here."

"Try to stop me. Try to throw me out, you ungrateful little toy soldier."

Without comment, Bill Talbot picked up the telephone and asked the operator to connect him with John Wilkinson at his home. Bill had spent some time with Wilkinson going over the company's situation, so they were, at Talbot's suggestion, on first name terms. "John, I hate to bother you," said Talbot. "I know what you're going through right now, and it's after office hours, but this is an urgent personal matter. The Talbot house, the one Father lived in and Harry and Grandfather and all the rest, it's full of termites. I want it torn down, leveled to the ground, and I want it done before I return in two weeks. Is that clear?"

He listened as Wilkinson objected that the house was a landmark, and couldn't they do something about the termites that was less drastic, and . . .

But Talbot cut in. "John, if that house isn't leveled to the ground before I get back, you will be fired. Do you understand? I'll explain more fully later. I don't have time now." He hung up, turned, and stared at his mother.

But to his consternation, he saw she had begun to weep. Then, he saw her put her head on the arm of her chair and sob. He had never felt so guilty in his life, or so cruel. He began to relent. He was just about to tell his mother she could stay in the house as long as she wanted to when it struck him that he'd seen this performance before. Many times before. She'd used it on his father whenever he had shown the least sign of not complying with her wishes or had rejected her demands for one good reason or another. Her strategy had never failed. But she didn't realize Bill had been there and taken it all in. She didn't realize she'd borne a smart son, who learned by what he saw and heard.

"You'd better stop all that blubbering and start thinking about where you're going to live," he said.

When she looked up at him, her face was a study in hate. Bill Talbot, captain, U.S. Army, was actually afraid. He feared she might attack him physically. He stepped backward. "Get out!" she spat the words. "Get out! And never come back!"

Talbot started to walk to the door. He stopped. He turned around. He shook his head. "No, Mother. This is my house. I'm staying."

Mrs. Endicott Talbot shot out of her chair. "You insolent, impudent, ungrateful ..." By now she was flying towards him, arms reaching out, fingernails first, to attack her son.

Bill grabbed both wrists. She kicked his shins, hard. Her frail body writhed in his grasp. She would have spit in his face except that ladies didn't do that. Kick, claw, slap, yes. Spit, no.

But she writhed and struggled until she was exhausted. Bill felt her go limp, as his hands continued to hold her wrists firmly. "Do you want to sit down now?" he asked.

She nodded, and he let her go. She sat on the sofa trying to catch her breath. When she did, she said, "My own son. Good God, what have I done to deserve this? My own son turning on me. Me, who's done so much for him. Me, his mother. Me . . ."

"You'd better ask God to forgive you for all the misery you've caused me," said Bill. "And Dad. And Harry. You never let Harry get married, did you? He was crazy about that Bradford girl. The year he got back from the war, he wanted to marry her in the worst way. It would have been a perfect match, too, and you knew it. But you wouldn't let him go, would you? You said that leg wound he got in France would make him a cripple one day, and it wouldn't be fair to the girl, right? You pulled out every trick you had in your hat, and you had a lot of them, too.

"If he'd married the Bradford girl, things might've been different for poor Harry. She might have sustained him when the situation got bad. Her father might have rallied the other bankers around to help Harry when he needed help. But, no. He had nobody, and he had no hope. So he got in his plane, flew it as high as it would go, then power-dived it into the ground. That's all he could think of doing. And I say you are to blame."

His mother's face was white. Nobody had ever spoken to her like that. Ever! She got up from the couch, threw her son a withering glance, and went up to her room.

After she left, Bill Talbot's entire body began to shake. He'd never defied his mother before, and he couldn't stop shaking. He'd been terrified of her all his life. He took a couple of deep breaths and told himself it was all over. If it hadn't been for the grief and resentment he felt over Harry's death, he might not have had the courage to do what he'd done. But he had, and he was glad. He was leaving in the morning, and when he got back his mother would be gone. He started to calm down. The shaking gradually diminished. He went to bed and slept like a rock.

He didn't know it, but all that night, his mother wept. She wept real tears for the first time since she was a little girl.

∞

They didn't have to tear down the Talbot mansion. Declaring she wouldn't stay another day under its roof, Mrs. Endicott Talbot departed the day after "that horrible evening with that repulsive, ungrateful, disgusting soldier—I don't know whose he is. He certainly isn't mine!" Bill had immediately cancelled the demolition order and had apologized to John Wilkinson for saying he'd fire him. In 1931, that was not an excusable threat. He also told John why he'd done it, and they both laughed, although the affair would never really be funny to Bill Talbot. He never saw his mother again. She died three years later at the estate of her Brewster relatives. In her will she left "William Endicott Brewster Talbot, who used to be my son, one penny (U.S.$0.01) to be used to kill a termite in the house where his mother and father lived so happily for so many years."

"Sir. There's somebody coming." It was Rosenberg's voice.

"What? Where?" Bill came back to reality. He was in Sicily on Santa Bianca, and the war was soon to come alive.

Rosenberg pointed below. The eastern slope of the ridge was flatter than the others. It was a gradual rise that even tanks could negotiate without trouble. And rumbling down the road was a column of German Tiger tanks, obviously headed towards Gela to repel the American landings.

We are in the right place at the right time, Talbot thought grimly; and if we do our job well, we'll all be dead before sunset.

"Ensign, can you contact the fleet yet?"

"Yes, sir."

"Good. Give them the coordinates for the east road just beyond our ridge. That dust you see is a column of enemy tanks. They're headed for the beaches, and if they make it, there'll be hell to pay. But tell them not to fire until we give the order. Understood?"

"Yes, sir!"

Talbot looked at the German tanks rolling down the eastern

road on their way to Gela. They were so close that he could hear their engines. The infantry trudged along beside the panzers to protect them from enemy close-range antitank weapons such as bazookas or rifle-grenades. They were almost past the ridge of Santa Bianca.

"Ready to fire?" Talbot asked the ensign, calmly.

"Yes, sir," replied Higginbottom. The ensign began talking into his radio fast.

Moments later, a shell from a cruiser roared in and exploded a short distance in front of the lead tank on the east road. Talbot heard the ensign talking into his radio again to correct the range and distance. His voice betrayed his excitement.

The second shell from the fleet hit the road between two tanks, missing them both but spraying hot steel shrapnel against their sides. Talbot saw the tanks pulling off the road into the fields alongside it.

"Tell them to pour on the fire," he yelled at the ensign. "Fire for effect! Fire for effect!" The ensign was already relaying this message into his radio.

Almost immediately, the cruisers in the harbor at Gela let loose. Talbot hit the dirt. Never before in his life had he heard such a roar.

The east road became a sheet of flame and flying rocks. For an instant it looked as if the entire road had disintegrated. When the smoke began to blow away, there were German tanks scattered all over, some upside down, some on their sides, some upright but burning furiously. And the ones that weren't hit were leaving the field as fast as they could move. It looked as though somebody had kicked over an ant hill.

All was quiet now. As Talbot turned to locate Rosenberg, an enemy shell landed right in the center of the ridge with a dry, dull CRACK, followed quickly by a dozen more in rapid succession.

"Hit the ground," Talbot screamed to his men. The shells all hit the center of the ridge. They blew it to pieces. That was where the German artillery decided the American command post would be. Luckily, Talbot figured that was what they would think and had positioned his men at one end of the ridge.

But the enemy had reacted faster than Talbot thought they could. After making large craters on the top of Santa Bianca, the enemy artillery gave the ridge a random shelling, as if to emphasize the fact they could hit any point on it.

∞

The shelling stopped. Warily, the men poked their heads out of the foxholes. At any moment now the shelling could begin again.

"Captain Rosenberg!" called Talbot. "Go see if we took casualties. And be careful."

A few minutes later, Ensign Higginbottom emerged from the command post and came over to Talbot. "Captain Rosenberg asked me to report no casualties from the artillery barrage, sir."

As an afterthought, he said, "Should we try to have the guns fire at the retreating German infantry, sir?"

"No. Let's save our thunder. The Germans know we're here.

They've got us zeroed in, and we're going to need everything the fleet's got real soon," he said, walking back to the hole in the ground that served as his command post.

"Have you heard any word about Colonel Gavin?" Talbot asked the radio operator in the hole.

Fernandez shook his head. "No word at all, sir. We're scattered all over Sicily, and troopers are just fighting wherever they got dropped." He smiled broadly. "It sure is confusing the enemy. They don't know what we're up to, and they think we're an airborne army, instead of just a combat team, we're in so many different places. Colonel Gavin is probably fighting like hell someplace."

Talbot hoped so. He liked Jim Gavin and prayed he wasn't dead. Behind him, Talbot could hear Ensign Higginbottom repeating grid coordinates into the radio.

"Sir, sir," he called to Talbot. "What did you say the name of this place was?"

"Santa Bianca. And make sure they zero in on the coordinates that we give them. The Jerries are starting to hit us, and if they take us out we won't be able to aim the navy's guns. But, if we stay here, we'll be able to give the fleet more targets than they'll be able to handle."

Talbot heard the explosions of shells and mortars hitting the ridge and hoped his men were in their holes.

"I'm going to go try to locate whatever it is that's shooting at us," said Talbot. "Tell them to stand by."

"Sir!" interrupted the ensign.

Talbot nodded impatiently at him.

"They say we can't be on Santa Bianca, sir. They say Santa Bianca's too heavily defended. Impregnable. We've got to be someplace else, sir."

"You gave them the position of the panzers on the east road on grid coordinates based on our being on Santa Bianca, didn't you?"

Higginbottom nodded.

"Then we're on Santa Bianca, because they hit those panzers dead on."

Higginbottom quickly relayed what Talbot had told him. He looked up.

"They've gone to talk to a general or something." He listened again. "Major, they want to speak to the senior military man in charge here."

Talbot took the headset. "Major Talbot here. Headquarters 505th Regimental Combat Team."

All Talbot could hear was the rasp of static. "What? What? I don't read you."

Seconds later a high-pitched voice blared through.

"Talbot? This is General George Patton."

"Hello, sir."

"Now, I don't know how in hell you took Santa Bianca, but now you got it, you hold it, do you hear? Keep in close contact with the fleet. Give them targets. Stop anything headed for our beaches. Stop every Goddamn Axis bastard that tries to get his ass anywhere near our beaches, you hear?"

"That is exactly what I had planned to do, sir."

There was silence at the other end for a moment, then Patton's squeaky voice again. "Talbot, were you a lieutenant in Hawaii in '25? All-American at West Point? Bill Talbot?"

"Yes, sir." He hadn't known whether or not Patton would remember him.

"Thank God," said Patton. "Thank God it's somebody I know I can count on. You hold on there, and we'll see you get all the support we can give you. Good luck, son."

"Thank you, sir." Talbot signed off.

As he did, Captain Rosenberg stuck his head over the top of the C.P. "Come and take a look, sir." Talbot got out of his hole. Rosenberg pointed to a cloud of dust rising from a field between the ridge and the sea. "Those panzers got past us, sir. Now they're spread out in the field in battle formation to attack the beaches."

"They must have come around the other side where we couldn't see them. Higginbottom!" Talbot yelled.

The ensign's head popped out of the C.P. Talbot pointed to the dust cloud.

"Panzers spread out south of us, headed towards Gela. Not an easy target, but let's try. Get fire onto those bastards, Ensign. That's what we're here for."

It wasn't long after Higginbottom's head disappeared into the hole of the C.P. that a single shell hit right in the middle of the field.

"That's got it! That's got it!" Talbot could see the panzers start to take evasive action. "Fire for effect!"

They did. They tore the field and everything in it to pieces. It took only fifteen minutes for twenty-six-ton Tiger tanks to realize they were no match for ten thousand-ton U.S. Navy cruisers. The

Mark IVs that survived headed inland, like rats running from a hungry cat. Rosenberg was smiling as he surveyed the field which was now dotted with blazing panzers, but Talbot's face was tense.

"What's wrong, sir?"

"They know what we can do now, so they have to get rid of us, no matter what. We've made it impossible for them to move on their main approaches to the beaches, and unless they get their armor down there fast, our forces will be too strong for them."

Just then a series of black puffs of smoke appeared high in the sky, followed by the unmistakable cracks of shells exploding.

Talbot and Rosenberg threw themselves to the ground. Talbot heard what sounded like somebody throwing a handful of rocks into a pile of mud.

"What the hell was that?" he asked.

"88 mm anti-aircraft shells," replied Rosenberg. "They're timed to explode in the air, so what they do is put a short timer on them so they'll explode above us and shower us with shrapnel. The hell of it is, we ain't got nothing to cover our holes with."

Rosenberg was right. They were vulnerable to shell bursts. "I'm going to the C.P.," said Talbot.

"Yes, sir," said Rosenberg.

At the big hole, as the men already called it, he asked, "How far inland have the assault troops gotten, Higginbottom? Are they heading our way yet?"

"They've made some progress, sir. 45th Division's moving well. First Infantry Division's met resistance at Gela. That's the one we're supporting from here. Some panzers must have broken through without our seeing them, and they're causing trouble. Third Division's landed at Licata and are already whipping the hell out of the Germans."

Good God, thought Talbot. This is still the first day of the invasion. It seems like months since I was thrown down onto this damn island.

The roar of airplane engines interrupted his thought. Talbot searched the sky. At first he couldn't see anything. Then he saw them. German bombers. This was it.

"They're going to bomb us off of here," someone yelled.

He saw the bombs detach themselves from underneath the fuselage of the first plane. They floated towards the ridge like hawks looking for prey.

"Get down!" Talbot screamed.

In the few seconds he had, he grabbed Higginbottom by his shoulders and pushed him down over the precious radio, then threw himself on top of the ensign.

The sharp crashing crescendo obliterated all other sounds as the ground shook beneath the C.P. Rocks and dirt rattled on the tops of their helmets. Talbot choked on the dust. Blood was running out of his nose. He tasted it in his mouth.

The concussion and explosions continued on and on, until suddenly there was nothing but a deafening silence.

☙

"Sir, sir, could you please . . ."

"Sorry." Talbot raised himself up off of the poor crushed

ensign, who had been pinned between him and the radio during the bombing.

"Is the radio safe?"

"It's fine, sir."

Talbot stood up and surveyed the ridge. It was pocked from end to end with bomb craters. Planes swooped over Gela, and flashes of fire came from the beach, but for the moment the Germans were not attacking the ridge. Men were screaming in pain and the medics rushed from one foxhole to the next. Though he knew it was futile, Talbot prayed that none of his men had been killed. He looked around for Rosenberg, Jones, and Vischer. He could see Jones on the far side of the hilltop checking his machine gun squads for casualties. Vischer was helping the medics tend to the wounded. Rosenberg was approaching the C.P. "We took casualties in the bombing, sir. Four men killed, twelve wounded." Rosenberg called out, as he neared.

"The medics are taking care of the wounded. I put the dead in an extra foxhole and covered them with ponchos, sir."

Talbot nodded sadly. All the years that he had trained in the military had not prepared him for this moment of reality. Men were dead, and it was his responsibility. For the first time he began to question whether he had been right to take command of these men. Perhaps they would have had a better chance of surviving on their own. Up here on the ridge there was no protection, and the bombing was sure to begin again.

He looked Rosenberg in the eye. "Are you sorry you joined up with me?"

"I'm proud to be fighting under you, sir. The men feel the same. We all knew that some of us was gonna get it today."

Before Rosenberg could finish, the two men were thrown to the ground by the force of an explosion only yards away. The most relentless shelling they'd experienced blew most of the top of the ridge to pieces for twenty minutes. As soon as it stopped, Talbot heard his machine guns firing and the ragged pops of rifles and grenades. He and Rosenberg jumped up and ran towards the firing. Talbot could see the German attackers coming up the east slope. They were spread out, and they stretched as far as he could see. Among the infantry were Tiger tanks, the new Mark IVs.

Talbot dashed back to his dugout command post, shouting to Higginbottom, "Get the fleet! Quick! Get the fleet! Have them lay down fire on the east slope and all the way back over the road and into the fields. We need saturation! Saturation!"

The ensign talked fast. But when he looked up, his face was chalk white. "The cruisers are out of range. They've been bombed heavily and are taking evasive action. It'll take them at least ten, maybe fifteen minutes to get back."

We don't have fifteen minutes, thought Talbot, we probably don't even have ten. "Just keep in contact with them. We'll do our best in the meantime."

Again, Talbot was out of the C.P. and running towards the shooting. The mortarmen were firing continuously, and Talbot wondered how long their ammunition would last. All at once he became aware of what sounded like a tremendous buzzing of bees.

Just in time he realized that they were German bullets flying over his head. He hit the ground and crawled forward to the line of men and machine guns. The firing was heavy. In front of him there were dead Germans on the slope. There must have been over a hundred of them. Others were writhing in agony. But the rest came on, dashing forward, hitting the ground, dashing forward again. One of the machine guns had stopped. It had either gotten too hot or had run out of ammunition. The other was shooting shorter bursts.

We don't have even five minutes, Talbot thought. They've got us.

An explosion! Rocks and dirt flying through the air, hot steel hissing over his head! The Tiger tanks were only a hundred yards away and advancing fast, firing their 88 mm cannon at the troopers' positions. Another explosion! Another! And the tanks continued creeping relentlessly forward. There were only three of them in the first group. But behind were three more, and behind them, even more. There was no chance they could survive this onslaught, Talbot realized in despair. Should he try to surrender? Should he try to give up and save his men?

He crawled to a hole and slid in. Poking his tommy gun over the top, he took aim at the attacking Germans and squeezed the trigger. To his disgust, he saw the Germans hit the ground a split second before he fired. He'd missed them completely. He picked out another group of Germans and fired again, but this time a mortar shell exploded in front of him and he missed seeing any effects his shots might have had. Instinctively, Talbot ducked into his hole. The Germans were using mortars too, and they were falling all along his line, among his foxholes.

Now the Tigers were so close that Talbot could hear their engines and feel their heat. He knew the end was near. Out of the sky came another sound. It was the roar of airplane motors, the rattle of machine guns, the dull boom of bombs exploding. If those are the Luftwaffe coming back to finish the job, we're gone, Talbot thought.

Looking over the lip of his hole, Talbot breathed for what seemed the first time since the attack started. The planes were American. Formation after formation of fighter planes were strafing and bombing the German attack. On the slope, the enemy losses were staggering. Talbot saw some German infantrymen running from the ridge, trying to escape the fighters' devastation. But he saw that the Tigers were still coming forward, and so were the German infantry closest to their line.

They know our planes can't go after them when they are this close, Talbot realized. They've still got us, no matter how many Krauts the airplanes slaughter out there. In a few seconds, the Germans would be inside the troopers' line and it would be man to man. Except for the damn Tiger tanks.

Talbot wished he could run back to the C.P. and tell Higginbottom to call the planes in to kill the Tigers, even if they were already on top of the ridge. But he'd never make it. The German infantry was too close. He'd be gunned down before he took two steps.

He reached deep into his pocket and took out a fresh clip for his tommy gun. He didn't know how many rounds he had left in the old one, but he knew he wouldn't have time to change clips when the Jerries came over the edge of the ridge and the hand-to-hand fighting began, and he intended to take as many of those bastards with him as he could before he went down.

The ground shuddered. Christ! Our planes are bombing us, thought Talbot. Out of his instinct for survival, he tried to sink further into the bottom of his hole as the concussion continued to rattle his teeth. Other explosions! Heat! Something burning like hell. And then he understood. The planes were doing exactly what he'd wanted to tell them to do. They were bombing the Tigers that had penetrated his positions. Talbot couldn't see it, but the bombs were slitting those Tigers open like ripe watermelons and setting them ablaze.

Then the six-inch guns of the fleet opened up, and the slope and the fields beyond disappeared in a sheet of flame. Even as the dirt and rocks rained down everywhere, Talbot was out of his hole. It looked to him like there were German soldiers all over the ridge. There were groups of men fighting up and down the line. Two Germans ran past him. Talbot pointed his Thompson and squeezed the trigger for a second, knocking both of them off their feet. He turned, sensing the approach of an enemy, and as he did he felt a flash of pain shoot down his leg. He was now face to face with a German whose bayonet was still stuck in his hip; Talbot jerked up his tommy gun, squeezed the trigger, felt the bayonet yanked out of him as the German, still clutching his rifle, fell backwards several feet, knocked over by the impact of Talbot's bullets.

Talbot felt blood trickling down his leg but he felt no pain. I could probably have my whole damn leg blown off and wouldn't feel it, he thought.

He limped towards the C.P., making his way around the edge of the ridge, instead of straight across it. Nothing on the north side. The fighting around him was intense. But a soldier's instinct told Talbot there was another danger someplace else. The Germans wouldn't launch a single-pronged attack now. At this point, they knew better. He cut across the corner of the ridge to the west side. There they were. Infantry and tank columns. Two of them. Headed straight towards the ridge. They'd be at the foot of it in about three minutes and the infantry would start up the slope with the panzers sitting below to blast the ridge with their 88 mm cannons.

He considered running but knew his right leg wouldn't function. It had gone completely stiff. He felt blood sloshing in his right boot. Slowly, he limped on, his lame foot dragging behind him. On the east side of the ridge the battle was still in progress.

Talbot moved slowly towards the C.P. If both those attacks had hit them at the same time, right after the bombing, the Germans would have taken the ridge by now. That's undoubtedly the way they'd planned it, but the shells from the fleet must have slowed the arrival of the second column. Talbot could feel his strength draining, his mind coming unglued. He shouted for the ensign and saw him pop up over the lip of the hole. Talbot yelled, "Call for fire on the west side. On the road. On the slope. Into the fields. Tanks and infantry on the west."

The ensign disappeared. Talbot heard the whine of a shell and started to throw himself to the ground, just as the shell exploded above and behind him. Something that felt like a red-hot whip lashed him across his back. He screamed involuntarily just before losing consciousness.

When he had arrived at Talbot Mills in 1931, Bill Talbot had his work cut out for him. But he had an analytical mind, and he used it. He quickly discovered that, under his mother's influence, both his father and Harry had bought second-hand equipment whenever they had to replace their antiquated machinery. The items they purchased were already worn out; they were inefficient; they broke down frequently and there were no parts available, so they had to have them specially manufactured. Then, there was the management. Instead of bright, competent, well-qualified but expensive executives, again at his mother's insistence, they had hired the people who would work for the lowest pay possible, and they got what they paid for.

Even John Wilkinson, the manager, was not capable of managing a firm the size and complexity of Talbot Mills. Bill liked the man, though, and called him in for a long talk, during which it turned out Wilkinson was acutely unhappy as manager and would be better suited for a lower-level job. They mutually agreed he should return to the shop floor as foreman, which was where he came from and where he'd been a much happier man. He was as delighted as a child who had just learned he was getting an electric train for Christmas.

Sitting in his office, Bill Talbot mentally summed up his situation: Talbot Mills had old, worn-out equipment that was expensive to operate and maintain. They had ineffectual management and practically no sales force. "The products sell themselves" had always been their motto. Most ominous of all, they had no money and owed considerable amounts not only to the banks but to their suppliers as well. To put it simply, the firm was in terrible shape and was getting worse every day. Bill shook his head. Then, he stood up and stretched. It was going to be a long, hard pull. But the army had taught him to solve problems, so he decided he would just have to put his mind to it and solve this one.

⟳

A week later, he invited the presidents of the four largest banks in the area to visit Talbot Mills. He met them at the gate and personally escorted them around the plant. He pointed out the state of the machinery, but he also showed them how proficient the workmen were at using it and fixing it. Then, he took them to the small room that had samples of every product the mill turned out. They were good products. Well-made. The tour ended in Talbot's board of directors room, which was sumptuously paneled with old mahogany that had such a rich patina it could be used as a mirror.

After the four men had settled into their chairs, Talbot stood at the head of the board table and began his presentation. "Gentlemen, this plant is either going to declare bankruptcy or it is going to become the most prosperous mill in New England, and the decision is going to be yours." He then went on to outline the plans he had for the company, which included replacing the oldest machinery immediately, the rest gradually, recruiting able young men with executive experience in well-run firms, and building up a sales force. There were many well-qualified men available, out of work because of the Great Depression. He detailed several other measures he intended to put into effect including the use of his personal contacts to get a few army contracts to help out during these depression days.

All four bankers listened quietly and politely. At the end, as he sat down, Talbot asked, "Well, what do you think of my plans?"

After a moment, Mr. William Bradford said, "I understand your mother has left Endicott?"

Talbot was surprised at the remark, but he answered, "Yes. She's left."

The four bankers exchanged glances. Mr. Bradford seemed to be the spokesman for them all. He said, "Then she won't be running Talbot Mills from her sitting room any more, will she?"

"No, sir," replied Talbot.

"Why did she leave?" The question was blunt. It was a question only a banker would dare ask.

Talbot didn't answer for a minute. Then he said, "I'm afraid I asked her to leave. You see, we have a rule in this family: Only one Talbot can run Talbot Mills. If she'd have stayed, I would have left."

Nobody spoke for a few minutes, but the bankers exchanged

glances back and forth. Several nodded at each other. Mr. Bradford said, "It'll take at least a million dollars to do what you want to do. Where do you expect to get it?"

"From you."

To Talbot's surprise, none of them jumped. They didn't start to shake their heads or wag their fingers or roll their eyes.

"A quarter of a million from each of you," continued Talbot. "That's not a lot to ask. It's small change for big banks like yours."

"If we don't lend you the money, though, you'll go under," commented one of the other four, a man named Peabody.

"And, if I go under, you'll lose the money you've already lent me," said Talbot.

"No," said Bradford. "We'll take over your mill and run it by the blueprint you just gave us. All we have to do is bring in our own man to take charge of things. And, as you said, there are plenty of able men available today."

Bill Talbot nodded. He'd outsmarted himself this time. What Bradford said was true. It was very true. His mind raced to find a way to repair the damage. "No," he said, "that won't work. No hired hand will ever be able to salvage Talbot Mills. I can do it because I am a Talbot, and I grew up here. The people at the mill will work their tails off for me. They know I can obtain enough business to salvage and even expand this company. The one thing you should do, if you go along with my plan, is to take out a life insurance policy on William Endicott Brewster Talbot, because if anything happens to me in the next year or two, this place will close down."

After that speech, Talbot was very much afraid they would all just get up and leave. Instead, Mr. Bradford said, "Bill, give us a little time now to discuss this thing among ourselves, will you?"

Bill Talbot rose from his chair. "Certainly. Please take as long as you like."

The waiting was torture. Talbot cursed. To himself, of course. Those four pompous jackasses in there are deciding whether we live or die. For a brief minute he longed to be back in the army. He sighed and shook his head. If only Harry had sent for him in time, they could have resolved this thing together. But, then, there was his mother. Oh, damn! He paced the reception room for the fiftieth time.

Finally, the old secretary, who had served both his father and Harry, came and told him the gentlemen were ready to see him now. Talbot's heart jumped. He walked as calmly as he could back to the board room, wishing his heart would stop thundering. Entering the room, he closed the door behind him and turned to the men sitting at the table. He forced himself to smile as he sat down. It wasn't meant to be a happy smile, just a smile to convey that there would be no hard feelings, whatever their decision turned out to be.

Mr. Bradford cleared his throat and said, "Bill, we're going to take a chance on you." Talbot's soul leaped. "We'll put together the loan for one million dollars between the four of us. Usual conditions."

"Thank you, sir. Thank you," said Talbot. "Thank you all."

The bankers smiled. "It was your presentation and salesmanship," said Mr. Peabody. "The fact you brought us here and showed us more than a bunch of figures. You showed us a working mill and explained what was wrong with it and why. Most important, you told us what the solutions are, and we agree with you. So, son, don't let us down."

"I won't," said Talbot. "I won't. I'll be your best account before long. You'll never regret your decision."

As they filed out, the four men seemed happy with the outcome of their visit to Talbot Mills. Bill Talbot said farewell to each in turn before they drove off. The last to leave was Mr. Bradford. As his chauffeur held the door to his car open, he turned to Talbot and said, "You know, I pushed the others hard to give you the loan, Bill. Do you know why? Because you threw your mother out of Endicott, that's why. Anybody with guts enough to do that is bound to be a winner. God bless you, my boy."

As he waved at the departing limousine, Talbot thought, yes, I got even for you, Mr. Bradford. I got even for mother's breaking up your daughter's engagement to Harry. I'll bet there are a lot of other people around here who'll back me to the hilt for the same reason.

∞

With the money from the banks, Talbot was able to try his new methods of production and marketing. They worked slowly at first. Then, he began to catch up with the competition, but it wasn't long before he passed them. Some of his competitors closed their doors forever, but Talbot Mills survived. Bill brought in top people and paid them so well they couldn't afford to leave. He based promotions on ability and performance instead of seniority. He instituted a research and development department, added new products. As the mill prospered, so did the town. Nobody said it, but everybody felt it: The removal of the malevolent presence of Mrs. Endicott Talbot had done more than anything else to lift their spirits and get people solidly behind Bill Talbot, heart and soul. He was the knight who had vanquished the dragon.

In 1932, Talbot was barely able to pay the interest on the loans, but he scraped up enough to do it. At first, he didn't think he would be able to, and it made him so sick he went to bed for the day. The next morning, though, he was up and ready with new ideas to raise cash. In 1933 he paid the interest and made a payment on the principal as well. From then on, he met all payments in advance, and by 1938 the debt was completely paid off. The company had a surplus, and the orders were pouring in faster than Talbot Mills could fill them. Bill Talbot felt absolutely euphoric.

After paying off the banks in 1938, Talbot Mills began to expand into military equipment. Talbot's instinct told him there was going to be a war in Europe and, he figured, the United States was too big to stay out of it and too democratic to turn their backs on the European democracies and let the totalitarian powers take over. He used his army contacts to the fullest. The joke among insiders was that Talbot Mills was a department of the Procurement Branch of the U.S. Army. Talbot made a reputation for himself, too, not only among the military, but in industry. Everybody knew Bill Talbot of Talbot Mills.

Talbot's eyes were closed, but he heard voices. Very slowly, he began to climb through the darkness of his unconscious mind. The voices were speaking English. He opened his eyes. It was late afternoon; the sun was in the West. The men on the ridge wore American uniforms, but they weren't paratroopers.

Vaguely he felt somebody grip him under his arms and try to lift him to a sitting position. He groaned. He heard the voice shout, "Get that medic over here. This one's hit bad."

"You be careful with him, dammit!" It was Rosenberg.

"Rosie?" he croaked.

"Yes, sir," replied the big captain. "Thank God."

Now that his eyes were focused, he saw the helmet bobbing up and down in front of him as the medic worked. The red cross stood out against the white circle. "Rosie, what's happening?"

"You got hit and put out of action. You were something out there, Major. A bit nuts, if you ask me, but pretty damn heroic. If I didn't know better, I'd say you wanted to get killed in this damn war! Thanks to you, we held out until the Rangers and a couple of rifle companies from the First Division arrived. The planes had reported we were being overrun, and somebody sent them to come grab the ridge before the enemy could get a firm hold on it. Our guys would have got here sooner, except a panzer division almost blew them off the beach. It was touch and go. If we hadn't stopped these other panzers from joining in, it'd be over."

"Look at that leg," Talbot heard the medic say. "Can you hear me, sir?" An unfamiliar voice.

Talbot nodded.

"Your leg's broke," said the medic. "It doesn't look too good. I'm going to give you some morphine."

"What happened to your hip?" the medic was asking.

Talbot's mouth was bone dry. "A Jerry stuck a bayonet into it," he whispered. "Back's hit too. Shrapnel from an 88."

The medic worked silently.

"Rosie, what about our men?" Talbot asked faintly.

Rosenberg was silent for a minute. "We've got us a lot of dead boys up here, sir. They fought like hell, though. Vischer's dead. The ones that ain't dead are all hit, except the ensign, Fernandez, and Jones. We guys from the 505th have been relieved by the Rangers and Big Red ONE Units, and we're all supposed to go down to the beach, but Jones wants to stay and fight."

"It's okay," said Talbot, wondering why he, of all people, had been spared. "Remind me to put everybody in for medals. I want you and Jones to get the big ones." Talbot could feel the morphine taking effect. He was drowsy and wanted to ask for more. "How bad are you hit, Rosie?"

"Broke arm is all," replied the big man. "That same 88 that

got you, sir." He sounded almost proud to have been hit by the same shell as Talbot.

Behind them the medic shouted, "Hey! We gotta get this one out of here! Bring a stretcher!"

⁂

In a field hospital in Sicily, Talbot lay on a stretcher, his right arm hooked up to a plasma bottle. He had no idea how long he'd been there. The stretcher was suspended between two trunks. He remembered a doctor working on him with the assistance of several medics, who handed him surgical instruments. Talbot had been so numb from the morphine, he didn't feel much of anything, but from where the doctor stood working, he knew he was doing something to his smashed leg.

"How bad's the leg, Doctor?" he had asked softly.

"If you're afraid you're going to lose it, relax. We'll save it. We're going to have to operate, but not here. We'll patch you up the best we can, then send you back to a hospital in North Africa. Right now, though, you're in no shape to make the trip, so you'll stay with us until you've recovered enough to be moved. After I finish with the leg, I'm going to cut the shrapnel out of your back. You won't feel it, but I've got to go in pretty deep."

Talbot nodded, then drifted off into semi-consciousness once more.

⁂

A fly lit on his nose and woke him. As he looked around, Talbot had become fully conscious and saw he was on a stretcher, surrounded by rows of other stretchers filled with wounded men.

Above was the canvas of a large tent, open at the sides to allow the air in, and the flies as well. It was hot. Talbot's leg was bound up in a metal rack to protect it, and it hurt. So did his hip and back, he thought, as he dropped off to sleep.

After eight years of intensive work to bring Talbot Mills back to prosperity, Talbot's doctor told him, "Bill, you have to start taking it easier. You aren't a teenager any more."

"No," Bill said, "I agree with you there."

"Slow down," continued the doctor. "Play some golf. Get married. Now that would do you good."

Talbot smiled and shook his head.

The doctor, whose name was Sam Adams, looked pensive. "Neither you nor your brother, Harry, ever married, did you, Bill?"

"No. Harry wanted to marry Marjorie Bradford in the worst way once. But he got over it, I guess."

It was Doctor Adams's turn to shake his head. "Your mother broke it up," he said matter-of-factly. "But how about you? Everybody here knows you refused to live in the same town with her, so I know I'm not being indelicate when I tell you my guess is that you're scared you'll end up with somebody like your mother for a wife. Or that she got you so emotionally screwed up you can't bear the idea of getting married. You need to work at getting over her influence, Bill. Go find a nice girl and marry her."

"Don't hold your breath, Doc, or you'll end up with higher blood pressure than mine," Talbot joked. But he knew that his doctor was right about one thing. It was time for a change. He had excellent people to run the mill. All he had to do was check in each day to make sure things continued as they were and to make his monthly trips to Washington to secure the military orders that were now flooding Talbot Mills.

After his conversation with the doctor, as a most prominent citizen of Endicott, Talbot had no trouble entering the social scene of country club dances and dinner parties. And soon, for the first time since his return to Endicott, he was enjoying himself. He no longer got headaches from his doubts and fears about the business and the repayment of the bank loans. Nor did he feel the driving urge to get up at five in the morning to work on papers at the mill, or to stay at the office until midnight trying to get the figures to balance.

But Sam Adams had gotten him thinking about something else, too. His love life had not been particularly fulfilling or even satisfactory, up to now. He'd lived practically like a monk. He told himself it was because he'd always been too busy doing other things. His education and athletic goals, his army career, Talbot Mills, his mother's influence. Yes, that would put him off women, make him fear them, even—or was that just an excuse? Talbot's lack of any significant love life was beginning to worry him. Was he sexually dysfunctional? He knew he was not. There had been that passionate interlude in Hawaii with Barbara Sommerville. But Barbara had rejected him for an older man.

Maybe that was what had put him off women? Anyway, thought Bill, I'm much better off without them. No strings, no commitments, no romance, no sex. I'm a free man! And I intend to stay that way.

∞

One Saturday evening in early June of 1941, at the first outdoor country club dance, Talbot spotted his old friend John Phillips Brown. J.P. was five years older than Bill, but had been a good friend of Harry's when they were kids. The Browns had been living in Washington for the past two years, since J.P., a Democrat, had been appointed an undersecretary of something-or-other by President Roosevelt. Recently he had returned to Endicott, having successfully completed his job in the capital. He was the area's leading attorney, and the word was that he would become a federal judge within the next few months.

Talbot made his way towards the Browns' table, stopping to chat with friends sitting at other tables along the way. The club was full and dinner tables lined the dance floor, which was large. Waiters in white mess jackets and black bowties served the tables as fast as they could. Wine bottles were examined by knowing connoisseurs and poured by head waiters. Finally reaching the Browns' table, Bill kissed Mrs. Brown on the cheek. Before she married J.P. she had been Marjorie Bradford, the girl his brother Harry had been so in love with. Talbot had always been fond of her.

"Bill, you remember our daughter, Clarissa." J.P. waved his hand at an extremely beautiful girl. She was slim and graceful; her thick brown hair was tied at the back of her neck in a soft bow to reveal her elegant neck and creamy skin.

"My God. You're little Clara Brown?" The last time he had seen her was at Harry's funeral. She couldn't have been more than nine or ten years old then.

"It's been a few years, Mr. Talbot," replied Clarissa, her lips breaking into a spectacular smile.

"Bill, you know young Winthrop Stanley?" J.P. interrupted, pointing to a young man sitting at their table. "He's been taking Clarissa out lately."

"Call me Win," the boy said, rising. "It's good to meet you, Mr. Talbot." Talbot had heard about Win Stanley, the local football hero who was now the star of the Harvard team. He was tall, well built, and classically handsome with clear blue eyes and wavy blond hair. A perfect Greek god.

Talbot felt a tinge of jealousy, not because the young man was taking out Clarissa, but because he was so handsome and so young. Bill knew Win's mother and father, of course, but he had been too busy to meet the younger generation.

He and Win shook hands. "You're the first and only All-American from Endicott, so far, sir. I hope to be the second." He turned to Clarissa. "Mr. Talbot was All-American at West Point in the class of 1922."

"1922!" exclaimed Clarissa. "Why, that's the year I was born!"

Talbot managed a sickly smile and was turning to go back to his own table where his friends were waiting for him, when Clarissa stopped him.

"Mr. Talbot? Win's going to be away all summer," she said, looking directly into his eyes. "Football camp," she explained. Obviously, this had been the subject of an acrimonious discussion at the Browns' table before Talbot's arrival.

Talbot hesitated. Clarissa was probably the most beautiful girl he'd ever seen, and it was natural for him to long to take her in his arms and kiss her. It would be for any man. Then he realized that this girl was half his age. He knew she was a sophomore at Smith, which would make her about nineteen. He was forty-one. He smiled slightly and said, "I feel quite certain a girl as beautiful as you will never be lonely."

∿

The following week, after Win Stanley had left for the summer, Bill telephoned J.P. Brown and invited him to join his table at the dance that Saturday. As a seeming afterthought he added, "And please bring Clarissa if she would like to come."

Talbot invited two other couples to join his table for eight. He dutifully danced with all the ladies, but the only times he enjoyed it was when he danced with Clarissa. Bill Talbot was still a handsome man, even though his brown hair had flashes of grey in it now, and he carried a few extra pounds. He'd confirmed that Clarissa was nineteen and a sophomore at Smith College. "Do you get home for weekends when you're at Smith?" he asked as they danced.

"Sometimes," she replied. "Sometimes I go watch Win play, if it's a home game."

That's right, thought Talbot. Stanley will be playing football every weekend. Aloud, he said, "It's going to be a lonely summer for you with Win away."

"I suppose so," she replied. "I've signed up to teach poor kids how to swim. That should make the days pass faster."

Bill thought that was just the sort of charitable thing she'd do, too. And, then, try to pretend it was just something to keep her occupied. "How about the evenings?" he asked.

She shrugged. "We have a library full of good books."

"That gets a little dull," he said. "I've tried it; I know."

"Do you have any better suggestions?"

"Sure, I'll take you out to dinner once in a while. After all, I'm a friend of the family; it's the least I can do."

"Win might not like that."

"What? A handsome young fellow like him, jealous of an old man like me? Don't be silly, Clara. He'll be delighted to know somebody like me is taking care of you, keeping you from being tempted to go out with somebody who could become his rival."

Clarissa didn't answer, and Talbot didn't push it. They danced in silence until the music stopped. As they returned to their table, she said, "I think it would be great fun to go to dinner with you once in a while."

Bill's heartbeat quickened. Could it be possible that this beautiful young girl would be interested in me?

∞

During that summer, he took her out more than once in a while. She acted as his hostess at dinner parties, and they sometimes attended the club dances together. Although she always left with other guests, the town began to buzz. Clarissa Brown, a nineteen-year-old college girl, seen all over town with Bill Talbot, a forty-one-year-old man. If it had been anybody other than Bill Talbot, it would have been a scandal.

Despite his better intentions, Bill had fallen head over heels in love with Clarissa and, while he knew it wasn't very sportsman-like of him to be wooing another man's girl behind his back, he couldn't help himself. Moreover, she was clearly warming up to him, seemingly flattered that the wealthy, mature, and cultivated Bill Talbot would be interested in her.

She was so young and vulnerable. For weeks he made sure never to make any physical advances. He didn't want to scare her away. An innocent like her was not used to the lusts of a forty-one-year-old man. Then one night, after a particularly romantic dinner-dance at the club, Bill could no longer restrain himself. As they got into his car to leave he saw the moonlight in her hair and the softness of her lips. It was too much to bear. Slowly he drew her to him and whispered, "You've grown up, Clara. You've become a most lovely and captivating young lady, and I find you irresistible. I fear, darling, that I am too susceptible to your charm." He was silent for a moment. There was no response from Clarissa. "What the hell," said Bill. "You're a beautiful woman, and I'm a normal flesh and blood man."

He kissed her. Kissed her hard and desperately.

Clarissa reached up her hand, and at first he thought she would push him away. Instead, she grabbed him and pulled him closer. "I think we should go somewhere else before one of my parents' friends sees us," she said softly. If Bill was shocked by her forwardness, he was careful to hide it. Wasn't this more than he had hoped for?

They took the long route back to the Browns' house, driving through woods and open fields which shone like silver in the moonlight. After the car rattled over the old bridge that spanned the river, Clarissa squeezed Bill's hand.

"Let's get out," she said impulsively.

Bill slowed the car and pulled off onto a small dirt track that led down to the water's edge. She was out of the car before it had stopped, and running towards the river. By the time Bill reached the bank, Clarissa had disappeared. Her gown lay in a crumpled heap on the grass. Bill stripped to his shorts and dove in after her. He could see her now, swimming upstream towards the knotted old willow that wept out over the river. Bill swam to catch up. Clarissa had stopped under the boughs of the tree, and was waiting for him. She stood up as he neared her, rising until the water reached only to her waist. Her thin silk slip was transparent now, clinging to her large, firm breasts, and he could see her hard nipples, straining against the cloth. She arched her back slightly, so that her breasts pushed towards him, and she smiled, letting Bill admire her openly. She put her finger to her lips, motioning him not to speak, not to move. Bill felt his erection growing under the water. It was all he could do not to grab her and take her right there. She took a step closer to him, so close now that he could feel her breath. The tips of her nipples grazed his bare chest. He sank down lower into the water, until his mouth was level with her breast, and then slowly, tentatively, he licked her nipples through the wet silk of her slip, his tongue rasping slightly against the cloth. The willow branches swayed above them, and moonlight fell on her, dappling and illuminating her body. Clarissa moaned softly. Bill stood and kissed her, pulling her violently towards him, crushing his erection against her. The river swirled around their legs, rushing past them, matching their urgency.

Without warning, Clarissa broke away and swam back downstream. She clambered up the bank, and pulled her dress over her head, then disappeared up the track towards the car.

Bill drove her home. He stopped the car before pulling into her driveway. Clarissa leaned forward and kissed him. And then she was gone. Not a word had passed between them.

∞

The silent ritual of kissing and fondling became part of every evening after that night. Often, they would sneak away from a party and go back to Bill's house, where they would lie on the thick fur rug before the unlit fire, drink liqueur, and stroke each other through thin layers of clothes, teasing, moaning, until Clarissa, finally, would pull away. They could not keep their hands off each other. After a while it was difficult for them even to go out together in public, and they would run for the privacy of Bill's car where Clarissa would stroke Bill, making him hard, as he drove, looking for a secluded place.

After one such night in the middle of July, Bill had a startling realization: He wanted to marry Clarissa Brown. Bill had known a few women over the years, but never one that really mattered. Unlike the others, this sensuous young woman plagued his thoughts. He wanted her to belong to him. The idea that she might give her body to another man drove him crazy. He wanted to be the first—he had to be the first man to take her fully. He also realized Clarissa's attraction for him was completely sexual. There was nothing spiritual or intellectual about it. But, he thought, what is love but sex?

The following evening he invited her to dinner, but when he picked her up he drove directly to his house.

"I thought we were going to a restaurant," she said in surprise, when they pulled up to his front door.

"I thought we'd eat at my house tonight, if that's all right with you."

She looked at him knowingly.

"You're in a rush tonight, Bill," she said, smiling.

It was a warm night, and Bill had had his housekeeper, Mildred, set up a table in the garden. The Japanese lanterns were lit, and candles flickered in the breeze.

"You look lovely by candlelight, darling," said Bill softly. "I'm only happy when I'm in your arms. But all we've done so far is kiss and hug each other. I want more than that. I want YOU."

Clarissa's expression, when she looked up at him was naive and unsuspecting, yet, at the same time, slightly enigmatic, as if she were pretending not to understand him but really did.

"I know you don't want to commit yourself to anything or compromise yourself in any way. But, you see, angel, I do."

She nodded shyly. "I'm really pretty young still, you know." That was all she said.

"Clara, what would you say if I asked your father if I could marry you?" Bill asked, pouring her a glass of champagne.

Her eyes widened.

"Why don't you ask me first?"

Talbot laughed. "You're right. Will you marry me, Clarissa? You'd make me very happy, and you'd be doing me a great honor."

Clarissa looked genuinely distressed.

"I don't know. Bill, I'm so thrilled. But can I wait? I can't decide now. There's college . . . and Win. What would I say to Win?"

Talbot wasn't surprised at her words. He had expected them. But he was surprised that Win Stanley was still in the picture. Surely Win was a fling of the past. "Clarissa, Win is a nice boy, but that is all he is—a boy. I'm a man. I have experience, I can take care of you as you should be taken care of. If you marry me you'll have everything you could ever want."

"But I already have everything I want. Why can't we just keep things the way they are?"

Bill reached across the table and touched her lips with his fingers. "Because I love you."

Clarissa was silent for a moment. Then, without preamble, she said, "You know, Bill, I think it would be a good idea for you to tell Dad you want to marry me. It'll ease his mind. He doesn't really approve of your taking me out. We've had some real arguments about it. I think he'd forbid me from seeing you if you were anybody else."

Talbot knew this was true. "Because of my age, I suppose?"

"Yes, exactly. Because you're so much older than I am. But

if you told Dad you wanted to marry me, that might make everything different."

"And Win?" asked Talbot.

"I won't tell him yet," she said quickly. "After all, I haven't said 'yes,' and all you're doing is telling Dad you want to marry me."

Bill wasn't exactly satisfied with that, but it would have to do for now.

※

A few days later Talbot paid a call on J.P. Brown. After a pleasant chat about the government and the chances of the United States getting involved in the war, he told J.P. he wanted to marry Clarissa, if she'd accept him. He was honest enough to admit that, so far, Clarissa had turned him down.

J.P. began to polish his eye-glasses. "Bill, I won't forbid you to propose to Clarissa, nor will I forbid her to accept you, if that is her desire."

"Thanks, J.P., I knew—"

"Wait a minute, Bill. I have a couple of conditions. The first is that you wait until Clarissa finishes college." Bill's heart sank. "The other is you allow her to go out with boys her own age until then, so that she can make up her mind when the time comes."

"Including Win Stanley, I suppose."

"Yes. Including Win. After all, he saw her first, Bill."

※

When Bill arrived to pick Clarissa up the next night, J.P. met him at the door.

"Good to see you, Bill," he said, embracing his friend. "I've spoken to Clarissa and given her my permission. She agrees to my terms."

"Thank you. I'll make her very happy, J.P. You have my word."

That night, Bill and Clarissa went back to his house after dinner. Sitting in the living room, Clarissa seemed strangely nervous. He'd never seen her like this. To put her at ease, he said, "Well, everything went just fine with your father, as you know by now."

She laughed as if he'd just told her the funniest joke she'd ever heard. She slapped her knee.

He put his arm around her shoulders and gave her a squeeze.

She squirmed out of his grasp, still laughing and stood up.

He wondered what life would be like after he married her.

As if reading his mind, Clarissa pirouetted around the room twice and said, "After we're married, Bill, darling, I shall put frilly pink cushions on all the chairs and have lavender curtains on the windows. And bric-a-brac. Lots of bric-a-brac. We'll have the most darling china horses and other animals. We'll have vases full of flowers all over the living room. Oh, Bill! I can hardly wait."

Talbot felt slightly sick. He looked around. Yes, he realized, in the last eight years he'd turned the Talbot mansion into a man's house. No pink or lavender, no bric-a-brac. Only tans and reds and blues. The furniture was substantial. Prints of ships and hunting scenes hung on the walls.

"And we'll get rid of all this heavy furniture," continued Clarissa. "Some really nice antiques will do just fine."

"Yes, of course," said Bill without a trace of sincerity. In fact, his brow was more than slightly furrowed.

Her laughter tinkled through the room. "Whatever happened to those lovely oil paintings that used to hang in the living room?"

"Oh, uh, Mother took them."

"But they were Talbot things and Endicott's. Oh, Bill, we'll just have to replace them." She laughed as if she'd said something extremely witty. Then she danced around the room again, waving her hands, pretending to hang imaginary paintings.

Bill tried to grab her, but she waltzed away from his advances. She's gone crazy, he thought. Fey as hell. "Are you all right, darling?" he asked.

Her reply was loud laughter, as she clapped her hands together. "Oh, Bill, you are so funny." She practically screeched the words.

He went to the pantry and poured himself a brandy and a very large creme de menthe for Clarissa. When he returned and sat down, he raised his glass and they both took deep swallows.

"What's wrong?" he asked finally.

"I'm scared." She sounded completely subdued now. The change had been sudden.

"I don't understand. Scared of what?"

Clarissa looked at him helplessly.

"How can I resist you now? It feels too good when you touch me."

They both continued drinking their liqueur, which seemed to steady Clarissa.

He kissed her, and she kissed him back. It was done naturally and spontaneously, although, to Bill, her kiss seemed more ardent than usual. They hugged each other tightly. Bill was trying to arouse Clarissa, but in the process he was becoming extremely impassioned himself. He paused so Clarissa could take a couple more sips of her liqueur. After that, the kissing became more fervent. His hand groped for her breast and found it. She didn't remove it. He fondled and stroked and put his hand inside her dress. She still didn't resist. They'd gone through this before. They continued kissing. He removed his hand and hugged her tightly. As she lay slightly back on the couch, he continued kissing her, and at the same time, his caresses became more intimate.

"Don't do that," she said.

"Why not?"

"Because it feels too good."

So, he kept caressing her. Clarissa was breathing as hard as he was. She continued to say, "No. No. No."

Breaking away for a minute, Bill Talbot said, "Look, Clara, we're acting like a couple of young kids, but we're not. We're adults." He stretched out his hands to her and she took them. He pulled her to her feet and led her upstairs. She didn't resist, even though upstairs had seemed taboo until now. He closed his bedroom door behind them and kissed her lustfully. The liqueur had removed her inhibitions. They both undressed rapidly and climbed into the large bed where they continued kissing and stroking each other, building up the intensity of their passion until it was unstoppable and the inevitable happened. It was sublime, absolute ecstacy for Bill. It was heaven. It was miraculous. He felt splendidly triumphant and relaxed at the same time.

As she rested her head on Bill's chest, Clarissa said, "I guess I'm not a virgin anymore, am I?"

Bill shook his head.

"I'm glad," she said. "Now I don't have to worry anymore about losing my virginity. What a relief."

"I hope it meant more to you than that."

"Of course, darling. At first you hurt me. After that, it was the most sensational feeling I've ever had in my life."

She kissed him again. He put his arms around her. She said she still hurt, but it wasn't long before they were making love again. "God, I adore this girl," was all Bill Talbot could think.

"I have to go home, you know," Clarissa said afterwards. "Let me go tidy myself up." She left for the bathroom with her clothes in her arms.

Bill got up and dressed. He looked at the clock. It was almost one, but that was all right. They usually got back to her parents' house late after a dance.

Clarissa returned, looking fine. He kissed her softly and said, "I love you."

"Will I have a baby?" she asked.

Bill smiled at her naïveté. "I think it's unlikely."

With Clarissa at his side, Talbot's summer had been perfect. Then Win Stanley came home for two weeks before returning to Harvard.

The night before he was to arrive in Endicott, Bill and Clarissa had an argument about whether or not she would see Win.

"Darling, how can you go out with him now?" asked Bill irritably. They had just made love and were still lying in bed together.

"Bill, be fair. You know I have to. Win is looking forward to it. I haven't had the heart to tell him about us yet. He still thinks I'm his girl."

"Well, you're not," Bill said sharply. "So forget him."

"He'll only be here for two weeks. And you promised my father."

"Well, I shouldn't have. I don't like this 'unofficial engagement' business at all," Bill said angrily. "I insist that you tell Win you are not going to marry him when you see him."

Clarissa rose and said indignantly, "Maybe I will, maybe I

won't. So please stop acting like my father." She didn't say anything else, even as he drove her home.

∽

The next two weeks were hell. Bill had to wait and watch while Clarissa and Win went everywhere together. He wondered if she was making love to him. It was driving him insane. But he knew that he had promised J.P. that he would not inhibit Clarissa's social life, so there was nothing he could do until Win left or Clarissa chose to stop dating him.

Bill waited a few days after Win had left for college before calling Clarissa. He was angry at her for ignoring him and thought it might be a good idea to give her a taste of her own medicine.

J.P. answered the telephone.

"She went back to Smith this morning," J.P. said. He seemed surprised when Bill asked for Clarissa.

"I thought you knew. I'm sorry, Bill."

"I must have gotten the dates mixed up," Talbot said, to cover his embarrassment. He hung up the phone. It didn't make any sense. Why would Clarissa have left like that?

For days Talbot brooded. He could not concentrate at the office. He had left several messages for Clarissa in her dormitory but she hadn't called him back. The last time he'd called, her proctor had answered.

"Yes, Mr. Talbot, she got the messages. I'm sure she'll return them when she has a chance," she said in a knowing voice. Humiliated and angry, Bill decided to drive up to Smith.

Early the next morning he got in his car. It was a beautiful fall day; the sky was a deep blue, and already the leaves were beginning to change. Talbot drove with the window open, the cold air rushing across his face, keeping him awake. It had been a sleepless night. What had he done to make Clarissa angry? There had to be some mistake.

He drove through the tall wrought-iron gates onto the Smith campus. A guard stopped him and asked to see his pass.

"The ladies aren't allowed visitors during the week without a special pass." He directed Talbot to a large red-brick building. Inside, an old woman at the desk eyed Talbot suspiciously.

"Is Miss Brown expecting you?"

"No, I wanted to surprise her. I'm her uncle," Bill lied smoothly.

"Just a moment, I'll telephone her dorm." The woman dialed Clarissa's hall. "Has Clarissa Brown gone to class yet? Her uncle is here to visit her." She paused. "What did you say your name was, sir?"

"Bill Talbot."

"Clarissa, is that you? Your uncle is here to see you. A Mr. Talbot." She listened then placed the phone down carefully. "Clarissa is unable to see you. I'm afraid you'll have to leave."

Talbot drove like hell back to Endicott. He had no idea what was going on, but he intended to find out.

☞

JAPANESE AIRPLANES ATTACK PEARL HARBOR!! The headline jumped out at Bill while he was having coffee in his sunny breakfast room. Outside, the ground was covered with snow and

Bill watched aimlessly as a lone sparrow looked for a lost seed. It had been two months since his disastrous trip to Smith, and he had thought of little else but Clarissa since then. She had never responded to any of his calls or letters, and eventually he had gotten the unspoken message: She didn't want to see him. Now, on this cold December day, Bill realized that he had ignored what was going on in the real world for far too long. That the Japanese had actually attacked the American fleet was incredible. He followed the news for the next few weeks, thinking about all his army friends and what they must be doing, when one day he noticed a photograph at the bottom of the front page. "Harvard Football Star joins U.S. Marines," the caption read. Underneath the photograph of Winthrop Peabody Stanley was a small article. Bill read the piece casually. Halfway through, he jumped. "Mr. Stanley, who became engaged to Miss Clarissa Bradford Brown over Labor Day . . ." He read no further. Now he understood why she had been avoiding him all this time. He put down the paper and went upstairs to lie down. When the office finally called, he said he was ill and wouldn't be in for a few days.

∞

Christmas was a strain that year. Everybody sat listening to the radio news reports about the war which the Japanese were clearly winning. Most of Endicott's so-called "society" attended the dance at the club on the Saturday after New Year's. It was a local tradition. Though Bill had no desire to go, he knew that his absence would be conspicuous. Perhaps, he prayed, the Browns were away. He had not spoken to them since his trip to Smith. He'd avoided them in town and had buried himself in work again, rarely accepting invitations. If he had ignored his doctor's advice, none of this would be happening, Bill thought bitterly. High blood pressure was much less dangerous than a broken heart.

The night of the dance, Bill dressed carefully. Just in case, he told himself. His tux was beautifully pressed, and he had to admit that he looked quite dashing. He put on his heavy cashmere overcoat and, taking a deep breath, left the house. Bill drove his father's old Buick down to the club. As he parked outside he saw the Browns' Lincoln a few yards away. They were here.

Bill joined a table of his married friends, all about his own age.

He spotted the Browns' table on the far side of the room. Clarissa was with them, looking ravishing. He quickly turned his attention to the woman next to him, hoping that Clarissa hadn't noticed him. The woman beside him chatted flirtatiously but it took all of Bill's power to concentrate on what she was saying. After a while he realized he would have to face up to the situation. Excusing himself, he walked over and greeted the Browns cordially, congratulating them on their daughter's fine match.

"Aren't you going to ask me to dance?" Clarissa asked, interrupting him. Talbot could see that the Browns were embarrassed, but he had no choice.

"May I have the pleasure?" He took her arm and led her to the dance floor.

"It's nice to see you, Clara. You look beautiful, as always,"

Talbot said, as he waltzed her around the floor. "Win is a lucky man."

There was a long silence between them, as they continued to dance.

"What happened, Clara?" Bill said finally, unable to contain himself. "Why did you do this to us?"

"I still adore you, Bill Talbot," Clarissa said evasively.

"That isn't an answer." Bill stopped dancing, took her elbow, and led her outside to a balcony overlooking the snowy grounds.

"I never could have married you, Bill. You know that. You're much too old for me."

"Then why did you tell me you would?"

"I never said yes. I said I would think about it. I thought about it and decided to marry Win."

"But I made love to you."

"Yes," she said softly. "You taught me everything I know." She brushed his lips with a kiss. "Win would kill me if he knew."

"What about me?" Talbot asked angrily.

"You'll be all right. You always are. And Win needs me. You don't."

"You're wrong, Clara, I do."

"Well, it's too late now."

"Break the damn engagement!" Talbot pleaded.

"You know I can't. Win is going off to war."

She turned to leave. As she got to the door she stopped and looked at him. "Forget about us. It was a lovely summer, but it's over. I'm going to marry Win. That was always the plan." She blew him a kiss and went inside.

∞

At the end of April, Talbot held a meeting of all his employees on the main shop floor of Talbot Mills. On a raised wooden platform at one end of the floor, Talbot stood flanked by several senior executives of the company, several army generals, and a few other well-dressed gentlemen from out of town. When everybody was assembled, Talbot cleared his throat and announced that he had sold Talbot Mills to a nationally famous manufacturing corporation which had promised to retain all the present employees of the company and to expand its production as part of the nation's war effort. "I have done this in your best interests," continued Talbot, "and to ensure a secure, productive company in these times of national emergency."

From the floor came a lone voice. It was that of the foreman, John Wilkinson. "What are you going to do now, Mr. Talbot?"

All eyes turned to Talbot. "Just as soon as I have signed the final papers transferring the mill, I am volunteering for active duty in the United States Army, where I plan to serve my country on the battlefield."

The announcement was greeted by silence at first. Then, a few people applauded politely. In a matter of seconds the applause rose to a crescendo, a groundswell that swept the mill floor and could be heard throughout the town. The applause swept over Bill and, for a moment, he even felt like a hero. But in truth, Talbot

knew he was a coward. He was not joining the army out of patrio-
tism. He was making no sacrifice. Hardly. He had sold the mill for
the huge amount of twenty million dollars. He was running away.

Running from the woman who had hurt him, running from
the shame and pain of a broken heart. And if he got killed it would
be a relief.

The next morning, every newspaper in New England carried the
story of William E.B. Talbot's selling Talbot Mills and enlisting
in the army. It was front page news. To his great surprise, Bill
Talbot received a telegram that same day from Clarissa. It said,
"BILL, DARLING, JUST READ THE NEWS. COMING HOME
FOR SPRING BREAK TOMORROW. CAN WE MEET?
LOVE, CLARA."

What the hell? thought Bill. Of course we can meet, but
why bother?

The next afternoon, he received a telephone call from Clarissa.
"Bill, I'm so glad you're still here," she began.

"Of course I'm still here. I have a lot of things to settle before
I go, and I have to stay at least a couple of weeks to train the new
people." He hoped his voice sounded friendly but not cordial.

"Can I see you this afternoon?"

Talbot hesitated before answering. "Sure. Go out and take a
walk in the woods by your house. I'll pick you up in the car."

After Clarissa got into Bill's front seat with him, she didn't say anything.

"Why did you want to see me?" asked Bill finally.

"Win's finished Marine boot camp and is in officer's training already . . . Oh Bill, I made an awful mistake. Win is not for me. You are. And, Bill, I'm so proud of you for selling the mill and enlisting. I can't tell you how proud I am." She took one of his hands off the steering wheel and squeezed it. "I love you terribly."

"Then, for God's sake, why in the hell did you go and get engaged to Win?" Bill continued driving. He had no destination. It was just that he felt that the inside of his car was the most private place there was to talk things out, and they needed a lot of time to do that.

"I don't know. I don't know what made me do that. I guess I was mad at you because you tried to bully me into not keeping the bargain we made with Dad . . ."

"How did I do that?"

"By raising hell about my going out with Win. You knew that was the arrangement! And you bullied me and talked down to me." At this point Clarissa pulled her small handkerchief from her pocket and dabbed her eyes. Before long, she was sobbing.

Bill pulled the car off the road and stopped. "There, there," he said, patting her shoulder.

Clarissa rested her head against his chest as he hugged her closer to him.

"Do you love me?" she asked.

"I never stopped loving you."

"I'm yours, Bill. I always have been and always will be. I

won't see Win anymore. I'll be waiting for you when you get back from this terrible war."

They kissed long and passionately. "I'm so happy, Bill."

"Let's go to my house and you can prove it to me there."

"I'd like that," she said. "And I'm going to ask Dad to invite you to join us at the dance tomorrow night, too."

∽

Bill Talbot didn't get Clarissa home until 7:30 that evening. Their late afternoon love-making had been exquisite and neither seemed to be able to get enough of the other.

At the dance the following evening, as they waltzed around the dance floor, Bill said, "Afterwards? My house?"

Clarissa smiled and nodded.

"You know, you're still engaged to Win." Bill had suddenly remembered that previously forgotten fact.

"Oh, I'll break the engagement," said Clarissa dreamily.

"And you'll be waiting for me when I return?"

"I told you I would."

In the army field hospital, Bill Talbot retrieved Clarissa's letter from his meager belongings and read it once more. It was clear. Short and *not* sweet.

Dear Bill,

I hope this letter finds you well. As I wrote you, Win Stanley landed on Guadalcanal. He was so heroic they made him a captain and awarded him a lot of medals. So, as you can see, he's doing very well.

You know, I never broke my engagement to Win. I saw no reason to. And now I'm glad I didn't. My Grandfather Bradford—the banker who helped you out, remember?—told me that now that Win is such a war hero in the Marines and was such a football star at Harvard, he won't have any trouble making his fortune when he comes back from the war. Then he'll probably go into politics and maybe become President of the U.S. some day. So, let's face it. When the war started everybody was scared and uncertain. Win went into the Marines right away, and I was afraid he might get killed and I'd be left with nobody. I wanted some security. You were in a position to give it to me. (Is it true you got $50 million for the mills? Everybody says so.) Now, I don't need you for my security anymore. Anyway, Win has survived the Battle of Guadalcanal, so I imagine he'll be coming home soon. And he can give me everything I want and then some. And he's young and handsome and more my age. I think I'd wear you out in about ten years, and I'd still be young.

So, Bill, I'm sorry to have to say it again: It's been fun, but it's over. I hope you'll come to the wedding. And don't forget to bring us a very nice present!

Yours truly,
Clara

Bill Talbot shook his head. How could he possibly have been involved with such a child and a shallow, inconsistent, fickle one at that.

∞

The field hospital depressed Talbot. Wounded men never stopped arriving. The doctors operated day and night to the sounds of shrieks and prayers. The floor was wet with the blood that seeped from saturated bandages. Lying on his back and staring at the canvas roof of the hospital tent, Bill listened to the groans that never seemed to stop.

On the stretcher beside Talbot was a young man who had been brought into the tent from the clearing station at the front sometime during the night. Talbot could hear the chaplain's voice. He looked over at the boy. He could not have been older than eighteen.

"I'm going to pray with you, son," the chaplain was saying. "Try to repeat after me." The chaplain bent his head and prayed, but the G.I. could only make bloody bubbles with his lips as he tried to say the words. Then, as Talbot watched through bleary eyes the chaplain made the sign of the cross over the boy, bowed his head, and left to minister to another dying man.

The boy lay there quietly, alive and breathing. Talbot could see the bubbles of blood still forming at his mouth. The boy knew he was dying. The chaplain's prayers had left no doubt. They were prayers for his salvation, not for his life. Two stretcher bearers walked past carrying a wounded man between them. A medical orderly stepped over the boy on his way from one aisle to another, as though he were already dead.

Talbot wanted desperately to reach out and grab the boy's hand and hold it, to let him know that it was all right, that he was not dying alone. He tried to move his arm to reach out, but it felt paralyzed, pinned to his side.

"The doctor will be here soon. You'll be okay," Talbot said softly. "Where you from, soldier?" Talbot knew that the boy couldn't answer, but perhaps he could still hear a friendly voice.

But the bubbles had stopped. The boy was completely still. He lay there for half an hour before a medical orderly noticed him, then stooped, felt his cheek, and put a piece of gauze over his face. There was no breath to disturb the light material; no breath to make it flutter, even slightly. The man stood and motioned to two others who put a blanket over the boy and took him away.

Talbot felt the hot tears roll down his face.

"Major Talbot." Talbot turned. His doctor was standing beside him. "We're moving you to the hospital today, Major. You're strong enough to travel, and you need better medical attention than we can give you here."

"Where am I going?"

"Back to North Africa."

Talbot still hurt as much as if he'd jumped from a thousand feet into a rock quarry without a parachute. The doctors told him he was lucky to be alive. He would walk with a limp for months.

☙

"Major." Talbot looked up and saw a pretty, young Red Cross girl sitting in a chair beside his bed in the North African hospital.

Bill tried to smile, but it hurt him. He nodded, and that hurt, too.

"I know you can't write yet, so I'm here to do it for you. Now, sir, whom would you like to send a letter to? Your wife, perhaps? Or a sweetheart? Your mother?"

"No," replied Talbot. "I have none of the above. No wife. No sweetheart. No mother. Nobody, really, even though I have relatives all down the eastern seaboard from Maine to Florida, and some, even, in California. But no *real* next of kin. Sorry, my dear."

The girl looked embarrassed.

"Don't feel dejected. There must be a lot of us."

She nodded. "Yes. But you're the first *officer* I've met who has nobody to write to."

☙

By the time Talbot was able to get up and walk short distances with a cane in the immaculately clean and fairly quiet hospital in North Africa, Sicily had fallen to the Allies.

It felt good to be mobile at last. Coming out of the john one morning, cane in hand, Bill was surprised to see that his ward was full of men. The wounded who could stand were out of their beds. Photographers were everywhere, and officers milled around.

"What's going on?"

"General Eisenhower himself is here," a captain he knew told him.

"What for?" asked Talbot. Surely the general would have more important things to do.

"No one knows," said the captain.

Now, through the crowd, Bill could see the general, flanked by several aides standing near his bed talking to some reporters. "Oh. There he is, General," said one of the nurses, pointing at Talbot. An aide detached himself and came over.

"Major Talbot?" he asked.

Bill nodded.

"The general's been waiting for you, sir. Please come with me."

Puzzled and embarrassed, Talbot followed him. Good Lord. General Eisenhower had come to see him? And on top of it the general was waiting for him while he finished in the john.

Thank goodness I shaved this morning, Talbot was thinking, as he shook hands with General Eisenhower. Ike's famous grin put him at ease immediately. The general leaned over and whispered in his ear. "Major, after the ceremony, I'd like to chat with you."

What ceremony, Talbot wondered.

"Quiet! Quiet!" an aide shouted. The murmur of voices died.

General Eisenhower cleared his throat. "Ladies and gentlemen, we're here today to honor an American hero who contributed immeasurably to the success of our recent campaign on the Island of Sicily. The official citation will be read by Colonel Johnson of my staff, but I wanted to say, personally, that I consider what Major William Talbot did on that first morning of the invasion to be one of the most valiant deeds of the entire war to date. You will all learn shortly of the feat of arms to which I refer, which took place on the morning of July 10th, but I would venture to say that were it not for the major's heroic action, things might have gone far differently that day. It gives me the greatest pleasure to pin the Distinguished Service Cross on the, uh, bathrobe of Major William Talbot."

Everybody in the ward laughed and applauded as the general pinned the medal on Talbot's bathrobe. Then, a colonel named Johnson read the official citation, which described in detail how Major Talbot had defended Santa Bianca and at all times acted in the best traditions of the United States Army.

Afterwards, General Eisenhower took Talbot by his arm and gently led him towards the small office at the end of the ward.

"That was a fine job you did, Major. Outstanding. We still aren't sure exactly how you got on Santa Bianca, but thank God you did. How are your wounds?" His eyes rested on Talbot's cane.

"All right under the circumstances, sir."

"You know, Talbot, that as a result of our successful landings, the allies are now in control of Sicily, and we're preparing to land in Italy, but we'd like to convince the new Italian government to join us and fight the Germans in Italy."

"Will they, sir, do you think?

"I'm very optimistic."

"Going into Italy's all very well, sir. But that leaves all the rest of Western Europe in the hands of the Nazis."

"That's what I've come to talk to you about. A lot of us have gone over your record, and we liked what we saw. You have all the qualities we're looking for: you're an Academy graduate, combat-experienced, and you've participated in an airborne landing. Omar Bradley, your old teacher from West Point, wants you. He's setting up a new headquarters, and I've already approved your assignment to it. He says he knows you well. Is that right?"

"Yes, sir," Talbot said. His heart sank. He wanted a combat command. He figured Eisenhower and Bradley were being nice to him. The doctors probably told them he'd never be fit for combat again, and this was their way of taking care of him for past services. He also knew it was no use protesting. "General, I'm a soldier. I'll go wherever you want me to go."

Ike smiled. "I knew you would. You're going to London just as soon as you're able to travel. General Bradley's already on his way there. So are a lot of other good men." He winked.

Now, Talbot returned the general's smile. He understood. It was the invasion of Europe they were talking about, and he'd be in on it from the planning stage. Ike wasn't putting him out to pasture. He was giving him the chance of a lifetime.

"I'm promoting you to full colonel, effective immediately," said Eisenhower. "You'll need the rank when you get to Bradley's headquarters, and you deserve it anyway. I'll have Johnson cut your orders, Colonel. General Marshall will be in overall command of the invasion of Europe, Bradley will command the U.S. First Army." Ike was walking out the door when he remembered something. "All of this is confidential, Talbot. Please keep it that way." And then he was gone.

∽

While writing up his recommendations for medals, Talbot had learned from Jones's actions that you didn't have to be likeable to be an excellent soldier. In his commendation letter for Captain Rosenberg, Talbot requested that he be assigned to him as an assistant. Ensign Higginbottom, he knew, had received the Navy Cross and been promoted to lieutenant. Fifteen other men had also survived, although they were all badly wounded. The rest of his force were either killed on the ridge or had died in hospitals.

Bill knew that he was very fortunate to be alive. He hadn't realized how lucky he was going to be when he jumped into Sicily. Now, he knew what war was, knew the horror of it. Yet, he hadn't flinched. He had come through with his honor intact. Leading men in battle had been exhilarating but assuming the awesome responsibility for their lives had been astonishingly depressing. Putting everything into perspective, he realized he'd completely outgrown Clarissa. Now, he couldn't understand how he had ever fallen for such a selfish, insincere little hypocrite. At last, he felt just as she did: It was fun, but it's over. It was never really meant to be, and Bill suddenly felt relieved, as if a great burden had been lifted from him and his life was only just about to begin.

Talbot's arrival in England was delayed slightly. His leg healed more slowly than anticipated. "That's why we don't like you forty-three-year-olds parachuting behind enemy lines and getting yourselves all shot up," the doctor told him. "A twenty-year-old would have been out of here and back with his unit a long time ago."

General Bradley had gone to London in September, and in November, while Talbot was still waiting to get out of the hospital, Brigadier General Jim Gavin had gone to London from Italy to take Bill's place. Gavin was seven years younger than Talbot.

Even though he was delayed, Talbot still had his orders to join General Bradley's headquarters in England. He arrived in December. General Bradley seemed pleased to see him, and congratulated him on his feats at Santa Bianca. The general held out his hand. "We'll get together some time soon to talk about old times." Talbot shook the hand of his chief. He knew the meeting was over, but he felt he had to have his say before he left. He took a deep breath.

"General, I don't think you're going to need me here now that you have Jim Gavin. Gavin doesn't need my help."

"Bill, do me a favor," said General Bradley. "Just sit tight for a while. Work with Jim. I've got some cogitating to do. You know, we all thought George Marshall was going to be the supreme commander for the invasion. Everything was set. Now, President Roosevelt says he can't do without Marshall; he needs him in Washington, can't sleep when he's out of the country, and Chief of Staff of the U.S. Army is a bigger job, anyway."

"Yes, sir. I'd heard General Marshall was going to lead the invasion. If he doesn't, then who will?"

"Eisenhower."

"You'll still command the U.S. First Army?" asked Talbot.

Bradley nodded. "Yes. Both Eisenhower and Marshall agreed on that."

☙

Back in his small room at the Dorchester Hotel where he was billeted with other senior U.S. officers, Talbot took off his overcoat and caught a glimpse of himself in the mirror. His row of ribbons surmounted by his paratroop wings were impressive. His tailored uniform and paratroop jump boots added to the image of a seasoned combat paratroop colonel. His day on Santa Bianca had taken him farther than he could ever have imagined possible. As a member of the Headquarters of the U.S. First Army, he'd know what was going on. When the time came he'd be able to pick his own assignment. What he really wanted was to lead an infantry unit in the field, bad leg and all.

By January, both Eisenhower and Montgomery had arrived in England, and things were moving fast. Bill Talbot did not become Jim Gavin's assistant. Even so, Talbot grew to like the cocky younger man. He was brilliant. A brigadier general at thirty-six, and completely fearless. The British wanted to run everything their way. But Gavin stood up to them. He had made combat jumps in Sicily and at Salerno, and had fought as a regimental commander in those campaigns. Everyone recognized that nothing could match combat experience in the field, so they deferred to Gavin's judgement.

Talbot liked London. It was one of those places you liked in spite of the wet fog and the bomb damage and other inconveniences of the war. By the time Talbot arrived, the Blitz was over. There were no more major air raids, but the barrage balloons were still up and in place. There were still occasional bombing raids.

At first Talbot was appalled by the extent of the devastation. Then, like everybody else around him, he began to take it for granted. The huge swathes of missing buildings all over the city no longer attracted his particular attention. The rubble piled up on the sides of the roads went unnoticed. Some of the mounds of debris shovelled into bomb craters already had weeds sprouting through the charred wood and crushed concrete. There were still large holes in the ground where landmarks once stood, but everybody simply walked around them. The worst holes were fenced in to keep pedestrians from falling into them at night.

Bill had made friends with a British major general named

Jocko D'Arcy with whom he worked on specific invasion projects, and the two of them would often go walking to relieve the stress of work. D'Arcy was a tall, well-built man who had been a great rugby player in his youth. His moustache bristled and he was so ruddy-faced that when Talbot first met him he feared D'Arcy was on the point of having a stroke. But as he got to know him, he learned that D'Arcy always looked that way.

They were walking towards St. James, just off Bruton Street near Berkeley Square one afternoon, when D'Arcy pointed out a particularly nasty-looking deep hole.

"That was once our most popular nightclub," he said sadly. "There was a telephone on every table and you could call up people on the other side of the dance floor. That was its claim to fame. Most of the officers I knew went there in the evenings with their ladies. I used to, and I probably would have been there that night, but I was in North Africa by then."

"It must've been bad."

"It was a massacre."

"Did you know anyone who was there that night?" Talbot asked.

D'Arcy nodded, and resumed his walk. It was obvious he didn't want to talk about it anymore.

"I was hit in Tunisia and sent home to recover," D'Arcy said, changing the subject abruptly. "I'll ride a desk for the duration, just like you. That's all we cripples are good for."

"Speak for yourself, D'Arcy. I expect to get a combat command."

They walked down to St. James Square past Norfolk House, which had been taken over as the Supreme Headquarters Allied Expeditionary Force.

"They say your General Eisenhower's going to move SHAEF down to Kingston," said D'Arcy.

"Why?" asked Talbot. "And where on earth is Kingston?"

"Kingston-On-Thames. It's a suburb of London. Your general wants more intermingling of his staff officers all in one place. Wants to weld his command into a really close-knit unit."

"Are there sufficient billets for us all?"

"I doubt it. Kingston's small."

"If I have to go down, can I commute?"

"Certainly. I intend to."

The two officers walked back to headquarters by way of Bond Street. There were large gaps between the shops where German bombs had obliterated many buildings, but the shops not hit were open, offering their expensive shoes and clothing, jewels and silver, and engraved stationery.

As they glimpsed Saville Row through a gap in the buildings on Bond Street, Bill snapped his fingers and said, "D'Arcy, would you mind stopping off with me at my tailor for a minute? I'm having a new uniform made."

"By all means. My tailor was killed during the Blitz," said D'Arcy. "Direct hit on his house. And the damned fool had some sort of a phobia about going underground, so he was inside the house when it was hit. I'd like to meet your chap for future reference."

Mr. James had been recommended to Bill right after he arrived in London. When he and D'Arcy entered the establishment, Mr. James was measuring a rather portly American. The tailor seemed harassed as he quickly measured the man's torso, all the while calling out numbers to his young assistant. He acknowledged Talbot's presence with a nod.

"That's fine for today, sir. Can you come back for a fitting in two weeks?" Mr. James said, after he called out the final measurements.

"Two weeks!" exclaimed the officer. "Can't you do it sooner than that? There's a war on, you know."

"Yes, sir. I'll do my best, but it will take two weeks."

When the American put his old uniform blouse back on, Talbot saw he was a major. Probably a re-tread from the First World War, he thought, or a politically appointed officer.

Talbot interrupted. "Two weeks, Mr. James? How come you're never able to do my work in less than four?" He winked broadly at the tailor.

Talbot's remark left the major with nothing further to say except, "Then, I'll see you in two weeks."

For the first time since he'd known him, Talbot had the satisfaction of seeing Mr. James smile. The poor man was badly overworked. All his regular old customers were having uniforms made, and now all these Yanks were coming in, recommended by their English friends. And, God knows, many of the tailors on Saville Row had been bombed out, leaving those who remained with more work than they could handle.

Back on Bond Street, Talbot commented on the variety of uniforms. Besides the usual British, American, and Canadian, there were Free French, Norwegian, Polish, Dutch, and a few Talbot had never seen before. "Place is crawling with damned foreigners," said D'Arcy.

Talbot couldn't help laughing.

"You Yanks are very naïve about these things. But you'll learn. Don't trust these foreigners any further than you can throw St. Paul's on a humid day." D'Arcy was obviously serious but Talbot still found the whole thing amusing.

"It's getting dark," he said. "Let's get a drink."

On the walk back to the SHAEF Officers Club on Charles Street, they passed a crew of laborers shovelling back some rubble that had apparently been sliding into the street. Talbot gestured at them. "Still?" he asked.

D'Arcy nodded. "Forever, I think. God only knows how many bombs the Huns dropped on this city. In some places there are blocks and blocks completely levelled, as you've no doubt noticed. They look more like open fields of concrete than city blocks."

"How many people were killed in the Blitz?"

"I don't know," said D'Arcy. "Thousands, tens of thousands, hundreds of thousands, perhaps. They never release figures on that kind of thing."

Pointing idly at an unusually large pile of scorched concrete, twisted steel, and charred wood, he continued, "There may even be bodies under all that. Ones they haven't been able to dig out yet."

⬬

At the club, after a few drinks, Jocko D'Arcy grew garrulous. "You know, Bill, I'm presently pursuing a rather beautiful widow. No success yet, but I think it will be soon. The problem is we've known each other all our lives."

"Good luck," said Bill raising his glass. "My sweetheart left me for the United States Marines. I'm certifiably single right now."

"We'll have to do something about that," said D'Arcy.

Bill smiled. "You've been trying already, you sly fox."

"Why, what makes you think that?"

"All the nice young ladies you've been introducing me to. WRENS and other lady officers in your offices and at the club we went to."

"Ah. You mentioned WRENS. So that must mean you liked the lady from the Royal Navy I presented to you the other day."

Bill laughed. "They're all very nice. I guess I just haven't gotten over losing my girl. And, besides, I'm still hurting from getting hit in Sicily." Talbot realized he liked to throw that in whenever he had the chance. He told himself he'd have to stop doing it. He was beginning to realize that he instinctively shied away from any relationship with the opposite sex. He thought he'd gotten over his fear of women when his mother left. Then, the breakup with the girl in Hawaii and the ending of his affair with Clarissa had hit him hard. No. No more. Besides, being unencumbered by love made him a better commander—no attachments, no one to leave behind.

In late January, Bill was surprised to get a letter from Clarissa. He hadn't heard from her since he'd received the letter telling him he was ancient history and she was going to marry Win Stanley. Naturally, he didn't expect to hear from her again.

Now she wrote to tell him that Win had been flown back from the Pacific in December. He had taken command of a company in the Second Marine Division after Guadalcanal. On November 20th, 1943, he led his men ashore in a combat landing on an island called Tarawa. He was hit by enemy machine gun bullets as soon as he left the landing craft. When they got him off the beach, they had to amputate his right leg. Now he was safely back in the States and would recover. Poor Stanley, Bill thought. Thank God he has Clarissa and she would never abandon him in his hour of need. That would be unthinkable. So, nothing's changed as far as Clarissa is concerned, said Bill to himself. Get on with your life. Get on with the war.

Talbot put the letter down and tried to go back to work, but he couldn't concentrate. He went to check on his request for Captain Rosenberg. It hadn't come through yet. Back in his office he still could not shake off the blue mood that Clarissa's letter had brought on. Perhaps he just needed to get away.

Bill went upstairs and asked for a few days off. Bradley took one look at Bill and granted him a three-day weekend pass. Big things were happening and Talbot couldn't be spared for longer. Bill wanted to go to a quiet place, so he picked the seashore. The beaches were reserved for practice landings by the military, and the area would be deserted.

∞

The beach hadn't been completely deserted. It was there that he had met the sad, blue-eyed blond gazing at the ocean. Now, he thought of her day and night, and when he did a glorious, warm feeling went all the way to his gut. There was none of the fear of women that his mother and Clarissa had bequeathed him. His trip to the seashore had at least accomplished that. Now, he immersed himself in his work in hopes of ridding himself of this new fascination. But it didn't work. He had to see her again. But how? He didn't know anything about her. He decided to find out, much like a detective trying to solve a mystery.

∞

Bill Talbot dropped in on his friend Jocko D'Arcy, hoping to catch him in his office after work. He was in luck. Jocko was just leaving, his beret on his head, his overcoat on his arm.

"Jocko! Got a minute?"

"Well, old boy, actually I'm on my way to have cocktails and dinner with the girl I told you about. Divine Sarah. I don't want to be late, either." He looked at his wristwatch. "No. I'm all right. What's your problem?"

"You know how you've been trying to fix me up with girls all over London? And none of them appealed to me? Well, guess what? I never thought it would happen for reasons known only to me, but I've met one that's just my cup of tea, as you would say."

"Congratulations, old boy! I couldn't be happier! Good luck and good hunting."

"Uh, Jocko. There's a problem."

D'Arcy nodded, as if to say, go on.

"I don't know her name. I don't know where she works. I don't know where she lives. I don't know anything about her."

"As you say, Bill, you have a problem. If it were a small problem, I'd stay and discuss it with you for the next five minutes. But, my friend, you have a problem so large that for you to even get started explaining it to me will take days, so it's going to have to wait. You see, I think tonight's the night! Cheerio."

And with a wave of his hand, D'Arcy was gone.

∞

For the next few days, Talbot buried himself in work. Everybody on Bradley's staff was working around the clock, knowing the invasion would take place sometime in the spring or summer. Talbot's task was to study aerial photographs of various sections of the European coasts and the areas behind any possible invasion beaches to select drop zones for the airborne landings. He had to examine photographs of the coasts from Cherbourg to Antwerp. He knew the work he was doing was valuable only as confirmation of decisions already made, but he also perceived that Bradley and his staff were evaluating his planning abilities, and he had to measure up to expectations.

❦

Unexpectedly, at the end of a particularly arduous day, Bill Talbot was surprised to receive a visit from Jocko D'Arcy. He rose and shook D'Arcy's hand, smiling.

"Bill," said Jocko without preliminaries, "I've come to apologize. I behaved rottenly the other afternoon. You came to me with a problem, and I cut you off and left you standing there. It was unforgivable."

"Forget it, Jocko. You had an important date. I can understand that."

"Thanks, old boy. That means a lot to me. Anyway, the date was a bust. Sarah obviously had her mind on other things. I don't know if she's met another man, or whether it's simply some female vagary, or I've done something to displease her. I don't know. Anyway, old chap, it didn't go well. Her mind was miles away. Her interest in me—nil."

"Sorry, Jocko. I really am."

"Look, Bill, yesterday I got an idea. I thought, perhaps if I could get her to go out with another couple, she'd relax and be more friendly. Maybe she was nervous. She hasn't gone out much since her husband got killed, and, even though I've known her all her life, she might have felt uncomfortable dining with me alone. She knew me in my salad days, of course, when I was quite a rake."

Bill nodded. "That makes sense. And it sounds like a good idea to have a couple of other people present. Make it a small dinner party. I'm sure she'll relax and loosen up. You're always

great around other people. You're the life of the party. She'll probably fall for you like a ton of bricks, if she hasn't already."

"I was sure you'd feel that way," said Jocko nodding vigorously. "Your date will be Edwina Beauchamp, one of Sarah's best
friends. A divorcee. Absolutely smashing . . ."

"Hey! Wait a minute. I didn't know you were considering
me for this party. Look, Jocko, I'm busy as hell right now—"

"Edwina," repeated D'Arcy. "Think you can remember that?
I'll pick you up at the Dorchester at eight. The ladies will meet
us at the restaurant. It'll be easier that way."

☙

It was pouring rain as their taxi moved through the dark London
streets. D'Arcy was jiggling his leg nervously. "Can't we move any
faster? We're going to be late."

Then he turned to Talbot. "I can't bear being late for Sarah.
She's such a lady and deserves to be treated like one."

"Tell me about the other girl."

"Edwina. She's fun. Always laughing. You'll love her."

Talbot felt suddenly tired and found himself wishing he was
crawling into bed for a good night's sleep.

They pulled in front of a French bistro and raced to the door
through the driving rain.

Once inside, Talbot removed his coat and quickly scanned
the crowded room.

Suddenly his heart leapt. Toward the back, seated at a table
for four was the blond, cornflower blue-eyed woman from the

beach. Talbot felt breathless and dizzy. It was so unexpected, so sudden. Had D'Arcy arranged it? How had he known?

D'Arcy swept up behind him and led him to the table. But in the next second, Bill Talbot's world crumbled when Jocko introduced the blue-eyed blond, now dressed in a WREN uniform, as his cherished friend, Sarah. The introduction to Edwina Beauchamp, whom Talbot hadn't noticed at all, went unheard.

Seconds later, Talbot was jerked back into consciousness. Sarah, he could tell, was just as dumb-struck as he was. She stared wide-eyed at him, confused and overwhelmed. A light went on in Bill's brain. He knew at that moment that she was every bit as interested in him as he was in her. Not only that, but she was just as afraid as he was. It was comforting and disturbing at the same time. And now, unwittingly, Jocko had brought them together. In that fraction of a second, Bill decided to act carefully. He extended his hand and shook Sarah's politely, murmuring, "Awfully nice to meet you," as if he'd never seen her before that moment.

"I believe we met before," said Sarah after the men had seated themselves. "Weren't you on the beach down in Surrey earlier this year?"

"Why, yes, I was," said Talbot smoothly. Then he snapped his fingers. "Of course. You were the girl sitting on the steps."

Since he was sitting next to Sarah on his left and Edwina on his right, he was able to wink at Sarah without the others noticing.

However, Jocko's antennae were out in an instant. "Is this the girl you were asking me about the other day?"

Talbot noticed Sarah smile slightly, then shook his head. "No. That one turned out to be a dud."

"In England," said Sarah, "a dud is a bomb that didn't explode."

Everybody laughed.

"Well," said Talbot, "this one certainly didn't go off."

The atmosphere relaxed, they ordered cocktails. Bill's mind was racing. How could he find out where to contact WREN First Officer Sarah ... Sarah, what? He hadn't heard her last name.

"Colonel Talbot, from your uniform, you're obviously an American, but even in civilian clothes I'd have known because you talk like an American."

It was Edwina who had spoken. Talbot had trouble taking his eyes off Sarah long enough to turn the other way.

"Massachusetts," he said blankly.

"Oh, you must be terribly homesick," Edwina continued.

"Actually," Talbot said, quickly meeting Sarah's eyes, "there's nowhere else on earth I'd rather be right now than here."

Edwina blushed slightly, assuming the compliment was meant for her.

After the waiter had delivered their drinks, they all raised their glasses and, like virtually every other diner in London, made the toast, "Here's to Victory!"

Edwina leaned forward to ask Talbot another question but her words were drowned out by a small swing band in the back of the restaurant. At once half the restaurant stood to dance.

Jocko reached for Sarah's hand. "Would you indulge me, darling?"

Sarah smiled awkwardly, then rose.

"Come on, Bill," Jocko shouted over his shoulder. "Turn a few with Edwina."

Bill realized he had momentarily forgotten his manners. He smiled at Edwina and asked for the pleasure of the next dance. As they danced, Bill realized Edwina Beauchamp was a wonderfully charming lady. Her ebony-black hair contrasted with her swan-white skin, and her face was distinctly Norman. She was one of those not very attractive women who managed to make herself beautiful. She was vivacious and made funny quips about everything. He was almost sorry when the music stopped and they returned to the table. If he hadn't been so smitten with Sarah, he'd have been interested in Edwina. She was great.

Finally, after consuming several courses of their dinner, Jocko invited Edwina onto the dance floor.

At last alone with Sarah, Bill gazed openly into her eyes. He didn't ask her to dance. Instead, he said, "I could look at you forever, you know."

Sarah laughed, her face as radiant as it had been on the beach. "It's nice to see you again," she said softly.

For a moment, there seemed nothing more to say. He simply wanted to sweep her into his arms and take her away.

"I was wondering," he began tentatively, "if you'd have lunch with me tomorrow."

She looked away and took a deep breath. When she turned

her eyes back to him, he was sure she was on the verge of crying. "I'm afraid I can't," she said quickly. "But thank you."

"Tea?" he asked, smiling boyishly.

"No."

"Sarah, please don't say no," Talbot said, reaching for her hand, then quickly pulling back. "I just want to talk. Nothing more."

She shook her head slowly and whispered, "I'm sorry."

"But why?" he asked. "Is it Jock—"

At that moment, Jocko and Edwina appeared, smiling and out of breath. "Well, that was jolly good fun," Jocko boomed. He sat down, full of life, and beckoned the waiter nearby to bring another bottle of claret. "You two have a nice chat?" he asked Talbot and Sarah.

They nodded half-heartedly and, for the rest of the meal, remained subdued and quiet. Jocko, cheerful and a bit too full of wine, led the conversation and hardly noticed their reticence. But Bill couldn't help noticing that Jocko and Edwina seemed so happy together, so spontaneous. Hell, thought Bill, Jocko thinks he's in love with Sarah, but I think it's Edwina he's crazy about. Oh, well, wishful thinking, I suppose.

At the end of the evening, Talbot said goodbye to them all, wanting to walk home alone, now that the rain had stopped. Inwardly, he was thinking, it's just as well she turned me down for tea and all that. I've gotten seriously involved with only two women in my life, and both affairs were disasters. They left me feeling rejected and devastated.

He reached for Sarah's hand, held it a moment too long, and said, "Goodbye. Good luck."

Sarah, it seemed, was unable to talk at all.

Walking home, Bill Talbot knew he had finally met a woman who was as scared of love as he was. He knew the reason for his fear. He didn't know hers. But it created a bond between them that was deeper than mere affectionate love. I must be careful, thought Bill. She is fragile. As for his own usual anxiety and reticence with women, he never gave a thought. Sarah was *different*. He knew it in his heart.

Talbot had been accepted as a sound planner and was now in on the actual invasion preparations. It was exciting to be a part of the largest invasion in history. Through Bradley, Talbot had managed to get a BIGOT card, which was essential for his new job. This top security classification entitled the card-holder to know all the details of the invasion, code-named OVERLORD, including the place and date of D-Day itself. Security was extremely tight. It had to be. Since he was now privy to the most confidential war planning secrets, Talbot attended meetings and briefings almost every day, and he learned something new every time he went.

Nobody seemed to know why the top-security pass was called a BIGOT. So Bill Talbot determined to find out. He discovered the name had been made up. It came from the English reference name for super-secret dispatches sent to North Africa via Gibraltar. Their code name was TOGIB, which stood for "To Gibraltar." Reversing the letters TOGIB to BIGOT was simply a matter of English whimsy.

The landing sites had been selected by the time Talbot arrived in London. After considering six possible areas from the North Sea to the Bay of Biscay, the planners narrowed the practical locations to two: The Pas de Calais, which was the shortest route from England to the mainland, and the Cotentin/Caen area in Normandy. Because the Pas de Calais was the ideal place for the landing, the Germans would be expecting the invasion there and were preparing accordingly, even though they were fortifying the entire coast in readiness for a landing anywhere. The Allies were, moreover, working on a top-secret plan to decoy the German High Command into believing the blow would come at the Pas de Calais, and it seemed to be working.

The main consideration for the Allies was that the area be close enough to England to guarantee air superiority at all times. The site had to be within easy range of British-based fighter support. It also had to have sufficient beaches to land an adequate number of assault divisions. For OVERLORD, all the beaches were referred to only by their code names. Two U.S. divisions, the First and the 29th, would land at Omaha Beach; another, the U.S. Fourth would land at Utah. The British 50th Infantry Division would invade at Gold Beach, the Canadian Third at Juno, and the British Third at Sword. The British Sixth Airborne Division would parachute into Normandy behind the beaches during the night before the invasion. At the same time, the American 82nd and 101st Airborne Divisions would jump into the area behind Utah Beach to link up with the Fourth Division. The U.S. Ranger and British

Commando units would also play vital roles. The invasion would be launched the first week of June.

⟨∞⟩

Talbot was working late one evening in the war room of General Bradley's headquarters in Bryanston Square when the air raid sirens wailed. Even though the Blitz was over, there were still intermittent night air raids by the Nazis. He shrugged his shoulders and continued to work, only interrupting himself to check once again to make sure the black-out curtains were securely pulled, which they always were, both day and night, in that particular room. The air raids were more of a nuisance than a threat these days. Talbot was reviewing the list of over 1,400 American units that would land in Normandy during the first fourteen days after the invasion. The meticulousness of the planning was awe-inspiring. Inside the war room, the walls were covered with TOP SECRET maps covered with acetate on which were drawn objectives, boundary lines between units, phase lines, and other secrets the enemy would have paid dearly to learn. Other maps were filled with symbols representing enemy emplacements and guns, with arcs marking their ranges. Outside the room an MP stood twenty-four-hour guard at the locked door. Only those with BIGOT cards were allowed inside.

Talbot never paid attention to the air raid sirens anymore. He'd gotten used to them. So, he was only vaguely listening to the wailing when there was a sudden loud crash, then the sound of broken glass hitting the black-out curtains and tumbling onto the rug as the air was sucked out of the room. A second crash was close and louder, and Bill Talbot found himself on the floor, gasping. He looked up and saw that the curtains had been blown away. Startled, he jumped to his feet. The lights had been knocked out, so there was no danger of exposure. He saw flames outside and felt the heat. Those were incendiary bombs. Striding to the door, he said in his normal tone of voice, "Sentry? Can you hear me?"

"Yes, sir," came the reply.

"Good. The buildings around us are on fire. We might be as well. I have no way of knowing."

"Yes, sir."

"It's essential to safeguard the security of this room. Do you understand?"

"I do, sir."

"Stay at your post no matter what. I'm not leaving this room."

As the fires raged in the row of flats that comprised Bradley's headquarters, the MP stayed impassively at his post outside the BIGOT room. From inside Talbot could hear the volunteers swarming into the building to fight the fires. He heard the stirrup pumps getting closer. But Talbot had only one thing on his mind. If any unauthorized person came into this room they would have to call off the invasion.

Talbot heard the sound of boots running down the hallway.

"You can't go in there," he heard the sentry say.

"We have to go in there, soldier. It might be on fire," somebody yelled.

Through the door, Talbot yelled back, "It's not on fire. I'm Colonel William Talbot, and I guarantee this room is not on fire.

I also order you not to enter. I'm armed and I shall shoot the first man who comes through that door." It was a bluff, and he prayed it would work.

"To hell with the bastard. Let him fry," said one of the men outside. The sound of boots faded. After that things were quiet. The heat diminished. Talbot looked out the window. The flames were almost out.

The MP unlocked the door. "Colonel Dickson, sir," he announced.

Monk Dickson was the head of Bradley's G-2 staff and was in charge of all the maps and overlays that covered the walls. Several of Dickson's men immediately started putting the blackout curtains back in place. Dickson looked more worried than Talbot had ever seen him.

"Monk, I was here the whole time. Nobody got in." Relief washed over Dickson's face.

"The guard at the door stuck it out, too. I'd appreciate it if you'd get him a decoration. It took guts to stand out there during all that bombing and fire."

Dickson nodded. "No problem," he said. "And, Bill . . . thanks."

The next day, Talbot joined several other American officers for a meeting with their British counterparts. He sat down at the large, polished table facing the panel board on which the maps and overlays would be shown, and was handed his briefing papers. Soon six other officers arrived. They were the English contingent. Talbot rose from his chair to greet the new arrivals and to introduce himself. In the next instant he found himself staring into the cornflower blue eyes of Jocko's desired Sarah. His jaw dropped. Her eyes widened. She stood, planted to the floor. He noted again that she was a WREN officer, and a very high-ranking one at that. An aide was saying, "May I present Colonel Talbot? Colonel, this is First Officer Lady Sarah Hayward."

Recovering quickly, Talbot said, "Oh, we're old friends."

"Yes. Yes, we are," stammered Lady Sarah, and at that moment Talbot knew she'd been thinking a great deal about him too.

Before they sat down, he asked quietly, "Is tea still out of the question?"

Sarah smiled. "No. I'd love it."

Bill could hardly wait for the briefing to end. Then, when it was finally over and the other officers began to discuss the different phases of their operations among themselves, he stood up and looked over at Sarah. She smiled at him, and he realized he was acting like a dumbstruck adolescent at his first dance. He regained his wits and strode over to her.

"There's a small lunchroom down the hall. It should be serving tea now."

She seemed to hesitate, then nodded and followed him out the door.

Seated at a table near the window, Sarah poured the tea and they both began to sip quietly from their cups.

Neither could think of anything to say. After all these weeks he'd spent thinking about her, Talbot suddenly felt frozen.

"I suppose you live in a barracks near here? Or on a battleship or something?" Talbot asked, breaking the silence.

Sarah shook her head. "The service allows me to continue to live in my old flat. I come to work early every day and go home late every night. I'm lucky the place wasn't bombed. They say the German High Command spared Mayfair because they expected to live there."

Talbot leaned back in his chair. "I doubt that even Hitler himself would be able to throw a beautiful lady like you out on the street."

Sarah laughed. "I'm afraid that's very far from the truth, but thank you, Colonel."

"So what exactly is your job?"

"I'm the liaison officer between the Royal Navy and the War Cabinet. I keep the cabinet advised, in a general way, of what the navy's up to. That's the reason I attended this morning's briefing. I wanted to be sure I understood everything accurately before I report to the Prime Minister this afternoon."

Talbot took another sip of tea. She reported directly to Winston Churchill?

He was way out of his depth. Who knew what her role in all this was? He might be treading on some important toes just having tea with her. But when he looked up from his teacup he realized that Sarah Hayward had already captivated him.

"I asked you before and you turned me down, but how about having lunch with me some day?"

Sarah looked away. "No," she said. "I'm afraid I can't."

Talbot's heart plummeted. "No?"

"Thank you for the tea. It was just what I needed." She gathered her papers and stood to leave.

"Is it something I said?" Talbot asked anxiously.

"No, you've been very kind."

"Oh, gosh," said Bill. "Of course. I forgot. You're Jocko D'Arcy's girl. Please forgive me. I really didn't mean to come poaching on another man's preserve. Stupid of me."

"Who said I was Jocko's girl?"

"Aren't you?"

"No. And I'm not a girl. I'm a woman. My own woman."

Bill laughed. He didn't know whether to believe Sarah or not, but he felt like laughing, anyway. Then, he realized he desperately hoped she was telling him the truth. He became silent, waiting for Sarah to say something.

Sarah looked flustered, as though the words she searched for were not the right ones. Finally, she said, "You see, Colonel Talbot, I've thought about you a lot ever since that day on the beach and after meeting you with Jocko. And seeing you now I realize that I don't want to put myself into the position of not being able to stand it if anything were to happen to you. I'm sorry." She turned abruptly and left him too dumbfounded to even get up out of his chair as courtesy and instinct demanded.

⨳

Hurt by Lady Sarah's attitude, Bill Talbot was once more on the verge of depression, and he knew it. But, try as he would, he still couldn't get her out of his mind. Luckily, his work was fascinating and he had the good sense to throw himself into it. The planning aspects of OVERLORD were spellbinding, the responsibility awesome. It required his complete concentration. Therefore, Colonel Talbot requested and was given a private office. In it were the tools of his trade: French railroad charts, maps, diagrams, photographs, terrain contours, and a hundred other minutely detailed miscellany—all important, but only if you knew their significance. In the late afternoon, Talbot liked to close his door and go over the new material that had arrived during the day. Sometimes he'd work until after midnight.

It was two days since he'd been rebuffed by Sarah Hayward,

and Bill had been in an unusually bad mood since then—snapping at his assistants, avoiding Jocko and the other officers. He'd been through that senseless rejection with Clarissa, and it angered him that, after all this time, he had fallen into the same trap again. He decided he would just have to accept the fact he would never be happy or successful with a woman. He closed his office door at five o'clock, as usual, and was studying the aerial photographs he'd just received, which were unusually good ones, when there was a knock on his door. Talbot looked up scowling. He had standing instructions that he was not to be disturbed.

"Who is it?" he growled.

His door opened a crack. Talbot rose, still scowling. "Well, dammit, either come in or stay out. I'm a busy man."

The face that peered shyly around the door had cornflower blue eyes and, as it emerged from the darkened hall, blonde hair. "I'm so sorry," stammered Lady Sarah. "It's just that I was told I could catch you in your office at this hour, and since I was passing by anyway, I thought I'd pop up and say hello."

Bill Talbot stood still and caught his breath. He didn't know how to respond, so he smiled.

Lady Sarah smiled back, and when she did it lit up the room.

"Sit down, won't you?" said Talbot, motioning towards one of the two side chairs in front of his desk.

Sarah came in hesitantly and sat in the chair, while Talbot came around his desk and sat in the other chair, pulling it at an angle so it faced hers.

"It's good to see you again," said Talbot. He smiled and hoped it didn't make him look foolish. "I can offer you tea, but I'll have to go fetch it."

"No. Thanks very much but I've had tea already."

Talbot couldn't think of anything to say. Finally he tried, "I'm sorry I was a little gruff when you knocked. I didn't know who it was."

"Are you terribly disappointed?"

"On the contrary. I'm delighted." His smile broadened. "You're a welcome relief from a lot of hard work."

She looked at her watch self-consciously. "I really must go," she said. "I . . . I know I behaved badly the other day, so I was wondering if you still wanted to invite me to lunch."

"Of course I do. How about tomorrow?"

"I'd love it," she replied, rising to go.

Talbot escorted her out of the office, locked his door behind him and saw her out of the building before he returned. He was thinking furiously: I really don't understand women at all.

∞

The next day, Talbot arrived at the Admiralty at noon, carrying a large package. An armed guard insisted on examining it before he would let Bill go up to Sarah's office. When he saw what was inside, he smiled.

"Good luck, sir," he said, laughing, as he let Talbot pass.

Sarah greeted him with a glowing smile.

"I'll just be a sec," she said as she put some closed files in a drawer and locked it. "Where to?" she asked, pulling on her heavy overcoat.

"I thought we could go across the street and into the park. If you can stand the cold. It's gorgeous out."

"That sounds lovely."

The park was beautiful even now on this typical raw winter day. They sat down on a bench, and Talbot opened his package. Inside, the benefits of being a U.S. colonel were evident. A thermos of scalding coffee; a jar of hot milk; chicken, turkey, and ham sandwiches; and thick slices of chocolate cake.

Watching her eat was fascinating. How, wondered Talbot, could she devour such quantities of food in such a lady-like manner. They made casual conversation during lunch and ate leisurely, paying no attention to the uniformed men and women rushing by, seemingly on errands of the utmost importance. It was as if Bill and Sarah had decided to take a short sabbatical from the preparations for the great invasion and were enjoying it in repose, as a lull in their hectic endeavors.

After they finished, Sarah said, unexpectedly, "I'd like to say something." He knew she was speaking seriously by her tone of voice. "We hardly know each other so I don't really understand why I made such a fuss the other day. It was childish of me. But more important, it was cowardly. I'm too old to run away from things anymore."

"We all have to run away sometimes," Bill said. "I've done it myself, but I'm not going to do it anymore." If I hadn't run away from Clarissa, though, I never would have met you, Talbot thought.

"You're very quiet, Colonel Talbot."

"I was thinking," said Bill.

"About some girl? A girl you left behind in America, perhaps?" Sarah asked the question casually, but there was a tightness in her voice.

"For several months in the summer and fall of 1941, I took out a girl twenty-two years younger than I am, and I even thought I was in love with her. But we fell out that same summer, and now she's engaged to a U.S. Marine Corps officer."

"I'm so sorry," Sarah said. But her smile betrayed her.

Bill looked at his watch. It was time to get back to work. Reluctantly, he packed up the picnic, throwing the last of the sandwich crusts to the pigeons. He helped Sarah to her feet.

"Back to business," she said smiling.

They made plans to have dinner the following night.

∽

Bill picked Sarah up at her flat. He was curious to see how a member of the British aristocracy lived. Her home was on a lovely street of red brick townhouses, not far from Berkeley Square. As she had said, nothing around her had been bombed. Sarah was on the top floor. Bill rang the bell downstairs, waiting to be let in by the maid. Instead, Sarah appeared.

"Hello there, come in." She led him inside and up three flights of stairs into a pretty but simply furnished living room. Bill had imagined something quite grand, and was relieved to find that it was not. He had been somewhat intimidated by her title.

Sarah produced a bottle of scotch, rare as hen's teeth in those days, and they had a drink before walking to the restaurant. The *Ecu de France* was a perfect little place that had thankfully been spared a hit.

They settled at a quiet corner table. Tonight Sarah seemed more relaxed.

Talbot impulsively reached for her hand and said, "Sarah, Jocko told me your husband was killed. I'm so sorry."

She shrugged, tears suddenly welling in her eyes.

"I shouldn't have said anything," Talbot whispered. "I'm sorry."

Lady Sarah shook her head. "It's not my husband," she said. ". . . It's my son."

"You have a son?" Talbot asked, amazed.

"I had a son. Ned. He died."

"Oh, Sarah. How awful for you."

She quickly wiped away a tear that had spilled onto her cheek. "Yes, for me. But mostly for him. He had just turned fourteen."

Talbot didn't want to press her so he simply reached for her hand again and said, "I'm sorry."

"Four years ago my husband and I put our son aboard a ship to take him to safety in America. He was going to live with some of our friends there and go to a prep school in New England. We wanted him out of danger, you see, and everyone thought then that the Germans would invade at any moment. But he was killed anyway. A German submarine sank the ship. There were no survivors, no bodies found."

Talbot had heard so many of these horror stories, and each time it broke his heart.

Later in the evening, after several glasses of wine, Sarah was composed and thoughtful. "You know," she said, "I've never told anybody this, but after Neddy drowned I used to wake up in the night unable to breathe. I felt like I was drowning. It was a terrible feeling, and afterwards I used to weep for hours. It was as if I were experiencing Ned's death-throes. I felt so guilty. I was the one who insisted he go to America. I wanted him safe," she said quietly. "Instead, I sent him to his death."

Then, obviously eager to move on, Sarah continued, "I didn't become a WREN until after Ned was lost. I felt that I had to do something, anything at all, to help fight the Nazis. My late husband, Scott, was against it at first; he was afraid I would become too independent. But gradually he came around. It's been my salvation." She was thoughtful for a moment. "Nothing ever really makes up for someone you lose. You just have to keep going, and try not to blame yourself too much."

She gazed across the table, looking into Bill's eyes for confirmation. Suddenly he found himself pouring out his soul, beginning with Harry's death. "I was in Georgia when I got the news. He committed suicide by power-diving his plane into the ground. I felt guilty about it for a very long time. You see, I had been able to leave home, but Harry was stuck, and I knew it. I was so afraid of getting trapped there myself that I rarely went home. Maybe if I had, I could have helped him." Bill paused, thinking about the day he had found out.

"I had to leave the military to take over the mill. It was in terrible shape. I had no experience, but I swore I wouldn't let all of Harry's work and my father's go down the drain."

"That must have been a frightening time for you." The sweetness in Sarah's voice drew Bill out, urging him to go on, to tell her everything.

"Those were hard times for everyone," he said finally. "But fixing the mill was nothing compared to standing up to my mother. That was the hardest thing I've ever done. She never forgave me, not even on her death bed."

Strangely, he found himself telling her the truth about his childhood, and about his mother's cruelty, something he had never told anyone before.

"So you see," Talbot said, "I really did know how Harry felt. If he had just talked to me first . . ."

It was almost midnight when he took Sarah home. She turned to him at her doorstep and held out her hand. Bill took it in his.

"Good night, Sarah. Can I see you this weekend?"

She nodded.

"Saturday?"

"I'd love that. And thank you for taking me into your life. I feel privileged that you shared it with me."

Bill leaned over and kissed her on the forehead. "Good night, sweet lady," he said.

After she disappeared into the building, he stood on the step, lost in thought before he finally turned and began to walk slowly back to the Dorchester. He and Sarah had become friends. For now that was enough. She was still grieving for her lost son—and her husband, too, he supposed. And how did he feel about Clarissa? Then there was Jocko D'Arcy who was crazy about Sarah, pursuing her, perhaps even hoping for a life with her. What in the world would he say to Jocko?

Talbot slowly shook his head. All he knew was that he thought constantly of Sarah Hayward, and it kept him in turmoil.

∞

First thing Monday morning Talbot was at the door of Jocko D'Arcy's office. He'd been feeling like a heel for not telling Jocko about his friendship with Sarah. Even though Sarah appeared to take her relationship with Jocko lightly, Talbot knew that D'Arcy had higher hopes.

D'Arcy greeted him warmly and offered a cup of coffee. "You're looking well, Bill."

"I don't know why. I haven't had much sleep for the last few weeks. Listen, Jocko, I need to talk to you about Lady Sarah."

"Sarah? What about?"

"I ran into her at a joint planning meeting. She seemed so subdued. I couldn't help but wondering what was wrong."

"I know," D'Arcy answered, shaking his head. "She's had a terrible time getting over her husband and son. I guess it's just a matter of time. It's kind of you to let me know though."

"Well . . ." Talbot started.

"Bill, I can only tell you I've known Sarah a long time. She's a strong woman and she'll recover. Our fathers were schoolmates. He's the Earl of Buckland, you know."

"Yes, I'd heard that," Bill said vaguely.

"Her family name's Fitz-William. Lady Sarah Fitz-William. Her family is landed but has no money. Her mother died when Sarah was young. She was raised by her father—he's a bit batty. But Sarah never seemed to feel sorry for herself."

Talbot nodded, curiosity getting the better of him. "What was her husband like?"

"Older man, pompous ass. Scott Hayward." D'Arcy paused, then added angrily, "He was a devil with the ladies . . . Never could understand why Sarah married him."

"The thing is, Jocko, I've—"

Suddenly a young officer appeared at the door. "General D'Arcy. Sorry to interrupt you, but General Eisenhower requests your presence immediately. He says you know what it's about."

D'Arcy slapped his forehead. "Oh my God, yes! Sorry, Bill, I have to run."

Bill watched helplessly as Jocko and the young officer disappeared into the hall.

☜

Although Sarah continued to go to dinner with Jocko, acting as his unofficial hostess, she also saw Bill Talbot more than either of them would admit. They had lunches in secluded little bistros and dinner sometimes at Sarah's flat, other times at out-of-the-way, obscure restaurants. Bill was beginning to feel like a thief in the night, even though there had been no mention of romance between them. Just chatting and joking, just being with Sarah, was sufficient, although Bill knew he had fallen hopelessly in love with her.

They took long walks in the many parks of London. Each had become familiar with the other's habits, knew each other's life history, hopes and fears, heartaches and joys. And, still, there was never enough time to say all the things they wanted to say.

On one particular Sunday afternoon, they walked through some pretty badly bombed-out areas. It was unseasonably warm for the end of March. Usually they would still be wearing layers of woolens, but today Bill and Sarah carried their overcoats over their arms as they strolled outdoors. Bill found himself holding her hand and noted with satisfaction that she didn't remove it. During the lifetime he felt he'd known Sarah Hayward, he had wrestled fervently with his emotions. He knew he had no obligation whatsoever to Clarissa Brown. She was engaged to Winthrop Stanley. He was head over heels in love with Sarah, and there wasn't anything he could do about it. The sight of her sent shivers down his back. Whenever she talked or sighed, she caused his heart to beat faster. She wasn't playing games with him the way Clarissa used to, either. Sarah was the most straightforward person he'd ever known. Yet, she'd never told him she loved him . . . Of course that would have been most improper. It was up to him to make the first move in that direction. She was much too reticent to express her emotions about how she felt about him. He didn't know if he had the courage to tell her he was just plain crazy about her. What if she rejected him? That would be the end of his seeing her and sharing her life. It would mean the end of the closest friendship he'd ever known. Could he take that chance? "Had we world enough and time . . ." But we don't. Time is running out. In a war, things happen fast. I'm sure Sarah knows that. I'm sure she loves me . . . That is, I'm fairly sure she does. I hope she does. She's become my life over these weeks and I hope I've become hers. But does she love me or does she consider me her best friend? Sooner or later, I'm going to have to summon up my courage and find out!

As they wandered through a series of bombed-out streets, Bill spotted a swathe of crocuses, growing in a crater between two buildings.

"Look."

Sarah peered down. "I've never seen them growing this early."

Stooping down, Bill picked one and presented it to Sarah with a bow.

"Why, thank you, kind sir," she laughed, with a curtsy. "May I ask what the occasion is?"

Talbot drew in his breath. "A very special occasion."

"Oh?"

"Yes. It's to help me tell you I'm terribly in love with you."

Sarah was silent. Bill had stopped breathing and was conscious of his heart beating in his throat like a kettle-drum.

Sarah put her arms around his waist, rested her head on his chest, and began to sob.

"I guess I said the wrong thing," said Bill. "I know it's probably too soon for you. But I can't help it. I wanted you to know."

She looked up into his face with the tears still streaming down her cheeks. "Oh, Bill, I love you *so* much . . . and I've been praying you loved me too. I'm unbelievably happy . . ."

He kissed her deeply. Wiping the tears from her face.

The sky was beginning to darken. People passing by hardly gave them a glance. In wartime London, lovers kissing in the streets were a common sight.

But their kiss was interrupted by the wail of an air raid siren.

"Good God. Another bombing raid?" Bill said.

"It is probably a false alarm."

"It may be, but we can't take a chance." He looked around for shelter. "Quick, darling, into this building. It'll give us some protection against anything but a direct hit."

They ran into the wrecked shell of what must once have been a beautiful townhouse. Bill could hear the throbbing of the bombers' engines directly above them now. This was no false alarm, and they were definitely German.

"They never give up, do they?" he said angrily.

He could hear Sarah breathing hard as she lay beside him on the remnant of an elegant floor, now pitted and dirty.

"God, I hate the Nazis," she said through clenched teeth.

With the crash of a thunderbolt, a bomb landed somewhere close by. Bill felt himself lifted up off the rutted floor by the explosion. Bricks fell from the shaken parapets around them, narrowly missing Sarah. Bill put his arm around her and held her tight. The engines still pulsated above. There would be more bombs. They might have to stay here all night, so it was lucky that the evening was warm.

"Are you all right?" he asked. Her face was ashen.

"I think so."

Bill drew her to him and kissed her fervently. She was shaking like a leaf, and he softly stroked her hair until she was still.

"I love you, Sarah."

"I know." She smiled. Bill put his heavy overcoat on the floor of the old mansion house. Then he lifted Sarah up in his arms and lay her on it. It was getting dark now, but he could still see her in the dusk.

"I want to make love to you," he whispered.

She nodded and tightened her arms around him. "I know, darling, but—"

"We'll wait," he said, finishing her thought. "I think you need to talk to D'Arcy. He's a good man."

"Yes, I was just having the same thought."

They lay on the pocked floor for a long time with their arms around each other. They could still hear the muffled explosions of more bombs, but they were dropping far away now.

"You can see the sky," Bill whispered, looking up through a hole where a roof had once been. A huge, yellow moon had risen.

"They call that a bomber's moon," Sarah said gazing at the sky.

"The call it a hunter's moon back home," Bill said.

"Same thing, I'm afraid," Sarah said grimly.

Bill stroked her hair gently.

At last he felt her head become heavy on his shoulder. She was asleep. Soon he would have to wake her; the night air was becoming chilly, and the sirens had stopped. But for now he would let her rest quietly in his arms.

M ajor General Jocko D'Arcy was in good spirits as he and Lady Sarah Hayward sat down at the table in a very elegant restaurant, dimly lit by candlelight. "We'll have a really good claret tonight," he said. "How would you like a Chateau Lafite '29? Nothing better."

"Except the '28?" suggested Sarah.

"You got that information from your father. He always goes for the '28, no matter what the wine."

Even as they ordered, Jocko could tell that Sarah was uneasy, tense.

"Everything all right with the Royal Navy?" he ventured. "We haven't lost any battleships lately?"

"Jocko, I've got to talk to you seriously."

D'Arcy nodded. He'd been expecting something, but he didn't know what.

"Jocko, I've fallen madly in love."

D'Arcy nodded, his face expressionless. "Not with me, I take it."

Sarah shook her head. "No, Jocko. I'm afraid not."

They sat in silence for a few minutes.

"I assume it's somebody I know," hazarded D'Arcy. "Would you mind telling me who?"

"I'd rather not."

"Oh? Why the big mystery? You're in love. I give you my blessing and am very happy for you, but I do expect an invitation to the wedding, so you might as well tell me who it is."

Sarah shook her head vigorously. Then, she smiled. "There's a war on, you know. Everything is supposed to be 'hush, hush,' remember? This is definitely classified information. It would give great comfort and assistance to the enemy were they to learn of it."

Jocko had to smile. "Same old Sarah," he said. He reached out and took her hand and gave it a squeeze. "I really do wish you the best of everything, my dear. And, if things don't work out for any reason, remember you always have me to fall back on, no matter what."

Sarah held back a tear, as she held D'Arcy's hand. "We'll still be best friends?"

"Haven't we always?"

⚮

At lunch the next day, Sarah said, "I've told him."

"How'd he take it?" asked Bill.

"Like an English gentleman, of course. Couldn't have been nicer. How would you like to get away from London for a few days?"

Talbot's face lit up. "I'd love it!"

"I have an idea, darling. Can you get some time off next weekend?"

Talbot nodded. He knew it would take some fast talking, but he could arrange it.

"Well then, dearest, down at the garage I still keep the old Bentley. The petrol tank is empty but if you could find some way to solve that problem, we could drive out to the country and spend some time alone together. At least a weekend, maybe longer, without the pressure of the war and the people and the bombings."

"Sounds glorious. But I don't know where the hell we'd go."

"Just leave that to me, darling," said Sarah. "All you have to do is get the petrol. Oh, and bring your ration cards."

⚬

There was a slight drizzle when Talbot pulled up in front of Sarah's flat that Friday morning in early April of 1944. He had been able to requisition for a week an army sedan, a Ford, which he knew would attract less attention than Sarah's Bentley.

Sarah was waiting with her small overnight bag. He kissed her quickly and took her to the car, then went back for the bag, which he put into the "boot" of the car. He smiled, realizing he already thought in English terms.

His own suitcase and an extra jerrycan of gasoline completed the contents of the car's trunk. A picnic basket and a car blanket sat on the back seat. Talbot's tan raincoat was wet from the shower which had become heavier. Jumping into the driver's seat, he kissed Sarah once more before starting off. "You're navigating," he told her. "I'm just the pilot."

They followed the Thames out of London, leaving behind the bombed-out buildings and flattened, charred blocks of tenements and warehouses along the river. Soon they were in the rolling countryside, which to Talbot seemed so pure, pristine, and undamaged. Everything was green in the spring of the year. After a while, he pointed and said, "Look. There's a cow. Imagine, angel, a cow."

"Now do you see why I wanted to get away from London?"

"Certainly. You're always right."

Sarah leaned against him and put her head on his shoulder. "I'm so happy just being with you."

He put his free arm around her shoulder and squeezed, then released her so he could use both hands to drive.

They continued in silence. Talbot wondered what she was thinking. He knew what he was thinking: I'd like to get out and make love right now. Driving this damned car is a pain in the neck. They were holding hands again. He squeezed hers and she squeezed back. Sarah smiled and gave him three quick squeezes. "Do you know what that means?" she asked.

Talbot shook his head.

"It means 'I love you.' That's what three squeezes mean."

He looked over at her quickly. Bill Talbot was happy to discover that, for all her vitality and character, Sarah Hayward still had the unsophisticated simplicity of a schoolgirl.

The fields had been going by quickly, and Sarah told him, "The farmers are the backbone of Britain, you know. And so many have gone into the army. Now, it's the older men and the Land Army girls who keep the country farms running."

Bill knew how Sarah hated the Germans and hoped the plight of the farmers wouldn't cause her to change the subject of their conversation from love to war. "We've left the rain behind us in London," Bill said.

"Why, so we have." Sarah smiled.

"Let's look for a place to have lunch. I can't wait to get at the basket in the back seat."

By the time they pulled off the small winding road into a wooded glade and spread out their blanket beside a stream, they had purchased a basket of fresh tomatoes, lettuce, and carrots. Before taking out the picnic things, Bill kissed Sarah as they stood beside the stream. Afterwards, she looked into his eyes and smiled. "My goodness," said Sarah. "This is a regular Victorian feast. I should be clutching a frilly parasol and wearing a large hat and hooped skirts down to my ankles."

As they dined on the good things Bill had brought and enjoyed a bottle of excellent claret, the only sound was the flowing of the stream. Otherwise it was as quiet as heaven. A bird trilled nearby. "What was that?" asked Talbot.

"Why, it sounds like a skylark."

Bill was silent a moment trying to bring back a memory. Softly, he said, "Hail to thee, blithe Spirit! Bird thou never wert ..."

Sarah turned her head quickly towards Bill. "That's Shelley. How in the world did a Yank colonel ever learn to quote Shelley?"

He smiled. "When I was young we were required to go to school. And there we were forced to learn poetry and other things I thought were quite unnecessary until today."

Sarah cocked her head. "Are you a romantic?"

"Of course," said Talbot. "If I weren't a romantic, you wouldn't have been able to put me off for so long. I'd have forced the issue or left. But I am a romantic, so here we are. Where are we going, by the way?"

Sarah put her arms around his neck and kissed him. "We're going to an old country inn. It's one of the only ones the military hasn't taken over, I suppose because it's out of the way and not near anything important."

"How did you find it? Or have you always known about it?" Talbot's tone of voice in no way implied he suspected she'd used the inn frequently for similar rendezvous.

Sarah's laugh was melodious. "I didn't find it, and I'd never heard of it before. So, my dearest one, I think it's time I divulged all. You see, Edwina Beauchamp had a dreadful marriage when she was young, got rid of the creep, and became the epitome of the gay divorcee. So, when you and I decided to go away for the weekend, I really didn't know how to arrange it, but I immediately thought of Edwina, and we got together for tea. She told me about this divine spot. She's stayed there many times and told me rooms 4 and 6 connect through a common bathroom. Apparently the proprietors always make a point of telling guests in those rooms to lock the other side when they're in the bathroom and to be sure to unlock it when they leave. She thinks they know perfectly well what goes on, but propriety is served. I asked her to arrange those accommodations for us, which she did."

"You mean she knows what's going on?" Talbot sounded surprised.

Sarah nodded. "Yes, and I think I went up in her estimation tremendously because of it." She finished putting things away and sat down on the blanket next to Bill. "Actually, I think Edwina and Jocko—well, they sort of go together as if they belong together. Edwina's crazy about him, and now that I'm out of his life, maybe things will begin to happen on that front."

Talbot smiled and shook his head. "I shall never understand women," he said slowly.

"You don't have to, darling. You only have to understand one of them—me!"

Spontaneously, the two moved towards each other and into each other's arms. He hugged her now, hugged the breath out of her, and she didn't mind. She was hugging him back. How long they lay together with their arms about each other they didn't know. After some time, they gradually loosened their hold on each other as if reluctant to do so. "I think you love me," breathed Sarah.

"You use a word I never knew the meaning of until now," he said after a pause. They lay on the cleared blanket in the early afternoon. Sarah untied Bill's tie and unbuttoned his shirt. She lay her head against his heart as he put his arm lightly around her shoulder. Without effort he rolled her onto her side and kissed her, then undid her blouse.

In the late afternoon, they still lay in each other's arms, with the blanket folded over them to cover their naked bodies. They had poured themselves into each other with a passion neither had ever known. Even now they continued to kiss. At last, Bill laughed lightly and said, "You know, we almost made it to that inn."

"Oh, my gosh! We've got to get going. We can't drive in the dark. And if we don't arrive in time, they're liable to give our rooms to somebody else."

"Ah," breathed Bill, "even in the midst of our pastoral solitude, the real world manages to intrude."

Registering at the inn went smoothly. Bill was glad they used their real names. Identification cards had to be produced, ration books presented. The older lady who checked them in had a kindly smile, the sort she reserved for newlyweds. She showed them to their separate rooms and explained about the bathroom they had to share. "Dinner's in half an hour," she told them.

"Oh, I think we still have plenty of food in our picnic basket. It'd be a shame to waste it," said Sarah, smiling brightly.

"All right, dearie, it's up to you," said the woman, imperturbably. It was, apparently, not uncommon for people staying in rooms 4 and 6 to bypass dinner their first evening at the inn.

After the bedroom doors were closed and locked and the bathroom doors permanently unlocked, Sarah and Bill inspected their respective rooms. Sarah's was small, with two single beds. Bill's was large with a double bed with its head set against the bathroom wall. Sarah couldn't help giggling.

∽

The picnic basket sat in the corner, unopened. Bill and Sarah lay in each other's arms. Their loving together put all other concerns aside. All unhappiness was forgotten. They'd put the war away. In Sarah's embrace, Bill Talbot felt he had finally reached home. "You are home, darling," said Sarah. Her words startled him. Had she read his mind or were they merely thinking the same thing?

At three in the morning, they were both awake and quiet. Then Bill turned toward Sarah and said, "Darling, are you familiar with Melville? Have you read *Moby-Dick*?"

"No," said Sarah. "It's an American classic, I know, but . . ."

"Well, there's a place where Ahab says something like, 'This whole act's been immutably decreed. It was rehearsed by thee and me ten million years before the oceans rolled.' And that's how I feel about us. I've existed up to now without design, without direction. But all the time I was aimed inexorably towards finding you and loving you, and whether you love me or not makes no difference. I am now where I belong, fulfilling the sole purpose for which I was created."

Sarah's hot tears splashed on his chest as she clung to him. Her arms enfolded him like a mother's around an infant, tenderly so as not to hurt, firmly so as not to lose her grip. Their two bodies as one, they dozed in quiet rapture.

∽

Talbot was aware of Sarah's disentangling herself from him and getting out of bed, but he was still half asleep and continued to lie where he was. It wasn't until Sarah came out of the bathroom that Bill opened an eye and tried to stretch his tired arms. Turning onto his side he watched Sarah walk to the open windows to check the blackout curtains. She did this out of habit, even though they'd remained open all night, since they'd never turned on the lights. She was completely naked and the simple act of walking to the window and back was a symphony in motion. Bill followed her every movement with delight. He realized he'd never given a thought to what a forty-year-old woman would look like without any clothes on and was thrilled to observe that Sarah Hayward had a perfect figure. Her skin was white as whipped cream and the nipples of her beautifully rounded breasts were the color of rose petals. She saw he was awake and got back into bed and snuggled up to him.

After breakfast, Bill and Sarah decided to take a walk. The country-side was beautiful in the spring of the year. As they strolled along a narrow path in the woods, Bill said, "I think we should be married as soon as possible."

Sarah hugged his arm tightly. "Oh, yes, dear Bill. Oh, yes! But shouldn't we wait until the war's over?"

Bill thought for a moment. "No," he said. "I'm not a young soldier going into battle, not knowing whether I'll return or not. I'm a forty-four-year-old colonel on Omar Bradley's staff, and I won't be in any danger. So, my darling Sarah, it doesn't make any difference at all whether the war is still going on or not."

"You'll have to meet my father, then," she said. But her smile was luminous. She stopped walking, gently turned Bill around so he faced her. Then, she kissed him on the lips. "I don't ever want to lose you," she breathed.

"You can't. We're one, now, and always shall be."

"Bill, darling, you're a strange and wonderful man. You love beautiful things. You're sensitive and kind and gentle. How did you ever decide to be a professional soldier?"

"It's a long story. I touched on it once. My father was kind and gentle, too, but he didn't have any steel in his backbone, and my mother trampled all over him."

"So, you decided to let the army put some steel into yours."

Bill smiled. "Something like that."

"What shall we do today, darling?"

"I thought we'd go have lunch in the same place we did yesterday."

Sarah giggled, and Bill realized it wasn't really a giggle, it was the happy little noise she made when she felt naughty and pleased at the same time.

Still making the happy sound, she said, "You mean you want to go back to the scene of the crime?"

"The criminal always strikes twice in the same place."

∞

While Sarah began to unpack the picnic lunch, Bill lay on his back beside the stream, as he had the day before. He mused, "You know, angel, I'm awfully lucky. After I got hit in Sicily, the army might very well have sent me back to the United States for further treatment and reassignment. I could have ended up being sent to the Pacific, or, more likely, running a training camp somewhere in the States. Or I could have been assigned to lead a combat unit into Italy. That's still a rough campaign, by the way. Nothing but mountains and rivers, the best defensive barriers in the world, and our boys are taking them one by one. The casualties are dreadful, though . . ."

Sarah had put her hand lightly over Bill's mouth. "Let's enjoy our picnic, darling. Italy's a long way off, and, besides, you already told me: you're too old and too shot up to lead troops in battle, so I doubt very much they'd send you into the Italian campaign, no matter what."

Bill smiled. "All I'm trying to say is, they didn't. I made an impression on General Eisenhower, and he brought me to England, where I met you."

"Santa Bianca," said Sarah. "Thank God for Santa Bianca."

They lay together on the blanket on the grass without moving. It was as if their minds continued to commune, each with the other. They knew their love would always be physical, but also at times would transcend them both and enter that spiritual realm known but to true lovers. It was in this ethereal state they lay motionless for most of that fine April afternoon.

After the weekend together, Bill and Sarah spent every night in each other's arms. Bill moved discreetly into Sarah's flat, keeping his own, which he had found when the Dorchester became too crowded, as his official residence. He obtained the necessary groceries through his U.S. Army sources, and they ate at home most nights. It was heaven. Bill marveled at the miracle that had brought him together with Sarah. It had been the salvation of them both.

Talbot's wounds actually stopped hurting, and he was happier than he had ever been in his life. He didn't remember when he had stopped caring about Clarissa. He occasionally wondered what she might be doing, but that was all. So, he was surprised to find a letter from a Miss C. Brown on his desk at work one morning. He read it slowly.

When he had finished, he stared out the window for a few minutes, trying to decipher its meaning. "Win lost more than his leg, so we can never marry," it said. "Win lost more than his leg . . ." He hesitated to even think it, but the only conclusion he could draw was that Stanley had his genitals shot off. The poor guy.

And now that he was crippled and impotent, Clarissa no longer wanted to marry him. Or perhaps Win had taken the honorable route and insisted she find another man. He hoped it was the latter.

The letter was short and, except for her few comments about the war and the weather, that was about all it said. It closed, "I still love you, Clara." She wants me back, Bill realized. All the times that he had prayed for this moment . . . And now, when he no longer wanted her, his prayers had been answered.

That evening Bill told Sarah about the letter. They had never talked about Clarissa before, but now it seemed important to get it off his chest and to explain what had happened between them.

"I wanted to marry her, and when she wouldn't have me, I fled town. I thought I had a broken heart, but I've since learned that the only thing that was wounded was my pride. I was a fool." He handed her the letter and watched silently as she read it.

"What a terrible thing for the young man," Sarah said finally. "Do you feel you ought to do the right thing by her?" Her voice betrayed her anxiety.

"No. I love *you*. And, if you'll have me, I want to marry you."

Sarah got up and came over to the fireplace, where Bill was standing.

He pulled her close and covered her face in kisses.

"This doesn't solve the question of the letter," she said, breaking away from him. "You have to write to her and tell her what has happened."

"Let's get married right now. Then we can simply send her an announcement."

Sarah shook her head. "You cared about her once. I think you owe it to her to let her down gently."

Bill wrote to Clarissa that evening, telling her that he had fallen in love with an English widow and planned to marry her. He made no reference to her letter.

∽

When Bill woke up the next morning, sunlight was streaming through the blinds, and it seemed as if the air was different—clearer and more alive. Sarah was still sleeping beside him, the sheets kicked down around her ankles. She was breathing softly, her thick blond lashes trembling slightly as she dreamed. I'm going to marry this beautiful creature, he thought in amazement, as he looked at her. Every day when he woke up she would be here next to him. He thought about the day he had met her, only a few months ago. It felt like years. She had been so sad that day, mysterious and distant.

Quietly, so as not to wake her, he crept out of bed and went to make breakfast. He had a meeting at ten o'clock and, though he and Sarah never discussed their confidential work, he knew that she had an appointment with Churchill that afternoon.

"Morning, love." Sarah was standing in the kitchen doorway, a white sheet wrapped around her, a sleepy smile on her lips.

"Do you want to get married today?"

"You have to meet my father first."

"By all means, my love."

"Bill, my father, he's . . ." she stopped.

He waited expectantly. "What about him?" he asked.

Sarah searched for the words. "My father is . . . strange. He had a tough time in the Great War."

"Darling, he is your father so I shall love him, however strange he is. Besides, darling, everybody's a little bit strange in one way or another. Before I met you, I tried to hang myself once, remember?" He hugged her to him. "We'll go down to Buckland as soon as we can get leave. Now I have to get ready for work."

Getting away to meet Sarah's father was not as easy as Talbot had hoped. All the military staffs in England were extremely busy. Time was passing too quickly for the hundreds of thousands of details that had to be worked out. On D-Day, which Talbot knew was scheduled for June 5th, the equivalent of 200 trainloads of troops would go ashore from the U.S. First Army alone. There were approximately 200 individual units going in, ranging from a division of 15,000 men to a photographic unit of two soldiers. And Colonel Bill Talbot was doing what he did best: planning, breaking down directives and orders to their lowest denominator, asking questions, studying minute details. His days were full and they were long. He remembered how awed he had felt when Sarah took him to meet the great Winston Churchill. Bill had been sure the encounter would be most awkward for all parties, but the tender rapport between Churchill and Sarah had made the whole affair both pleasant and friendly. Unexpectedly, it turned into a most agreeable visit, and Bill Talbot had felt completely at ease with the Prime Minister and Churchill had felt the same way about Talbot. Their personalities were mutually compatible. They had become friends the moment they met.

Nevertheless, Bill was determined to meet Sarah's father, if that was what she wanted. He concocted a scheme to inspect some units stationed near Buckland and asked Sarah to arrange for Saturday afternoon and Sunday off from her Admiralty duties. He took the train up early Saturday morning and was met by an army car and driver, as arranged. He was conscientious in doing his duty until mid-afternoon, when he had the driver deliver him to the railroad station. There he waited until Sarah's train arrived, and they took a taxi to the Buckland Estate.

The drive from the station took longer than Talbot expected, as the taxi wound through some of the most beautiful countryside he'd ever seen. Rolling, cultivated, green fields seemed to stretch for miles, their splendor pleasantly interrupted by stands of trees— stately oaks, majestic pines, and shimmering beeches. Finally, the taxi turned into a driveway flanked by two large pillars on which sat heraldic beasts. Talbot did not catch sight of the house until they had almost reached the end of its mile-long private road, and to him it looked like a palace. Two stories high, it was an enormous, turreted building with large wings at both ends, each one as imposing as the original manor-house that joined them. Talbot tried to count the chimneys but stopped at a dozen. Arriving at the ornate front doors, Bill paid the driver and asked him to pick them up the next afternoon. He looked around. The house was impressive, but in dire need of repairs and maintenance. The garden, which must have been beautiful once, was now overgrown with weeds. Dead flowers hung on their stems. Grass was growing in the driveway.

"I told you, darling, so don't be so dismayed," Sarah said, seeing the look on Bill's face.

"I think it's very grand," Bill reassured her. "Does your father still have a staff? If not, how do we get in?"

"We just open the door." Sarah turned the massive iron handle, and one of the doors swung open. "Daddy!" she shouted. "It's Sarah."

Her words echoed through the dark, cavernous hall. Bill smelled mildew as they entered. The late afternoon sunlight streamed through the open door and the leaded glass windows, enabling them to see well enough to make their way through the hall. Sarah took them through the maze of rooms to the rear terrace. Beyond the terrace, they spotted several people working in a vegetable garden.

"Oh, there they are."

Walking down the path, they came to an old man resting on his knees, a small garden trowel in his hand. When he saw Sarah, he smiled and slowly rose to his feet. He was tall and handsome, with white hair and the same blue eyes as his daughter.

"Daddy, this is Colonel Bill Talbot. Bill, my father."

"Your Lordship," said Bill with a slight bow.

"Please. Call me Ned, Colonel. Ned Fitz-William."

"Thank you, sir."

The Earl of Buckland passed a hand across his brow. "Whatever happened to Scott Hayward?" he asked Sarah. "You and he used to be great friends."

"Oh, Dad, you remember. He was killed a long time ago. In North Africa."

"Too bad," said the earl. "Though I never liked him, I knew his father well."

A large woman in an old cotton print dress approached with two small children in tow.

"This is the Flynn family," Sarah said. "They were evacuees from London during the Blitz, and luckily they've stayed on. They're a great help to my father." She smiled at the children. "I want you to meet Colonel Talbot. The colonel is an American paratrooper."

The children's eyes widened.

"Colonel Talbot and I are going to be married."

"Imagine that," said Mrs. Flynn, smiling.

The earl seemed confused. "You're going to marry? I thought you were married to that Hayward fellow." Sarah ignored her father's memory lapse.

"Daddy, Bill is my fiancé."

"Congratulations, Colonel."

Bill suggested to Sarah that she and her father have tea on their own to catch up on things.

Then, while they were at tea, he intended to have a long chat with Mrs. Flynn in the kitchen, in hopes of discreetly finding out the situation at Buckland.

After offering her an entire box of chocolates and watching

her eyes shine, he pulled an orange out of his bag and gave it to her. Such items were like gold and, to return the favor, she probably would have told him anything he wanted to know.

"You must like it here to have stayed," said Talbot.

"Well, sir, it's not that we like it so good. But, you see, my Willie got himself killed at Dunkirk during the evacuation from France, you know."

"Yes, I understand." As Talbot knew, the Germans thought they'd won the war after they'd overrun Europe in that summer of 1940. Thank God, the British army got away at Dunkirk and lived to fight another day, except for a few good men who held off the German army so their comrades could escape. "Your husband must have been a brave man to have stayed and fought."

"Oh, no, sir. Willie was one of the first to get aboard a ship and leave Dunkirk, sir. Only trouble was the ship got itself sunk, it did, and that was that. Willie went to the bottom. Anyway, the main reason we stayed on was to help his lordship."

"I understand he's also a little bit hard up these days."

"Yes, sir. Like all of us. His lordship explained he can't pay us nothing for helping out, but we helps out anyway. He's a kind man, a bit confused now and again, but a lovely man."

"Yes, I noticed that," Talbot said.

"The earl was gassed in the Great War, sir, and was in real bad shape, they says. He was the youngest of three brothers. His two brothers and his father, they got themselves killed in the Great War, and the death duties took all the money. And his lordship, like I say, got gassed bad, and he had to take over the title then, which was wicked because he didn't have no money to support this place or nothing, and he couldn't sell it. Has something to do with the old laws of the land. But he couldn't work on account of the gassing and what it done to his head."

Bill shook his head. "Sad," he said.

"Yes, sir. In the village they remembers his father, sir. They say there must have been twenty servants in the house, gardeners, butlers, footmen, maids, cooks, chauffeurs, and all the rest. But now all the money's gone and there ain't hardly nothing coming in, since all the rents and other income goes to pay the debts what's due."

"And the earl's wife, his countess?" said Bill. "I understand she died?"

Mrs. Flynn nodded. "In the village they says she couldn't stand living in this place, especially without money." She leaned over and whispered to Talbot, "They says she done away with herself, they do. His lordship is the one what found her, and that's one of the reasons he's a little . . . forgetful and all, don't you see. They say he loved her very much . . ."

"There you are." Sarah's voice startled them both. Bill sprang to his feet.

"I thought I'd have my tea with Mrs. Flynn," he said. "How'd it go with you and your father?"

Instead of answering, Sarah turned to Mrs. Flynn abruptly. "His lordship wants me to sleep in the upstairs north wing, in the queen's room."

"Yes, ma'am."

"And he wants the colonel to sleep in the south wing, in the Cecil suite."

"Very good, ma'am."

Bill extended his hand to Mrs. Flynn. "Thanks for joining me for tea," he said smiling.

Before Mrs. Flynn could shake his proffered hand, Sarah said, "Come, darling, it's time we both joined Dad."

Bill didn't have an opportunity to talk to Sarah before dinner. Their rooms were at opposite ends of the manor, and the earl's quarters were between them. The place was a wreck. A layer of dust covered the furniture and floor. The sheets were musty. Idly, he wondered if there was a good hotel or inn somewhere in the neighborhood. He decided he'd slip Mrs. Flynn a tenner to clean things up before he went to bed.

The stairway was rather grand, Talbot thought as he descended, bathed and dressed in a clean uniform. In the hall, the Earl of Buckland sat waiting for him. He was in dinner dress, a tuxedo with black bow tie. Talbot smiled and presented his lordship with a bottle of twelve-year-old scotch whiskey, which he had brought especially for the occasion.

"Oh, I say, I can't accept this," said the earl. "It's worth its weight in gold."

"Please take it as a favor to me," said Bill.

"Sarah says you and she are engaged," said the earl pleasantly, as he scrutinized the label on the bottle.

"Yes, sir. We hope you approve."

The earl waved his hand. "Sarah's over twenty-one. I don't think we've ever married any Americans before, but I understand people do it all the time, so why not." He smiled again. "Let's open this, do you mind?"

Before Bill could ask where the pantry was, Sarah came downstairs, looking so stunning she took Bill's breath away.

"You look lovely, my dear," said her father.

Sarah kissed them each on the cheek. She took the bottle from her father. "I'll go get Mrs. Flynn and have her mix us all a drink."

After a stiff scotch and soda, the earl seemed to pick up considerably. "Thank God for Mrs. Flynn," he said. "I don't know what I'd do without her. But, do you know, at one time, we had thousands of people living here. All from London. When the Boche stopped bombing London every night, they all went back, except for Mrs. Flynn and her two little boys. Now, the damned government wants to take over Buckland Manor to billet troops of some kind. I tell you, son, we've got to do something."

Sarah said very quietly, "Daddy, there were not thousands of people living here. There were four or five families. But, you see, Bill, my father's not used to having people around."

"That reminds me," said the earl. "When are you coming back? I miss you, my dear."

"There's a war on, Daddy," said Sarah. "I miss you too. Now, let's go have dinner."

The dining room was huge and elegant. Oil portraits lined

the wood-panelled walls. The long table was bare except for the three places set at the end nearest the kitchen. Two exquisite silver candelabra gave off more than enough light to see by. The food was bland, but when the earl poured the claret from a decanter, Talbot took a tentative sip and leaned back in his chair with a sigh of contentment. It was the best wine he'd ever tasted, and he'd tasted quite a few.

"Buckland has always been well known for its cellars," the earl explained.

By the time the wine was finished and Mrs. Flynn had been sent to fetch another bottle from the cellar, Bill and the Earl of Buckland were telling each other anecdotes and laughing together as if they had known each other for years. Bill had noticed that the earl's confusion seemed to come and go. But tonight he was perfect company, and Sarah seemed overjoyed to see her father in such good form.

Bill and Sarah slept apart that night, and the next morning Bill woke up tired. He dressed and went downstairs to the kitchen. Restored after his coffee, which he'd brought with him and donated to the house, Talbot went walking with Sarah. She pointed out various plants and flowers that were still growing and in bloom. She showed him the small chapel, which had been locked up for some time now. "That's where I'd like us to get married," she said happily.

"If we're going to be married soon, darling, I'm afraid it won't be here. We can't possibly get away again. We were lucky this time."

"But after the troops have left to invade Europe, you'll still be here, and we'll get married."

"All right," he said. "If you really want to wait."

"There's Dad," she said, pointing. "He's up. I wanted to wait to let him show you the rest of the house. I knew he'd want to."

The Earl of Buckland didn't seem any the worse for his evening's frolic. "Hello, hello, hello," he greeted them on the front steps of the manor. "How did you sleep?" he asked Talbot.

"Just fine, sir."

"Good. Good. Nothing like a fine claret to make a man sleep well, I always say."

"Dad, would you like to show Bill around inside?"

"By all means."

Buckland Manor was like a museum. Talbot had never seen so many paintings by Joshua Reynolds, Gainsborough, Lawrence, and Romney, to say nothing of the Rembrandts, van Dykes, Constables, and Turners. The earl passed them all by rather offhandedly and became enthusiastic only when they got to the Stubbs paintings of horses and dogs, where he spent half an hour admiring and directing Bill's attention to their fine points. The furniture was shabby, but its quality was still discernible. Bill's first impression had been right. Buckland was a palace. But it was neglected and run-down. Well, Bill thought, if this war ever ends, the first thing I'm going to do is fix this place up for Sarah's father.

The study was large and lined from floor to ceiling with volumes of literary works, all on mahogany shelves. The windows were closed, and even after the earl opened them, there remained the moldy smell of mildewing old books. His lordship began coughing and couldn't stop for a good ten minutes. "Are you all right, sir?" asked Bill.

"Yes, yes," replied the earl between coughs. "I was gassed, you see."

Bill was about to start coughing, too. The air was close, and he knew the musty smell as much as the gassing was bothering his host.

After the earl caught his breath, Bill decided to get right to the point. "Sir, I'd like your permission to marry your daughter."

"Sarah? You want to marry Sarah?" His lordship sounded as though this was the first time he'd heard about it. Talbot wondered if the coughing had somehow confused his brain again.

"Yes, sir. I believe she might have mentioned it to you . . ."

"You know, I think Sarah's married already."

"He was killed, sir. In the war. Sarah's a widow, and I want to marry her."

"She doesn't inherit, you know. Buckland, title and all, goes to a male cousin. You know that?"

Bill shrugged. "Money isn't a problem."

The earl scratched his head.

"Sir. May I marry your daughter?"

"Well, yes, if it's all right with her . . . No dowry, I'm afraid."

Bill rose from his chair. "Thank you, sir," he said. "Thank you very much."

∞

The train was packed returning to London, but Bill had purchased first-class tickets, so their compartment was not as crowded as the other coaches. Sitting beside the window, Sarah turned and pretended to be looking at the scenery, even though they were still in the station. But Bill could see by the shaking of her shoulders that she was weeping softly. As the train began moving, he was unsure whether to leave her alone or try to comfort her. In the end, he put a hand on each of her shoulders and turned her towards him. She didn't resist. Tears were rolling down her cheeks.

"I never dreamed it would be so bad."

"Oh, come, darling, it wasn't that bad. I like your father. He and I got on just fine. His memory fails him once in a while, but at his age, that's quite forgivable."

Sarah nodded. "Thanks."

"I gave Mrs. Flynn three hundred pounds to air out the study, clean the books, and make sure your father's room is clean and the sheets washed. I asked her to make your father as comfortable as possible as long as the money lasts, and when it's gone I'll send some more."

Sarah was shocked. "But you can't afford to do that."

"Sarah, my darling, I could buy Buckland Manor if you wanted it." He laughed at her expression. "I'm what you English call 'an American millionaire.'"

Sarah just stared at him, speechless.

In London, springtime was thought to be the most heavenly time of year. The tulips were out in Hyde Park, and the constant rains were replaced with sunny days. But Bill hardly noticed the change. By May, his workload had become so great that he was rarely home before midnight. It was exhausting and he missed Sarah. He hoped that he would spend a lot more time with her after the troops had left for the continent.

Tonight, Bill was exuberant. It was only six o'clock and he was finished working for the day. More importantly, he'd learned that Bradley was planning to leave part of his staff in London, at least for several months after the invasion, perhaps permanently, as a rear echelon, and Bill was already beginning to pull strings to get assigned to that staff.

He felt on top of the world again as he opened the door, anxious to tell Sarah the good news. Sarah was sitting beside the fireplace and Bill sensed immediately that something was wrong. Her face was pale, even in the fire's glow, and reflected a sadness he'd never seen in her before, not even on that day he first met her on the beach.

"Is something wrong, darling?"

"My father died this morning."

Bill sat down and took her hand in his. "How did it happen?"

"It was so nice today that Dad decided he'd take a swim in the brook." She shook her head. "The water must have been colder than he expected. He had a heart attack."

"Oh, darling . . ."

"I have to go to Buckland tomorrow. As soon as I can get things arranged at the Admiralty."

"I'll come with you."

"You know you can't get away now."

"Bradley will have to give me a few days off."

"No, I'll go on my own. I'll be fine."

Bill knew she was right. There was almost no chance that he could be spared.

"How long do you think you'll be gone?"

"No idea. There'll be a lot to do though, and I'm the only one who's in a position to do it."

Sarah put her arms around Bill's neck and said softly, "You see, you're all I've got now. I couldn't stand any of this if I didn't have you."

"Don't worry, you have me forever."

As he leaned down to kiss her, there was a knock at the door. Sarah looked at Bill, inquiringly. He shrugged his shoulders.

"It's not my house. Not yet, anyway," he smiled.

"Who is it?" she called.

"It's Jocko," came the reply from the other side of the door.

Bill immediately started grabbing all the masculine items he could spot in the living room—his officer's cap, his raincoat, his sweater and scarf. Sarah quickly tidied up the cushions and pillows.

"Hold on, Jocko. I have to make myself presentable."

"If it's not convenient, I'll come back later."

"Of course it's convenient. I'll be right there."

Bill was already on his way into the safety of the bedroom. They had continued to keep their love affair a secret at Bill's insistence. There would be time enough to let people know, and Bill wanted to secure a more permanent post in London in the meantime.

Opening the door, Sarah greeted Jocko warmly.

"The door was open downstairs, so I came up. I just heard about your father. I'm so sorry. Do you need anything?"

Behind the door of the bedroom, Bill could hear them clearly.

"Thank you, Jocko. You're always so considerate. I'm all right at the moment. I'm going to Buckland in the morning."

"What will you do now?" D'Arcy asked kindly.

"What do you mean?"

"Who will take care of you?"

"I've been getting along pretty well on my own for some time now."

"Sarah, you don't have to put on a brave front for me. You lost your son, your husband, now your father. It's too much for one person to bear."

"No, I'll pull though. You know that. And Scott was never much help to me anyway."

"Your husband was a son of a bitch. I hated the way he treated you."

"So did I," Sarah said, looking away in embarrassment.

"Sarah, if you need me, any time at all, I'm here for you."

"You're sweet, but you shouldn't worry about me, Jocko. You should find a nice lady and marry her."

"There's only one woman who I want as my wife," D'Arcy said softly. "It's you."

"I'm flattered, truly. And it means a lot to me that you are my friend. But I can't marry you."

"I understand," D'Arcy said flatly.

"No, Jocko, I don't think you do." Sarah took a deep breath. "It isn't you. I think you are wonderful. But I'm in love with someone else."

"So you told me," said D'Arcy. After a long silence, he asked, "But you never told me who. Is it anyone I know?"

"Yes. It is." D'Arcy stood there expectantly. Sarah knew that she and Bill had agreed to say nothing, but suddenly she didn't have the energy for any more secrets. If she told D'Arcy he wouldn't dare make things difficult for Bill.

"I'm going to marry Bill Talbot, Jocko. As soon as possible."

"I see." Even through the bedroom door, Bill Talbot could sense the resentment in D'Arcy's voice. "When did this happen?"

"Recently."

"So the best man won again," said Jocko facetiously, his voice laden with ill-concealed malice. "Well, I guess I'll be going. Wouldn't want Bill to drop in and find me here."

Bill heard Sarah escorting D'Arcy to the door. He heard the door close and came out of the bedroom.

"Well, I guess it's official now," she said. "I'd better start packing."

"Not so fast."

"Bill, don't be angry. I had to tell him about us. I wanted him to hear it from me first. It was wrong of me not to have told him sooner."

"I'm not talking about D'Arcy, darling." She looked at him in confusion. "Now, tell me about what a bastard Scott Hayward really was."

Sarah breathed a sigh of relief. "I guess I should have talked about it, but I didn't think it was nice to speak ill of the dead."

"What was D'Arcy talking about?"

"Scott was a womanizer. He left me for long periods of time. Everyone knew. Even Neddy knew. And he and D'Arcy's wife were lovers at one time. D'Arcy tried to kill him once." She paused. "I've never said this before, but a part of me was actually relieved when he died. I thought that I'd be free of all the pain he brought me. I felt so guilty for even thinking that way that I kept away from men after he died just to punish myself. But the truth is, he was a real bastard, and I should have left him. When Neddy died, all he could say was 'stiff upper lip.' I loathed him for that."

Sarah stopped and looked at Talbot. "I wish you could have known Neddy."

"I do too, Sarah." Bill cupped her face in his hands. "I'm going to make sure nothing ever hurts you again, darling." He kissed her softly.

"The only reason I married Scott, I think, was because he'd been in the Great War just like Dad, even though Scotty was in it for only a short time at the end. Afterwards, he had a few low-paying Foreign Office jobs with big titles. He was, apparently, good at soldiering. He went back into the army when the war started and rose to the rank of brigadier fairly fast."

Bill decided to change the subject. He had heard quite enough about the late departed Scott Hayward. He got the picture very clearly. "I didn't know Jocko was married."

"It was the same kind of marriage mine was. Her name was Anne de Warenne, but she was fairly discreet as long as Jocko was around. She was a little bit afraid of him, I believe. But she flaunted her affairs just as soon as Jocko left for North Africa. She was killed while dining out with another man at a night club which was quite famous for having telephones on the tables. Everybody in the place was killed . . ."

Bill nodded. Now he understood Jocko's reluctance to discuss that particular bombing.

∞

General Bradley and Field Marshal Montgomery rose to their feet signalling that the high-level staff meeting was coming to a close. Major General Jocko D'Arcy knew that he had to act quickly. A sly, almost crafty, expression flitted unwittingly across his face.

"I'd like to make a suggestion," D'Arcy said slowly.

Bradley nodded for him to proceed.

"I think it would be an excellent idea if several of our senior planning officers were to go to France after the invasion to see how well the troops followed our plans in actual combat situations. Whether or not, in practice, they were able to conform to our overall strategy."

"Sounds sensible," Montgomery agreed.

"What sort of officer do you recommend we send over?" Bradley asked.

"A combat veteran, possibly one out of action due to wounds, somebody who's been in on the strategic preparations from the beginning. Somebody like your Colonel Bill Talbot." He paused to let his words sink in.

"Yes, he'd be perfect," said General Bradley. "He's smart, conscientious, and completely dependable."

D'Arcy's expression didn't change, but if any of the other officers had looked in his eyes, they would have seen a cold glint of triumph shining through.

∞

Bill was careful to avoid D'Arcy after his call on Sarah. He knew that sooner or later he would have to see him, but he wanted to put it off until Sarah returned from Buckland. Anyway, D'Arcy had no idea that Talbot had been listening, so perhaps he wouldn't mention a thing.

As it turned out, Talbot didn't have to hide from his friend. A few days later, five minutes after he'd arrived at the office one of his aides, a lieutenant named Jackson, knocked on his door.

"Sir. You're to take a physical this morning."

He thrust a paper into Talbot's hand. "Everything's here, Colonel."

"Why the hurry?" Talbot asked. "They checked me out last month."

Jackson shook his head. "I don't know, sir. But it's marked 'Rush.' "

Talbot looked at the paper he held in his hand. It was a directive to Colonel William E.B. Talbot, D.S.C., to report at once to the head medical examiner at the nearest army hospital. The names of the doctor and the hospital were also written on the paper.

The doctor was a man named Marks whom Bill knew and liked. At the end of the examination, which consisted mainly of testing Bill's ability to use his right leg, Doctor Marks seemed satisfied. "No more trouble with the leg, then?"

Talbot shook his head. "No. I get along fine. Haven't had to use the cane for a couple of months now, not even in the damp weather."

The doctor felt along the entire leg, pushing here and there. He glanced up at the X-rays taken on previous visits.

"You're okay, Colonel," he said finally. "Completely and perfectly healed."

"That's great," said Talbot, "but I could've told you that, myself. Anyway, why all the hurry? You usually give me a week or two's notice."

"I don't know. We got orders to find out immediately—if not sooner—if you're fit for combat duty."

Talbot's heart sank. He was afraid his voice would tremble as he asked, "Well, am I?"

"I don't see why not," replied the doctor, smiling.

Bill Talbot was crushed. The very last thing he wanted right now was to go back into combat again.

∞

"What's all this about my getting a combat command?" asked Talbot as calmly as he could. General Bradley looked up from his desk and smiled at him.

"That's what you said you wanted when you first got here. What we have in mind isn't much of a 'command,' but you sure will get shot at. That's why we had the medicos give you a going over. If the slot opens up, we want to know whether you can fill it or not. It's comforting to know you can."

"Thank you, sir."

"To be honest, we hadn't even considered shipping you out until someone suggested that you go over after the invasion to see how things were progressing from the planning angle. We saw immediately from your record that you are far too qualified for anything like that. You're a West Point graduate; you trained as a paratrooper; you jumped into Sicily, were awarded the D.S.C, to say nothing of the exceptional work you've done here in London.

"It got us thinking. There's another mission that's absolutely perfect for you, but it can only be handled by somebody qualified for combat. Since you were already in the pipeline to France when this new proposal came up, it was obvious that you were our man.

I can't give you any details yet, but it's almost certain you'll be shipping out soon. I knew you'd be pleased."

Bill looked puzzled. "So if I hadn't already been in the pipeline to France, as you put it, you wouldn't have given me this other assignment?"

Bradley shook his head. "It probably never would have occurred to me. I'd have kept you in my headquarters, possibly in London, for the duration."

Talbot smiled, saluted and left. What else could he do? There was no way he could tell General Bradley that he had changed his mind.

When he returned to his small office, Lieutenant Jackson was waiting for him.

"How did it go, sir?"

"Fine. Just fine," said Talbot. Before he entered his office and closed the door, he said, "Please get me Lady Sarah on the phone, will you? She's in Buckland."

It took Mrs. Flynn some time to find Sarah. Finally she came to the phone. "I was just packing to come back, darling. I feel I've been here too long as it is."

She gave him the details of the quiet funeral and how sad it was. Finally, Bill told her about the medical exam and the possibility of a combat command.

Sarah was quiet. "Look, darling, I don't want you to leave me. Ever. And we'll try to do everything we can to prevent it. But, if you have to, then you have to, and that's that. You can't just run out. You couldn't do it, and I wouldn't let you. Tell me this, is your leg well enough for you to parachute out of an airplane? I think you told me it wasn't."

"No," he said. "I think my jumping days are over."

"I'm certainly glad of that. Let's wait and see what happens," she said. "Right now, we're just guessing. This whole thing might be a false alarm. Mightn't it? Besides, colonels lead pretty safe lives behind the lines. They aren't supposed to get killed. As long as you don't go leading any charges, you'll be all right." But she knew colonels could be killed. Her husband had gotten killed, and he was a brigadier.

∞

Talbot was summoned once more to General Omar Bradley's office. The general was cordial.

"Sit down, Bill, sit down. Let's get back to the assignment we have for you. I've been talking to Max Taylor and Matt Ridgway. As you know, their two airborne divisions jump into France the night before the invasion. They want airborne landing parties to come ashore with the beach assault troops to act as liaison between the paratroopers and the infantry, so they won't shoot each other up when they meet. One of them has to be commanded by a fairly high ranking, experienced officer, preferably one who's made at least one combat jump. Do you know anybody who fills those requirements?"

Talbot smiled. "I think I do, sir," he said.

"You can handle it, then?"

"Yes, sir. I can handle it fine. But there are paratroop officers with a lot more experience than I have. Younger, quicker men, maybe. I just want you to know that."

"I know it already. I also know they're all parachuting into France with their units. This is the ideal job for you. Do you accept it, Bill?"

General Bradley's question was mere courtesy. It was unthinkable for Talbot to refuse or even give a qualified answer. His only response could be a crisp, "Yes, sir."

Bradley stood and extended his hand. The meeting was over.

In the days that followed, Talbot learned there would be several similar parties landing with the assault troops on the beaches codenamed Omaha and Utah. The other groups were commanded by captains. When Talbot discovered this, he went to talk to General Bradley about it.

"Why am I the only colonel to lead a liaison group?" he asked as soon as he entered Bradley's office.

"I guess the time has come to tell you, Bill. You're going in on Omaha Beach, the others on Utah. As you know better than anybody, Omaha's going to be tough, a lot tougher than Utah, so we want somebody with a little more rank and experience. We also want an Academy man. You see, Bill, men are going to get killed on that beach. Their leaders will get killed, too. You'll act as a spare senior officer. You'll have no command responsibility until some unit larger than a company loses its commander. Then, you take charge. Anything up to and including a regiment. Even a division. If an assistant division commander, who'll be a brigadier general, gets it and there aren't any regimental commanders left in that division, take over. Understand?"

Talbot nodded. "You feel it's going to be that rough?" he asked.

"It's going to be that rough. But, remember, this operation is being planned as a success. There can be no thought of failure. D-Day is going to be 'do or die.' On those beaches we shall win or we shall lose this war."

"Yes, sir."

☙

Talbot knew from previous briefings why General Bradley expected trouble on Omaha. If there had been another beach available, they wouldn't even have considered landing there. Sheer cliffs, 100 feet high, dominated each end of the beach, which was 300 yards wide at low tide and shelved up to a steep bank, behind which were sand dunes and a sea wall. Beyond the dunes the ground sloped up to a 150-foot-high plateau. Each of the four exit roads from Omaha Beach led to a town fortified by the Germans to block any Allied route off the beach.

Besides the natural obstacles, the Germans had planted the area between high and low water with upright iron frames and heavy wooden stakes angled toward the sea, plus steel hedgehogs that would stave in the bottoms of the landing craft. All the various barriers were mined. In addition, the Germans had the usual barbed wire barricades and antitank ditches, and their weapons were sighted so they could cover every inch of the beach. Artillery consisting of high velocity 88 and 75 mm guns could rake the beach at will; concrete pillboxes, mortar pits, gun casements, firing trenches, bunkers, mine fields, underground bunkers, rocket launchers, and antitank gun emplacements completed the German defensive preparations. A week before the invasion, a first-rate, battle-hardened infantry division from the Russian Front was moved into the area to bolster the troops already in place.

Bill knew he would have preferred to take his chances parachuting behind the enemy lines the night before D-Day instead of landing on Omaha Beach. Going in on D-Day, at this point in his life, was the absolute worst thing that could happen to him. It was the last thing he'd expected, the last thing he wanted. As General Bradley had told him, "It's going to be rough. Men are going to die on those beaches." Planning the assault was one thing; actually landing on Omaha Beach was something else altogether.

After telling Sarah about the physical, he hadn't brought up the subject of combat again. She knew, though. How could she not know? Since she had returned from Buckland he had been in confidential meetings from sunrise until the moon came up. Leaving her, even for a few days, was intolerable to him. The thought that he could be killed and never see her again was inadmissible.

On the night before he was to leave to board his ship for the invasion, Bill left work early. While Sarah cooked dinner, Talbot fixed himself a drink. "I won't be able to come home tomorrow night, darling. I have to work late at the office," he said as casually as he could.

Sarah came into the living room, a cooking spoon in her hand.

"So, it's on." It was a statement, not a question. "And you're going."

She came over to Talbot, put her arms around his waist and pulled herself tightly to him. For several moments they stood still, embracing each other wordlessly.

"Look, darling," he said at last. "I'm going as a sort of liaison officer, an observer, almost. I'll be so far to the rear that I might as well have stayed in London."

"You never did tell me what your job is," she said. "But they checked you out physically for a combat command, didn't they?" She jerked her head away and looked Talbot in the eye. "They wouldn't have done that if you were going to stay in the rear. Please, darling, don't try to protect me."

God, how he loved this woman. And she was right. She deserved to know the truth.

"I'm going into battle. It will be very, very bad, and I may not come back to you," he said at last. "When I fought at Santa Bianca I had nothing to lose. I was running away from a broken heart, and that made me fearless. Now I have everything to lose and I'm afraid. Before, they called me a hero and gave me a medal for bravery. But I wasn't brave . . . just careless. Leaving you tomorrow will be the first courageous thing I have ever done."

Sarah rested her head on his shoulder. "Don't worry. I won't cry. I won't make it hard for you. There's a monstrous war on, and you're in it. I understand that all too well. Just be sure to write."

The last sentence almost didn't come out. For all her brave words, she sank into his arms and wept.

Talbot stood by the ship's railing, field glasses to his eyes, watching the invasion of Normandy get torn to pieces on Omaha Beach. He could see boats being blown out of the water, tanks blazing at the water line, and bodies strewn over the beach. He shuddered involuntarily and removed the glasses from his eyes. Even without them, he could still see columns of smoke rising from the shore. There must have been thirty or forty boats still standing offshore waiting to get through the maze of broken landing craft, smashed vehicles, and the remaining mined German obstacles. The German artillery was picking them off like ducks in a shooting gallery.

"Colonel Talbot, sir."

Talbot turned. A young infantry captain saluted smartly. "Please get your party ready, sir. We're going in now."

Talbot looked at his watch. It wasn't yet ten o'clock. That meant they would be going in way ahead of schedule. "Things are bad on the beach, sir," the captain said, as if he read his mind. "They don't want any more matériel. They want combat troops and tanks, and they want them fast."

Talbot nodded. Besides Captain Rosenberg, whose assignment he had demanded before he left, he had two radio men, both sergeants, one named Blackstone, the other O'Leary. All three were standing nearby.

"We're ready," said Talbot. The captain saluted again and departed.

As his boat began its race for shore, Talbot sensed that the battle for Omaha Beach had reached the crisis stage. The guns of the *Texas* were firing as fast as they could be loaded; destroyers were running in so close to the shore they seemed to be trying to beach themselves. But, at the last moment, they turned and fired salvo after salvo at the German strong points on the shore. Yes, thought Talbot, things are getting hot. The guns of the U.S. fleet were probably the only artillery the infantry on shore could count on.

Bill Talbot had never deceived himself that this would be an easy landing, but the actuality was far worse than even he could have imagined. When his boat got into the debris of war, and the shells started to hurl geysers of water into the air around him, drenching him with salt water, Talbot became convinced he wouldn't live to see the sun go down. Wrecked boats floated past, life preservers, bodies, pieces of canvas, first aid kits, cartridge belts. Talbot felt his skin prickle. It was the tremendous size of the invasion that made the confusion so ghastly. The slaughter of men and the destruction of equipment were on a scale heretofore unimaginable. Yet the boats continued to grind into the shore in reasonably good order. Then, as the shells and machine-gun bullets began to break up the formations, they became a wild jumble of watercraft, each boat trying to make the beach any way possible, passing the sinking, the burning, the damaged and shattered, sometimes colliding with them and becoming casualties in their turn. Some, trying to take evasive action, strayed from the paths cleared by the engineers and blew up on the mined stakes or were gutted by the steel girders placed in the water for that purpose. By the way the crew handled her, Talbot knew this was not the boat's first combat landing, and she might have an even chance of making the beach in one piece.

They were almost there now. The shallow water swirled beneath them, red with the blood of the wounded and the dead. The crunch on the sand almost threw Talbot off his feet. The ramp splashed into the breaking surf.

The infantrymen lunged forward, for an instant happy to have something solid beneath their feet. For most, that comfort was short-lived. Some fell thrashing in the water adding their blood to its spreading crimson stain; others made the dry land only to fall hard, knocked off their feet by the enemy's machine guns, their helmets flying in one direction, their rifles in another.

Talbot stood frozen to the deck of the landing craft, watching the panorama unfold. If he'd been a private, somebody would have shoved him hard and told him to move his ass. He took a deep breath and turned to Rosenberg.

"Okay, soldier," he said calmly. "It's time to get off the boat."

Wading through the surf, Talbot tried to move fast. But the water made his progress terrifyingly slow. The sounds of firing came from all directions. A stream of machine gun bullets stitched the water to his right, slightly off the mark. The wind, he thought. It was the wind that blew those bullets away from us. Next time we might not be so lucky. He passed a man lying in the water, helmet off, face gray, floating out to sea. Another had raised himself on his hands to get his head above water. Talbot grabbed him under his arm and dragged him shoreward. Rosenberg churned up beside him and hooked his free arm around the man's other armpit. On the beach, a few yards from the water's edge they dropped him. At least he wouldn't drown. Somebody was sure to pick him up before the tide covered him.

Talbot hit the ground just as a German mortar shell exploded.

He looked to his rear. Rosenberg was lying flat behind him, and beyond him were the two radio men. Good. Shells and machine gun bullets thudded and pounded all over the beach. For a moment, Talbot lost his composure. He couldn't think or move. His mind became numb until it suddenly awoke and told him to get moving or he'd be killed just as surely as one day followed another.

He had to get away from the beach. That's where the Germans were concentrating their fire now. When he thought the enemy fire had gotten momentarily lighter, he rose to his feet and dashed forward. He knew Rosenberg would lead the other men, and they would follow him. Talbot didn't look back. He zigzagged for a few yards, then hit the ground, trying to make himself as difficult a target as possible for the German gunners. Up again, he zigged right and left, raced forward, then hit the ground. He wondered if he'd been hit and knew he wouldn't feel it if he had. He was too pumped up. Only a killing or disabling blow would even slow him down. The danger would be bleeding to death before he knew he was struck.

Halfway up the beach, he lay panting on the shale. Talbot could feel the ground shake as large shells exploded nearby. He could feel the sting of broken shale hitting his body. He looked behind him. His team had followed him and lay flat a few yards away. The radio men had been chosen by Rosenberg from the paratroops. Thank God my men are all combat-experienced, Talbot thought.

He was on his feet again, running forward, trying to get to the rise in the ground ahead of him. There was protection there. He knew the terrain. He just hoped he had the stamina to make it.

Almost as soon as he flopped down on the beach after his last dash forward, he felt a tug on his ankle. He turned. Rosenberg was pointing to his rear and trying to say something. Through the smoke and exploding shells, Talbot saw the two radio men lying on their backs, their stomachs ripped open. He gasped. Now at his side, Rosenberg was pulling his arm. "I'm hit," he croaked. "Leg. Don't think I can go . . ."

Rosenberg's leg was sopping with blood.

"Medic!" Talbot yelled above the din of battle. A G.I. with the distinctive red crosses on large white circles on his helmet and on his white armband came jogging up to them. Talbot patted Rosenberg on the back and got ready to move forward again.

"See you in Paris."

He looked back. There were so many bodies, so many dead G.I.s. And the enemy fire continued to rake the troops coming in. They couldn't miss. Yet the men kept coming. God, how brave they were. Inexperienced draftees were charging into almost certain death and never looking back. In that moment, despite the carnage and the destruction on the beach at Omaha, Bill Talbot took renewed courage from the bravery of the men around him. In his heart he knew men like that could be killed but could never be defeated.

With newfound vigor, he leapt forward, his legs churning, his rifle at high port. Once more, he was a determined, purposeful leader. He motioned other men to follow him wherever he saw them—in groups, alone, he didn't care. He was running towards the plateau. He was going up that plateau through the draw in front of him. He was going over it, and he was going to take as many men with him as he could. To hell with this beach. We're going up there where we have a fighting chance to make those damned Germans pay for what they've done. We're going to skin their Nazi hides!

∞

Talbot was still panting as he lay on the top of the rise. G.I.s all around him were firing, holding a line while other men kept coming up the ridge in small groups to join them. A blond major without a helmet flopped down beside him. "I'm Kelly. Third Battalion. Somebody told me there was a colonel up here with us."

"Colonel Talbot. On detached service from SHAEF to liaison with the paratroops."

"Well, sir," said the major. "You just brought our First Battalion up the hill."

"You've got two battalions," said Talbot. "If you can find one more, you'll have a regiment."

Kelly didn't answer right away. Then he said, "The second was supposed to be the reserve battalion, sir. But they had to come in sooner than anybody planned. The German guns shot their boats out of the water. They never made it to shore."

"What happened to the First Battalion commander? And what happened to your colonel?"

"Major Sims, First Battalion, got cut almost in half by a Jerry machine gun, sir. Our colonel got hit on the beach. The medic said he had to get first aid or he'd bleed to death, but the colonel said he'd catch up later."

Talbot was silent for a moment. As the senior infantry officer on top of the rise in front of Omaha Beach, he was going to have to take over. Mentally, he began organizing the two-battalion unit to be an effective force against the enemy. "How long have you been with the division?" he asked Major Kelly.

"Since Sicily."

Talbot nodded. That was good. Kelly was battle-experienced. "Which of the company commanders of the First Battalion can take over the battalion?"

The major didn't hesitate. "Captain Irving," he replied, "Company B. Been company commander since North Africa. Would've been battalion except we got some new majors and light colonels when we got to England to train for the invasion."

"Send for him," said Talbot. Kelly motioned to one of his men, told him what to do, and returned his attention to Talbot.

"You'll lead your Third Battalion. Irving will lead the First. As soon as we can, we jump off for Colleville. What time is it, Major?"

"Almost 1330."

"Has anybody bothered to tell the *Augusta* we're off the beach and moving inland? If they haven't, General Bradley must be about to jump overboard." Kelly told his radio men to put the message into the division network for relaying to corps and army on board the *Augusta*.

Bullets and shells had continued to rain in on them while they spoke. Talbot knew they had to move quickly. They had to convert their fingerhold into a solid fighting line that could meet the enemy on his own terms. Then, they could kick his ass all the way back to Berlin. But first they had to get away from Omaha.

"I'm Irving, sir." The words, coming from behind him, startled Talbot. He turned and saw a rather handsome young man hunched down behind him. The man was tall and lean, and he looked intelligent. Talbot did not recognize him, so the man had made it off the beach on his own.

"How long have you commanded B Company?" asked Talbot without preliminaries.

"Since our original company commander got killed in Tunisia."

"Can you take over the First Battalion?" asked Talbot.

"Yes, sir. I think so," replied Irving.

"Good. You're a major now. Take over the battalion, and good luck."

Irving nodded.

"We're going for Colleville. Can you jump off with your three rifle companies in ten minutes? Less?"

"Yes, sir," said Irving. "What's the signal?"

"When we go, you go."

Both battalions now commanded by Talbot had been badly shot up on the beach and were about half strength when he took over. Many of the men were wounded. But by late afternoon, they were rooting German infantry out of Colleville in vicious house-to-house fighting. Talbot marvelled that troops who had taken such punishment on the beach that morning were still able not only to fight offensively but to drive the enemy before them. It was getting dark. His radios weren't functioning yet, but the linemen were out stringing wires. A grimy messenger came through the blown-out door of the stone house that he had set up as his command post. He saw the colonel's insignia on Talbot's collar and saluted. "Message, sir. I'm to tell you: 29th Division is off of Omaha Beach, too. They already cleared Vierville and they're holding the outskirts of Saint Laurent. So, we hold the Colleville-Saint Laurent Road. That's the message, sir."

They'd made it. They were off the beach. The days ahead were sure to be bloody. The Germans were certain to fight hard.

Now it was only a matter of time and casualties, battles and hardships, misery and suffering. Allied victory was assured in that decisive moment when the first American assault troops broke out of Omaha Beach.

Talbot remained in command of the regiment for only two more days. Then the regular regimental commander, despite his wounds, caught up with his outfit, thanked Talbot for all he had done, and offered to provide him with transportation to the rear.

First Army Headquarters was located in tents in an orchard behind the Pointe du Hoc. Communications wires seemed to flow in every direction.

"Congratulations," Bradley said, when Talbot reported back. "General Heubner told me what a great job you did. He's put you in for another Distinguished Service Cross."

"Thank you, sir."

"I'm going to keep you here in headquarters for now," continued Bradley. "But as soon as one comes up I want you to assume a combat command. We may get a request in a day or so, or it might take weeks. It all depends on who screws up and when they get relieved."

It occurred to Talbot that it might also depend on who got killed and when.

In London, the tremendous workload and stress of the D-Day invasion of Normandy were finally winding down, and Major General D'Arcy had at last been able to get a full night's sleep. Instead of going directly to his office the next morning, he decided to go by to see Bill Talbot. They had not spoken since D'Arcy's visit to Sarah's that evening, and he didn't want his jealousy to be too obvious.

Lieutenant Jackson was at his desk outside Talbot's office.

"I say. Can I see Colonel Talbot for a moment?" D'Arcy asked casually.

Jackson looked up, startled. "No, sir," he stammered awkwardly, as he rose to attention, not knowing exactly how he should handle the question.

"Due soon?"

Jackson shook his head. "I thought you'd know, sir. Colonel Talbot landed on Omaha Beach on D-Day."

D'Arcy sucked in his breath, momentarily losing his aplomb before he was able to ask, "He's all right?"

"I'm afraid we have no news at all, sir."

❧

General Bradley couldn't very well get away from his headquarters to visit the First Army's infantry divisions in the field, so he assigned Talbot to do this for him, with strict orders to report any problems. This would enable the high command to take steps to correct trouble before it got out of hand. As a result, Colonel Talbot became well known among the divisional commanders and got to know most of them. They were good men. There was only one division, the 20th, that really bothered him. The commanding general was Talbot's classmate from West Point, General Philip Sheridan Smith, with whom he was very congenial. Smith was quiet and unassuming, but, Talbot imagined, far too compassionate and gentle to command a division of infantry. Checking the records, he discovered that General Smith had taken over the 20th when it was nothing but a bunch of raw recruits and a few National Guardsmen and had trained it to perfection. Shortly after landing in Normandy, the 20th fought its first battle at St. Anselm against a larger unit of veteran, elite German troops and stopped them cold. It was a magnificent feat of arms. After that, the division performed badly. It couldn't take its assigned objectives. It retreated for no discernible reason. It requested to be placed in reserve to regroup. It caused Talbot to shake his head.

Finally, he sought out the assistant divisional commander, Brigadier General Sam Bingham, a former National Guard officer he knew and liked. Almost the exact opposite of Bill Talbot, Sam Bingham was overweight, red-faced, outgoing, informal, a typical civilian-soldier. He was also bright, and had the confidence of the men under him. Half-way through their conversation, hoping to catch Sam off-guard, Talbot asked bluntly, "Sam, what's wrong with the 20th?"

Bingham hesitated. Finally, he said, "You know, Phil Smith wasn't with us when we came over to Normandy."

"Why?" asked Talbot, trying to hide his astonishment.

"He got sick," said Bingham. "We were combat loaded and ready to go, so we went."

"And in that first battle, at St. Anselm, which you won against all odds?"

"I'm afraid I was the one who took command at St. Anselm. I had to, as ranking officer. When Phil finally arrived, he wanted to fire me. Said we suffered too many casualties."

"What's Smith's problem?"

"He trained this division, Colonel. It's his baby. But, instead of Philip Sheridan Smith, his family should have named him George B. McClellan Smith. He is McClellan to a 'T.' As you'll remember from your Civil War history, General McClellan trained his troops to perfection but failed to use them properly in battle. Failed to press his advantage, refused to take the offensive if he thought he'd suffer casualties that would weaken or destroy any of his units. Phil is just like him. Wants to keep his troops unharmed and intact, a complete unit."

"How do you feel about your boys getting killed? You came from the National Guard. You knew a lot of them."

"You can't win a war without doing some hard-knuckle fighting. Sure, we took our licks when we first got here. But we stopped the German army cold, too. Actually, Colonel, our men are good. They're proud of what they did. But now, they're hanging their heads in shame."

"Why haven't you reported any of this?"

"I've been in the National Guard most of my life and in the army since '41. That's long enough to learn you don't ever report your commanding officer."

However, Talbot was under orders from the top to report

any emergency situations he encountered. He followed his orders
and made his report.

ᚗ

Talbot had just finished his breakfast and was sitting in his tent,
rather satisfied and happy. For three weeks he had waited for a
new command, but he'd decided not to go asking for it. The longer
he was safely away from the front, the better, he thought, as he
took out a piece of paper and started a letter to Sarah. He'd learned
from Sarah's letters that D'Arcy was still in London as he had
anticipated. He had started to reread the letters from Sarah again
when his tent flap opened and a young captain stepped in.

"Colonel Talbot, sir, please report to General Bradley."

ᚗ

General Bradley stood in the middle of his operations tent, surrounded by officers, as he pointed to different areas. "For God's
sake, get moving," were the words he was using most. But he didn't
raise his voice. He didn't berate his officers. He spoke quietly,
urgently, and with authority. But the message was still the same:
"You've got to press harder. Our drive is being slowed down.
You've got to push more aggressively."

He looked up finally and saw Talbot standing beside the tent
flap. He smiled and came over, leading Talbot outside the tent.

"Bill, I need to talk to you in private. I got your report on
the 20th Division, and I've already relieved General Smith."

"Yes, sir. You know, I actually like Phil Smith, sir. It's just
that I'm afraid he's not cut out to be a soldier."

"He'll retain his rank and return to the States to train infantry replacements. It's what he's good at."

Talbot nodded. "I'm glad," he said.

Bradley nodded. "You know Sam Bingham. I've promoted him to major general and given him command of the 20th Division."

Talbot nodded. "A good choice, sir. Sam Bingham is the ideal man for the job. He knows the division inside out."

"I told him the same thing, and we discussed it in detail. Bingham is taking over, but he's going to need help—a good assistant who is an Academy man, knows the army, and has the military experience and the contacts to ensure the competent leadership of the division."

"That makes a lot of sense," said Talbot.

"Do you accept the job?"

Talbot was genuinely startled. The offer was completely unexpected. He had always assumed he'd eventually assume command of a regiment, but now he was being offered a promotion to brigadier general and the post of assistant divisional commander. He nodded. "Yes, sir, of course I accept."

"I assume you get along well with Bingham," commented General Bradley. "He's the one who recommended you for the job, but, I must say, I agree with his judgement."

The two men shook hands, smiling.

∞

Talbot sat in the rear of the command car taking him to his new job. On the front bumper was the red square with the single silver star, indicating it was the vehicle of a brigadier general. The 20th

Division, The Bloody Bayonets, mused Talbot. Officially, they're called the Red Bayonets.

Bill knew they'd earned their distinctive shoulder patch in the Argonne in the Great War. It was a red circle on a neutral background with two parallel red bayonets inside it, both pointing forward. It commemorated a victorious attack they made even though they were completely out of ammunition.

Bradley's words came back to Talbot: speaking slowly, obviously thinking as he spoke, the general had said, "As you know, for the first few days in combat most new divisions suffer a disorder resulting from acute mental shock. Until troops can acclimate themselves to the agony of the wounded, the finality of death, and the realization beyond any doubt that the enemy is trying to kill them, they herd by instinct in fear and confusion. They can't be driven to attack but must be led, and sometimes even coaxed, by their commanders. Whenever possible we try to relieve the severity of that shock by conditioning a new unit in a 'quiet' sector before committing it to attack. Here in Normandy there are no 'quiet' sectors. Every outfit that comes across the beach gets thrown right into the attack, under the most appalling conditions. Yet most of them weather the ordeal with distinction. They recover in a short time. But so far the 20th hasn't recovered as it should have. Now that we've found the problem, I expect you and Sam Bingham to bring the division up to its fighting potential. Otherwise, I'm going to break it up and distribute the men as infantry replacements— which we sorely need right now."

Talbot scratched his head. The 20th got their guts kicked out before their boots were even dry, he thought, stopping that German offensive at St. Anselm. They won the day, though, and they were proud of that. Then, their commanding general arrived and wouldn't let them fight. So, my friend, General Bradley's, evaluation is wrong as far as it concerns the 20th Division. They're like a fast race horse pulled up short by a jockey.

∞

One of the first things Sam Bingham and Bill Talbot did was to call a meeting of their three regimental commanders. The 483rd Regiment's commander was Colonel Leonard Franks, a stocky, tough-looking soldier, the type Talbot was glad to have serving under him. The 484th Regiment was commanded by Colonel Reginald deWitt, tall, slim, and ascetic-looking. DeWitt had a large nose and practically no chin. He always wore a long raincoat which made him appear even taller than he was. The 485th Regiment was commanded by Colonel Red Parks, a pugnacious-looking redhead of about 45. He reminded Talbot of Lieutenant Jones with whom he fought at Santa Bianca. All three expressed the same sentiments. Their men were good, well-trained, and able to defeat anything or anybody who got in their way. Give them their heads, and the generals would see how quickly the division could turn around. Talbot nodded. He liked them all. Bingham said, "All right. Make sure your battalion commanders know there's been a complete change in the command of this division. Our primary mission now is to engage the enemy and beat his tail off. Have them pass it down to the companies and platoons. Prepare your men. We're moving up tomorrow."

Sarah wasn't expecting company, so she was slightly surprised when the buzzer rang, and even more surprised to discover that Jocko D'Arcy was downstairs. After their last awkward conversation she had not heard from him. Sarah opened the door nervously. She sucked in her breath. It must be bad news about Bill.

"What is it, Jocko?"

D'Arcy seemed uncomfortable.

"Has something happened to Bill?" Sarah spoke resolutely, forcing herself to be brave.

D'Arcy didn't answer right away. Powerful emotions were coursing through him. "I did something really awful," he said at last.

Sarah remained silent.

"I have to tell you. I have to tell you it was I who recommended Bill for duty in France . . ."

Sarah clutched her throat.

"But I didn't know the stupid Americans would send him ashore on D-Day at Omaha. I swear I didn't. That wasn't what I wanted."

"What did you want?" Sarah asked, trying desperately to regain her composure. "What could you possibly have been thinking of?"

"I wanted to get Bill out of London. I didn't want him killed."

"Has he been killed?"

D'Arcy shrugged sadly. "I don't know. The casualty lists aren't in from Omaha yet. But Jackson says that no one's heard news of him, and we lost so many men that day. I'm sorry, Sarah."

Sarah felt her anxiety dissipate. That morning, she had received a letter from Bill, so she knew he had survived the landing and, at least at the time he wrote the letter, was alive and well and safely back at General Bradley's headquarters. "Just why did you want Bill Talbot out of London?" she asked finally.

"Because I'm in love with you, and I thought if he were out of the picture for a while I might have a chance of winning you."

"You know me better than that, Jocko."

D'Arcy nodded. "I feel unspeakably guilty. I've never done anything like this before. I don't know what malevolent spirit got into me. I suppose all of us have some element of evil in us, and being in love makes us do irrational things. Especially when we've lost the person we love."

"I understand, Jocko." Sarah paused. "Bill landed safely. His letter arrived this morning."

"Thank God," D'Arcy turned to go. At the door he hesitated. "Forgive me," he said. Then, he was gone.

⚮

Bill Talbot's heart pounded. He was watching one of his regiments go into combat. As the sun began to rise, Talbot's 20th Division riflemen slogged up the road into their attack positions. They had been on the march since three o'clock that morning. Along the hedgerow on their left, a few battle-stained survivors from the division they were relieving sat watching them. Beside the road, Brigadier General Talbot stood in his command car surveying his troops and making sure they saw him there. The booming of artillery could be heard clearly, but nothing was coming into this particular sector. Rifle and machine-gun fire sounded on both flanks, but Talbot was pleased to note that his infantry moved normally, without the jitters usually apparent in second-rate troops. They didn't pause to listen to the firing. They didn't jump into ditches without reason. They simply filed into their positions as ordered. They were obviously crack, well-trained riflemen.

Half an hour later, stunned by the ferocity of the American attack, the Germans were running. Talbot's troops had swept all before them. The officers' attitude had changed quickly. Without the restrictions imposed by General Smith, all regiments attacked successfully. Their casualty rates rose, but the division took its objectives, and the casualty rates of the Germans opposing them soared. Under the command of Bingham and Talbot, the 20th Division rose high on the list of the most dependable, elite units in the U.S. Army.

Bill thought of Sarah constantly. He remembered their last evening together, and his promise to stay far from the action. He had broken that promise, risking his life on Omaha Beach and beyond. Now, though, he was pretty safe in a division's headquarters far from the front—except when he decided to go up to see for himself what was going on, which was often. His heart battled with his soul. He wanted a life with Sarah after this damn war was over. Wanted it so badly he could taste it. But he knew that he was facing his demons for the first time now—he faced death voluntarily now when, more than anything, he wanted to live. And each time he survived he felt stronger, more peaceful.

Progress against the enemy was now slow. The hedgerows were devastating, and the Germans fought well. The Allied timetables were weeks behind schedule. Still, the buildup continued. Troops and vehicles continued to cross the beach and proceed inland like endless sea snakes emerging from the ocean. Talbot made it a point to chat with Sam Bingham regularly to find out on an informal basis whatever he could about the overall situation. Arriving back at division headquarters from the front one afternoon, Talbot proceeded to Sam's office, as usual. The two men had become close friends as well as colleagues.

Bingham was walking up and down distractedly, but he smiled when Talbot entered. "Sit down, Bill. Sit down. I have a bottle of sour mash here, and I was just wondering who I could share it with." He poured two drinks. "It's rough going, isn't it, Bill?"

Talbot nodded.

"Have you heard the latest?" asked Bingham.

"I don't think so. That's why I'm here. I thought you'd tell me." Talbot smiled.

"We're going to break out. We're going to crack the German line and take objectives far beyond our present positions. The air corps is going to carpet the other side of the Periers-Saint Lo Road with tons of bombs, then away we go."

"I hadn't heard the details."

"George Patton's Third Army becomes operational on August 1st. I've heard that his style of fighting is to attack, attack, attack, no matter what the cost."

"He'll shake things up," Talbot agreed.

"The 20th Division's going over to the Third Army after the breakout."

Talbot took a sip of bourbon.

"You were in Sicily," said Bingham. "You fought under Patton. So, what do you think?"

"I served with him in Hawaii, too. Years ago. He's a military genius. But working for a genius is awfully tough, Sam. Let me put it to you this way: We both knew Phil Smith. He was a nice guy. Compassionate, kind and timid. No fire in him. Now, imagine his complete opposite. That's Patton."

Bingham nodded his understanding.

"Bill, if anything happens to me, I want you to take command of the 20th. I've told Bradley, and he agrees."

Talbot laughed. "Nothing will happen to you, Sam. At least, I certainly hope not!"

☞

Talbot wrote to Sarah that night, as usual, to assure her he was not in any danger. The fact was he worried about her now that the buzz bombs were falling on London. He pleaded with her to resign her commission and go live in the country. "Go anywhere that's safe," he wrote. But he knew it was out of the question. He could hardly expect Sarah to abandon her duty when she had quietly agreed that he had to land on Omaha Beach.

☞

One day, when he was doing his routine duties at headquarters, Talbot received a letter from Endicott. He turned it over and saw the address was that of Judge John Phillips Brown. Why would J.P. Brown be writing him? Had something happened to Clarissa?

Dear Bill,

I hope I have your right address. Anyway, I'll take a chance on it. We are all very proud of you, Bill. Everybody in Endicott knows you landed in Normandy on D-Day and have been fighting hard ever since. It must be hell, and if there is anything any of us can do for you to make life more tolerable, please let us know.

As you are aware, Clarissa graduated from Smith last month. And, since I promised you could marry her when she graduated, I intend to make good on that promise. Needless to say, Clarissa is thrilled.

Therefore, Bill, if you can get leave to come to Endicott for the wedding ceremony, that would be wonderful. I'll see what I can do from my end. We probably won't have time for anything fancy because of the war and all that. We'll have a small, family wedding. You request permission from your end, and, as I say, I shall see what I can do from here.

Let me hear from you as soon as you have a chance.

Warm regards, J.P.

Bill scratched his head and read the letter again. Something very peculiar was going on here. Why hadn't Clarissa written to him herself? Had she gotten his last letter? He had made it very clear that he was engaged to marry Sarah.

"Bullshit!"

The words made Talbot jump. It was Sam Bingham.

"Why are you doing this?" he demanded, handing Bill an official-looking piece of paper.

Talbot began to read. In his hand was a directive granting special leave to Brigadier General William E.B. Talbot to proceed to the United States (referred to as the "Zone of the Interior" in the directive) for the purpose of getting married and thereafter assignment to a training unit in the Z.I.

"I'll be damned!" said Talbot. "They must be desperate. Ignore it, Sam."

"You didn't have anything to do with this?"

"What do you think? Of course, I didn't. It's the work of

one Judge John Phillips Brown, who happens to be a personal friend of the President. For some reason, he wants me to marry his daughter. What do we do to squash this thing?"

Sam Bingham's scowl had already been replaced by a smile. "What did you do, Bill? Knock the girl up?"

Talbot had to laugh. "Not unless you can do it by proxy," he replied. Then, he stopped laughing as a very nasty suspicion entered his mind. But he shrugged it off. Impossible. Win had his balls shot off, hadn't he?

"I'll tell them I can't spare you," said Bingham.

And that was that. Except Bill still worried. If J.P. Brown had this kind of power with the President, could he get mad enough at Bill Talbot to get him sacked?

Bill was uneasy. And baffled. That night, he wrote a very long letter to Sarah, telling her what had happened. He hoped it reached her before she got wind of any rumors.

◌

Lieutenant General Lesley McNair had been appointed Chief of Staff of the U.S. Army General Headquarters in 1940 and had completely reorganized the army's training methods. The G.H.Q. concept gave way to McNair's Army Ground Forces, which was responsible for the training of every soldier in the United States Army. McNair created the best-prepared U.S. Army ever to take the field. For Talbot, meeting him was a privilege. The occasion was the briefing of the senior officers who were involved in the operation, code-named COBRA, which it was hoped would enable the American army to break out of Normandy. The attack was to be preceded by the U.S. carpet bombing of the area on the far side of the Periers-Saint Lo Road. At the briefing, Talbot learned that 1,500 heavy bombers, B-17s and B-24s, were going to be used plus about 400 medium bombers and 550 fighter-bombers. It was going to be awesome.

There were questions about the bombers' air route that needed to be discussed during today's meeting. General Bradley insisted they were to fly parallel to the American line, not over it. Flying over the heads of the infantry to drop bombs ahead of them created the danger of some bombs falling on Allied troops. General McNair was fully in accord with Bradley on this. Bradley assured everybody present that the air corps understood the risk and had promised to fly the parallel pattern, reducing the possibility of bombing their own troops.

"I'm glad we were there," Sam Bingham said to Talbot as they left the briefing. "Tell me, though, who is this General Brereton they mentioned a couple of times."

"Brereton." The words leapt from Talbot's lips. "What's he got to do with this?"

"Well, he's the head of the Ninth Air Force, and . . ."

"Good God. Then, he'll be in charge of this operation from the air corps side."

"You sound upset," said Bingham. "Weren't you listening in there?"

"They must've briefed you about Brereton while I was out of the hall. I had to talk to that new group of officers who came over with McNair." Talbot paced anxiously. "General Lewis Hyde

Brereton was in charge of the Far East Air Force in the Philippines under MacArthur. In spite of the fact that the Japanese had hit Pearl Harbor on December 7th, and MacArthur had ordered Brereton to get his planes dispersed and away from Clark Field, Brereton still hadn't complied with the order by the afternoon of December 8th when the Jap planes arrived and happily bombed Clark Field and all the planes massed on the ground there. Brereton lost two entire squadrons of B-17s without getting one plane into the air. MacArthur's bomber force was destroyed."

"Why wasn't Brereton court-martialled?"

"I don't know. MacArthur fired him, of course. The army sent him to the Mediterranean. I do know this: In the invasion of Sicily, Brereton was instructed that under no circumstances was he to fly his troop carriers loaded with our paratroopers over the fleet. We knew the navy would be heavily engaged, and we didn't want them shooting down our own planes. I was with the 82nd Airborne and helped plan the invasion, so I know how strongly General Ridgway felt about this."

Bingham looked distressed.

"I went in with the first drop, the night before the infantry came ashore," Talbot continued. "The second drop was supposed to arrive the next evening, but we'd been so mis-dropped by the air transport, they postponed it a day. Then, Brereton flew them in from the sea. The ships had just fought off a German air attack when the transports appeared overhead. The navy shot them out of the sky. Slaughtered over 20 percent of our paratroopers along with the planes."

"Jesus," said Bingham.

"While we were in England preparing for the invasion, Brereton's tactical fighter squadrons were supposed to practice working with the ground troops in close support. They never showed up. Brereton didn't even apologize. Just said they had other things to do. When he finally told Bradley he was ready to do his practice runs with the assault troops, it was too late. Our men were already in their departure areas for the real thing. God knows how many guys got killed because of that jackass. All I can say is I'm damned glad we're one of the followup divisions and won't be on the Periers-Saint Lo Road when Brereton's planes come over."

"Uh, Bill," Bingham was clearing his throat. "Our orders are being changed."

"How?"

"We're moving up onto the road. At the far end, though. The bombers aren't coming anywhere near us. We'll just be holding the hinge, so to speak. The Ninth Division, the 30th, and the Fourth will be jumping off in the main attack."

"Maybe I should have taken that leave to the Zone of the Interior, after all," said Talbot.

∞

On the afternoon of July 24th a box of heavy bombers flew over the infantry positions, perpendicular to them. They were the only unit that was still unaware that the mission had been cancelled because of bad weather. In spite of the poor visibility the heavy bombers dropped their bombs before returning. The bombs fell on American positions a mile and a half short of the target area and killed or wounded about 150 G.I.s.

∞

"Did you hear about what happened?" asked Sam Bingham that evening.

Talbot nodded. "Brereton flew his planes over our lines, which he had agreed not to do, and they clobbered our own troops. But let's look on the bright side. This afternoon's mission had been cancelled and only a few squadrons failed to get the message. Think of how much worse it could have been. Now, at least, we can correct things and make sure the air corps flies parallel to the road, not over it. Anyway, now maybe we'll get rid of that bastard, Brereton."

Talbot was asleep in an army cot at five o'clock the next morning when he was abruptly awakened. Someone was shaking him. He opened his eyes and sat up. Sam Bingham had lit a candle.

"What's up, Sam?"

Bingham answered in short sentences. "The saturation bombing is on for this morning. Eleven hundred hours. The air corps says they have to make their run over our lines. They say the corridor on the other side of the Periers-Saint Lo Road is too narrow. They'd have to fly too close together and be over the German anti-aircraft guns too long."

"You mean yesterday wasn't a mistake?"

Bingham shook his head. "No mistake. That's the way it's got to be or the air corps won't fly the mission. If they don't help us break the German line with their bombing, there's no telling how long it'll take us to break out of Normandy."

"The bastards."

"Anyway, Bill, since the 20th isn't jumping off right after the planes hit the Germans, I've been assigned to accompany General McNair to watch the show."

"You lucky son of a gun," said Talbot. "You'll have the great man all to yourself. You'll be able to tell him how to run the army ground forces. What I wouldn't give to be in your shoes."

"Yeah," Bingham said with satisfaction. "But you are in my shoes, Bill. While I'm gone, you're in command of the 20th."

The planes were majestic as they flew in, wave after wave. Standing in an open field, Talbot tilted his head back until his steel helmet fell off. Beyond the bombers flying overhead, the noise and the smoke gave proof of the devastation their predecessors were inflicting on the enemy. Now Bill could see the bombs. They hurtled into the smoke that had enveloped the German lines. Talbot felt relieved. Things were going to be all right, after all. Then, something in the picture gave him pause. He couldn't put his finger on it, but there was something that disturbed him. Gradually, his mind began to grasp it. The bombers were using the smoke as their target. They were bombing on the smoke, something they'd been told not to do. And now, to Talbot's consternation, a gentle wind was blowing the smoke back towards the American lines. He knew the feeling of terror the rest of the troops on the ground were feeling at that very moment. There was nothing they could do to avoid their fate. They were going to be slaughtered mercilessly like animals trapped in a pen—by American bombs.

☞

Talbot picked up the field phone. It was a call from headquarters. "Yes?" said Talbot. The bombing had been going on for what seemed a long time, and Bill was worried. He listened for a few moments, then said, "Sure. We can get into jump-off positions in about half an hour, if we start things rolling now . . . Yes, sir."

As he handed the phone back to the young officer who had summoned him to take the call, Talbot said slowly, "They've done it again. The air corps battered our attack divisions. They bombed on the smoke that drifted back over our lines. They hit our guys hard. HQ figures over a thousand casualties and they want to know if we can move up and jump off in case some of the units just can't make it. The casualties are nothing compared to the confusion. It's incredible."

The field phone was buzzing again. Talbot picked it up.

"General Talbot?" asked the voice at the other end of the line.

"Yes?"

There was a brief pause, then another man got on the line. "Oh, Bill, I'm glad I got you so fast. A lot of our lines are out because of the bombing." Talbot recognized General Omar Bradley's voice.

"Yes, sir," he said.

"I have some bad news, Bill. General McNair was killed by our own bombers."

"What?!" The words flew from Talbot's lips. "General McNair? That's not possible."

"I'm afraid it is, Bill." Bradley sounded sad. "And, Bill . . . Sam Bingham was with him."

"Was Sam hit?"

"He was killed, Bill."

Talbot felt sick to his stomach.

"I'm sorry about Bingham. I know you were friends. Bill, Sam always told me he wanted you to take over if anything happened to him. So, the 20th is yours if you want it."

"Of course I want it," said Talbot slowly. "But I never wanted to get it this way."

"Ike will forward the recommendation to Washington for approval."

"Thank you, sir." There was no elation in Talbot's voice. The command of a division was what he had always dreamed about. But Talbot felt only sadness. He would gladly have given up his new stars to have Sam Bingham back.

☙

In a press conference in London two days after the COBRA bombing, General Brereton stated that the delay of the offensive was due to the slow start and the sluggishness of the troops on the ground. He neglected to add that this delay was due to his planes bombing the hell out of those troops on the ground, forcing them to have to untangle the wreckage of vehicles and equipment and remove dead and wounded Americans hit by U.S. bombs before they could begin their attack.

A dejected General Eisenhower declared privately he would never again employ heavy bombers against tactical targets. He transferred General Brereton from the Ninth Air Force to command the newly formed First Allied Airborne Army.

That unit went on to lose almost the entire British First Airborne Division at Arnhem a month later due to Brereton's refusal to drop the paratroopers closer than six miles from the bridge that was their objective.

In spite of the American casualties caused by the bombs, the overall operation had been a huge success. The German side of the Periers-Saint Lo Road looked like the face of the moon. Seventy percent of the German troops were out of action—dead, wounded, crazed, or numbed. All their forward tanks were knocked out and the roads were impassable. Command posts simply vanished along with entire regiments. When the American infantry divisions began to move forward, bomb craters, wrecked vehicles, and congestion hindered the advance, but by that evening, General Bradley knew COBRA was achieving its purpose. The German army was in disarray. The breakout had begun.

Bill was still grieving for Sam Bingham, but the sight of a letter from Sarah cheered him up—until he opened it. It was short.

> Bill,
>
> You told me to keep in touch with the American SHAEF people here in London to get news of you whenever you were unable to write. I'm glad you did that, Bill. Otherwise I'd never have learned of your returning to the United States to get married. By now, I'm sure you've left, and when this

catches up with you, please accept my congratulations and best wishes.

Yours, Sarah

Her letter left Bill stunned. He'd forgotten he'd told Sarah to check with SHAEF. Why hadn't she received his letter? He realized how badly mail was delayed, especially within Europe, but he had written to her weeks ago.

He checked the army postal system and found out that when their transport system was strained, as it was most of the time, mail to and from the Z.I. (U.S.) took priority, which was logical. Mail to civilian addresses within Europe was in mailbags, piled in warehouses, where it remained for long periods of time. Only now was this type of mail beginning to move. It seemed almost as if the army were trying to break up liaisons between its soldiers and the local European girls. If too much mail to local civilians piled up, they sent it back stamped "Undeliverable," which to their little rear echelon minds, it was. That situation was corrected from time to time, but Bill's letter had never been sent. He knew he had to do something and do it fast before things got completely out of control.

✥

"General Talbot to see General Bradley," announced the sergeant on duty outside Bradley's headquarters.

"It's good to see you, Bill," said Bradley. "What can I do for you?"

"I've come to ask a favor."

"Name it."

"Omar, I've got a personal problem . . ."

After he'd finished, General Bradley burst out laughing. "I don't know which is harder, fighting a war, or dealing with a woman who thinks she's been jilted."

"How about sending a signal to SHAEF, London, to be delivered by your most senior officer, saying that Major General William E.B. Talbot wishes to marry WREN First Officer Lady Sarah Hayward by proxy, immediately if not sooner?"

"You say Lady Sarah is a widow?"

"Yes, sir. Her husband was killed in North Africa."

"Was his body recovered?"

"Not to my knowledge. But someone saw him shot, I believe."

"That's not good enough. The Enoch Arden law applies in England, too."

"Enoch Arden?" Talbot asked in confusion.

"The law states that a person has to be missing for seven years before being considered dead, and, only then, is his or her survivor free to marry somebody else."

"Brad, can't we ignore it for now. We aren't breaking any laws by sending a signal, are we?"

Without answering, General Bradley called in his clerk and dictated the message for immediate delivery to SHAEF, London, over his signature. "There," he said after he finished.

"Thank you, Omar." Talbot said. He hoped it would work.

∞

A week later, Talbot received a letter from Sarah.

A very nice general had come to the Admiralty to visit her

with a message from General Bradley, himself, saying Major General Talbot was asking her to marry him by proxy, immediately. She told Bill she didn't think she had time to get married right now but later would be fine and that she was sorry for writing such a nasty letter. She should have known Bill would never do a thing like that, that she should have checked the information instead of accepting it, and she missed him desperately.

General George S. Patton loved the press, and the press loved Patton. The general gloried in headlines. According to him, they were the voice of the people, therefore, the voice of God. He entertained the newspaper reporters royally and told them what he was doing and what they could do to help him. Whenever he came across a cache of particularly good wine, he'd invite them to dinner. He'd pose for their photographers, making sure they got pictures of his pearl-handled pistols. The reporters couldn't get enough of him. However, their publishers didn't appreciate their writing stories exclusively about General Patton. They were quick to point out that there were other men fighting the war. Men like Eisenhower and Bradley. The correspondents got the message.

After the 20th Infantry Division was assigned to Patton's Third Army, it seemed that nothing could stop them. Talbot did all the right things. In addition, Talbot was handsome and charismatic. And he treated the reporters cordially, the same way he treated everybody else. He cooperated with them without asking for, or even wanting, mention in their news stories. Therefore, they liked him. At first, the newspapers referred to "the lightning thrusts of the 20th Division." These subcaptions soon became "The 20th Division, under General William Talbot sweeps forward." Then, with the Third Army making its historic dash across France, headlines began proclaiming, "TALBOT'S 20TH CROSSES SEINE," then "TALBOT LEADS DRIVE" and "TALBOT'S TERRIFIC 20th ENTERS CHALONS." Inevitably, Patton called Bill to his headquarters.

"Look, Bill, when you talk to those newspaper guys, don't forget who's running this show."

"Sir, I don't ask for this stuff. I even discourage the press correspondents," Bill responded truthfully.

"Oh, yeah? You had a briefing for the bastards yesterday."

"They asked for it. One of them had interviewed me in North Africa after I'd gotten hit at Santa Bianca. What could I do?"

"Tell them to see me, dammit."

Talbot started to tell his boss that he'd been doing exactly that. Instead, he simply said, "Yes, sir."

Bill knew that he was doing a great job. It was almost as if he had been born to lead the 20th Infantry Division to victory after victory.

These were heady days. After the breakout, German resistance in France was crumbling. The armored divisions raced ahead as much as fifty miles a day. Talbot loaded his men onto the tanks, loaded them in trucks and jeeps and any motor vehicles he could lay his hands on, and flung his columns forward. To his leading armored cars, his orders were the same every day: "Drive on until fired upon." Then, whenever one of his units hit a hastily constructed German roadblock, usually just a heap of logs thrown across the road or a pile of dead horses or wrecked vehicles, there would be a short, vicious skirmish, then on they'd go to the next obstacle. Each insignificant firefight was reported by the press, written up as an example of the fast-moving, fighting-on-the-run tactics of Talbot's Terrific 20th, whose favorite words were, "GO, GO, GO!"

Unsolicited by Talbot, the newspaper correspondents had made his name a household word.

At the same time, General Patton was becoming a little less enthusiastic about the successes of William E.B. Talbot, especially as reported in the newspapers. One of these days he planned to put a stop to it. But he had other things on his mind now. His army was running out of gasoline. His tanks were beginning to grind to a halt, and his infantry had no fuel for their trucks.

☙

Talbot rode in the front seat of his jeep, sitting beside the driver. He much preferred to travel this way instead of by the usual command car reserved for him. He liked to keep up with his troops, and a jeep made a much smaller target should he blunder into the fighting line, which he sometimes did. The 20th was following one of Patton's most famous armored divisions in order to secure a town named Le Petit Jean, which the armor was going to bypass. Hearing firing, Talbot ordered his driver to speed ahead to see what was going on. He discovered that when the armored division had arrived at the town, they met so little resistance that they had decided to go ahead and take it. The 20th wasn't needed. The tanks were already rolling down the road. Checking out the town, Talbot spotted several junior officers and a sergeant conferring beside a wire fence. Talbot stopped his jeep and strode over to them.

"I'm General Talbot of the 20th Division."

"Yes, sir, General, we recognize you, sir," said a young lieutenant.

"Anything I can do for you?"

"There is something, maybe, sir. You see, our division went through here pretty fast. Nobody paid much attention to this German warehouse complex. We think we should probably blow it up. It looks like some sort of an ammunition dump, and we're wondering what to do about it."

"Don't worry about it, son," said Talbot. "You've already taken the objective we were meant to take, so why don't you just leave it to us. It'll give us something to do."

"Thank you, sir," the men said in unison. General Talbot had taken the responsibility of blowing up the warehouses off their hands, and they were happy to leave to go catch up with their unit.

As soon as they were gone, Talbot stopped the next truck in the 20th Division's convoy. The markings on the bumper indicated the vehicle was from Company E of the 485th Infantry. "Where's your company commander?" asked Talbot.

"Up ahead, sir," replied the lieutenant sitting next to the driver.

"Take my jeep and go get him," said Talbot, talking fast. "Unload your men here. Park the truck over there in the field."

To the men who had been in the truck and who now stood beside the road, Talbot said, "I'm assigning Easy Company to guard this dump. Until the rest get here, you men spread out around the perimeter fence. Don't let anybody in without my authorization. Understood?"

The men nodded and mumbled, "Yes, sir." Most had never been addressed directly by a general before and were a little nervous.

In quick order, Talbot had the dump completely surrounded by the men of Easy Company. Their captain, a wiry young man named Schwartz, seemed most competent. After giving the necessary orders, Schwartz stayed with General Talbot to see what else would be required of him. Entering the compound with the captain, Talbot began to inspect the insides of the buildings. Each time he came out of a warehouse, he was smiling more broadly than before. In a few minutes, Colonel Red Parks, commander of the 485th joined him. "Do you know what we have here?" asked Talbot.

Parks shook his head.

"We have here what must have been the entire fuel supply for a German panzer army."

Now it was Parks's turn to grin broadly.

"And do you know what a couple of idiot tank officers were about to do when I arrived? They were going to blow it up."

Parks laughed out loud. "What are you going to do with it, sir?"

"I have two choices, don't I, Red? I can keep it all to myself so the 20th can continue rolling after everybody else has ground to a halt for lack of fuel. Or I can tell Patton what I've got and let him allocate it where he needs it the most."

Parks didn't say anything. He knew what Talbot's decision would be.

"You know," Talbot said finally, "Patton's a little sore at me these days for all the publicity I've been getting. I don't think I'll push my luck. Are your communications working?"

∞

Getting in touch with an army commander was not easy. Corps Headquarters wanted to know why the 20th Division wanted to communicate directly with the Third Army command. "This is strictly a social call," Talbot said. "Just send this message to General Patton: General Talbot invites General Patton to join him in Le Petit Jean for dinner. Be sure to tell him the dinner might be as good as the one at Gela. All right? That's G-E-L-A. Thanks."

There was nothing slow about George Patton's mind. He understood Talbot's message immediately, and by dusk his entourage of armored cars came screaming into Le Petit Jean, antennas whipping the air and dust billowing up around them like smoldering volcanos.

Talbot stood waiting for him. "Welcome, General."

"Let's have it, Talbot," snapped Patton. "You didn't get me over here for nothing."

"How's your gasoline supply?" asked Talbot.

"You know damned well how it is. We're almost dry, and

we can't get any more because that bastard, Monty, insists on getting his share . . ."

"Then, sir, come with me for a few minutes." The two generals entered the depot.

When they emerged, Patton's belligerent mood had turned around completely. He was jovial. "We're going to keep this our little secret, you hear, Billy? Nobody's going to know about this but us. They'll all wonder how in the hell Third Army's able to travel so far on what they've dribbled out to us. We'll set them on their ear, by God. I'll make you a corps commander. Got an opening coming up real soon, and its yours if you want it, you hear?"

☙

Even with the unexpected bonus, on the far bank of the Meuse River the gas tanks went dry. Talbot's 20th finally halted, exhausted at the end of August.

The 20th Division was already 150 miles east of Paris, which had been liberated on the 25th. Patton was blue in the face with frustration. "Dammit, Brad," he pleaded with his boss. "Just give me 400,000 gallons of gasoline and I'll be inside Germany in two days." But General Bradley had to shake his head sadly. "You might as well ask for the moon, George. There is no gas."

Talbot knew, as did Bradley and Patton, that for infantry to go forward without the support of tanks or artillery would be suicide. They just had to sit it out. Patton had warned that the delay would permit the enemy to regroup and fight. And it wasn't long before Talbot noted that the Germans were becoming more aggressive.

The Germans were reorganizing.

By the middle of September, the Third Army was receiving gasoline in limited supply once again, but by then the front had stabilized. The supplies received by the U.S. armies in the field were not nearly enough to mount an offensive. They were barely enough to keep them operative. Enemy resistance increased.

The weather had also changed. It was getting colder, and there was rain and drizzle constantly. Mist and fog came and went. The skies were overcast. The high spirits of the American armies that had carried them all the way across France that bright summer were falling with the temperature. The battles that autumn were appallingly bloody—Aachen, the Hurtgen Forest, Metz, and a dozen others just as savage. Casualties mounted. Armies fought stubbornly for yards, not miles.

The supply route extended 350 miles from Normandy to the front. Antwerp had been taken by the British on September 4th, but couldn't be used until the end of November, after they finally cleared the Germans out of the Schelde Estuary. The failure of the Allied airborne landings in Holland meant that the war would not end in 1944 but would continue at least until the late spring of '45.

⁂

During the hard fighting, Bill Talbot discovered he had an excellent team. His artillery commander, Brigadier General Pat O'Hara, was a cultured and well-educated gentleman who complained constantly about not having enough ammunition but always seemed able to support the infantry when they most needed help. Talbot's three regimental commanders were just as proficient. Red Parks of the 485th was a perfect combat leader, strict, yet friendly with his men. The 484th's Colonel Reginald deWitt was a genius who moved his units as he would chess pieces on a board. And the 483rd's Leonard Franks was probably the best of them all. Tough and brave were the adjectives Talbot thought of every time they met. He reminded Bill of Rosenberg.

Rosie had written to tell him that his leg wound had been worse than Talbot had thought, and he had been sent back to a hospital in England, then to the "Zone of the Interior" for further hospitalization in Boston. Now, he wrote, he was the commanding officer of a training company at the Infantry Replacement Training Center at Camp Blanding in Florida. Most of the other officers and non-commissioned officers in his training battalion had served in the Aleutians. He explained that, because of his leg, he couldn't parachute anymore. But he could stay in the army, and keep his rank of captain, at least until the war was over. Then, he'd go back to being a sergeant, he supposed. His friends in the 82nd wrote him that Captain Jones had broken his legs jumping into Normandy, survived, and was also back in the Z.I., where he'd been honorably discharged from the army for disability. Rosenberg mentioned that having been wounded on Omaha Beach on D-Day made him something of a celebrity in the camp. Bill was happy for Rosie, secure now in the States. People came and went in a war. Nothing and nobody stayed long.

A few of Sarah's letters caught up with Talbot near Metz. He opened the ones with the most recent postmarks first. "The way they write, darling, at least here in London, you and Montgomery are winning the war all alone. Be careful. You sound much too heroic to suit me. I'd rather know you were safe somewhere far behind the lines ..." He read Sarah's early letters last. She told him that D'Arcy had returned from Normandy, where he had gone as an observer, after being shot in the shoulder by a sniper shortly after the breakout. He had just left the hospital.

Bill also picked up a letter postmarked from Endicott. It was from John Wilkinson, the shop foreman at Talbot Mills.

Dear General Talbot:

We have all been reading about you in the newspapers. Congratulations, sir. You are a credit to us all, and we are working very hard to manufacture the things the army needs to help you and men like you win the war against those Nazis. Please keep it up, sir. God bless you and we pray for you all the time. You are the hero of Endicott.

The mill is doing very well. The people who bought it from you are four-square. We are double the size we were when you left. They wanted to promote me to the front office, but I told them I was happier on the floor, so they made me the manager of production operations. It is a big title, and I get more money, but I am still the shop foreman.

If you will excuse me for taking a liberty, sir, I thought if you don't already have the news, I should tell you, since I do not believe any of your friends in Endicott will particularly want to inform you. I remember you used to take out Miss Clarissa Brown before she got engaged to Mr. Stanley, the one who went to the Marines and got wounded at Tarawa. Well, Miss Brown went out to the West Coast to see him after he got sent back from the Pacific to the hospital there.

She went several times. Well, now, last Saturday, she got married. But not to Mr. Stanley. She married a Navy Pharmacist's Mate she met out there. A very nice young man, from his pictures. He is nineteen, and is a very handsome and clean-cut boy. I know I shouldn't say this, Mr. Talbot, but the rumor is that Miss Brown, Mrs. Erikson, as she is now, is going to have a baby in a few months, but I suppose these things happen in wartime. Such a high spirited young lady. A shame you are so far away and Mr. Stanley got injured so terribly. Young Erikson is from the mid-west, Iowa I think, where his family has a very nice drug store and soda fountain, so the young couple have something to look forward to after the war. Anyway, sir, now I must close.

Yours very truly, John Wilkinson

So, Clarissa had gotten herself knocked up by a navy enlisted man.

And she and her father were going to get me to marry her before the news got out, Talbot mused. He felt sorry for her, and more than a little responsible. Perhaps she would still be a virgin now if he hadn't seduced her. But he had meant to marry her, he reminded himself. And it was Clarissa who had left him. She had wanted too much. Now she was paying for her fickleness. Beautiful, lovely little Clara. It pained him to think of her trapped and unhappy. She had always been a wild thing.

Bill put Wilkinson's letter back in its envelope.

It was time for reviewing the daily orders to his 20th Infantry Division.

CHAPTER

In London, when Edwina Beauchamp and Jocko D'Arcy returned to her Mayfair townhouse after having dinner, her telephone was ringing. Edwina picked it up. "Oh, Sarah," she said, looking at her wristwatch. "Isn't this late for you to be up?"

"I've got to see you," said Sarah. Her voice was urgent. "I know it's too late tonight. How about lunch tomorrow?"

"Done," said Edwina. "You've gotten my curiosity up."

D'Arcy looked at Edwina and raised his eyebrows.

She shrugged and shook her head. "No idea," she said.

The next day, Sarah and Edwina sat together in a small French restaurant they both liked. Without preliminaries, Edwina said, "Tell me all."

Sarah smiled. "This isn't going to be a gossip session, Weena. It's serious."

"You haven't called me that in years. It has to be serious."

"The main thing is: I don't know how to tell Bill." Sarah's voice was plaintive.

"You really are in a state. What is it you don't know how

to tell Bill? I assume you mean Bill Talbot. Jocko told me all about you two, so you don't have to be reticent, dear."

"That I'm married," wailed Sarah.

Edwina looked stunned. "You're married? When the hell did this happen?"

"You know. You were there. I married Scott Hayward. It was 1925."

Edwina shook her head, noting her friend's agitation. "Please calm down, Sarah, dear. I think the war's getting to you. And with Bill Talbot so far away, fighting in battle after battle, I don't wonder you're a little distraught."

But Sarah was shaking her head vigorously. Tears welled in her eyes. "No. No. No. You don't understand. I'm a married lady." She fumbled in her handbag, extracted a letter, and handed it to Edwina.

Edwina read it with her growing consternation showing clearly. At last, she handed the letter back and said, "I understand. It's plain. Scott's alive in a German prison camp."

Sarah took out a handkerchief and dabbed her eyes.

Edwina couldn't think of anything to say.

"How will Bill react, do you think?" asked Sarah.

Edwina was silent, which was unusual. "I suppose you've got to tell him," she said finally.

"I love him," said Sarah. "I'm a married woman terribly in love with another man. And I'm married to somebody I can't stand the sight of."

Edwina took a deep breath. "All right, my dear. Write to Bill and tell him about Scott being alive."

Sarah sucked in her breath, shaking her head at the same time.

"Hear me out," continued Edwina, now as calm and resourceful as ever. "In the same letter, tell him you intend to divorce Scott just as soon as that's decently possible. You do, don't you?"

"Yes, of course," said Sarah. "But suppose Bill doesn't like the idea of my having a living husband? Suppose he will want to break our engagement?"

"Give him an escape clause. Tell him that if he can't accept things as they are, then he doesn't have to answer your letter."

Sarah nodded, then said, "Suppose he doesn't answer my letter."

"Oh, he will, darling. You don't have a thing to worry about."

✺

That evening, Jocko D'Arcy came by Edwina's for cocktails before dinner. They chatted amiably as usual. Jocko gave her a hug and a kiss as they raised their glasses.

Turning serious, Edwina said, "Jocko, dear, tell me something. If Sarah Hayward were free, if Bill Talbot were out of the picture, would you still pursue her?"

Jocko shook his head. "That's an infatuation of the past. We all grew up together. You two were the brightest and most fun of all the girls that season of the '20s. You both married most unsuitable men, and I didn't do so well myself. After Scott was killed, I did fall in love with Sarah. I admit it. But it's over and done.

Now, it's you and me. It always should have been from the start. Thank God I know that now."

"Scott Hayward's alive. Sarah got word from the Red Cross. She'll divorce him, of course, but suppose that happens and suppose Bill Talbot gets killed. Would you want her then?"

"Scott alive? Good God! How?"

Edwina explained.

Jocko drew her to him, put his arm completely around her and gave her a heartfelt kiss. "No, darling. Nothing would change. I love you with all my heart. We go together like roast beef and claret, and we always will."

The German army was, once again, a formidable fighting force on their Western Front. The American progress was slow and costly. The weather was getting colder and darker. In late November, Patton ordered the 20th to attack the enemy at a village near Metz. Instead, Talbot on instinct, formed defensive positions below the village and, when the enemy attacked at that precise point, he was able to throw them back with heavy losses. It was ascertained later that the Germans had a copy of Patton's order and had decided to hit the 20th on the move when they were most vulnerable, but Talbot had thwarted them by changing the plan. It was intuitive on his part, and it had worked.

Patton didn't like it. He let it be known that, in his opinion and that of others, Talbot was getting a little too cocksure of himself.

Talbot had been extremely lucky this time. Disobeying direct orders was a dangerous sport, and next time he might not be so blessed.

∞

The 20th Division was encountering only dirty, hard, brutal, bloody fighting. Talbot preferred to let his regimental commanders handle the day-to-day operations. This was not his sort of warfare. What he desperately wanted to do was go back to England for a week or so to be with Sarah. And he probably could have arranged it, but his sense of duty simply would not permit him to go off to London and leave his men dying in the mud of France.

God, but this had been a hard war. Again and again, Talbot sent his men into battle, watched them come back tired and bloody, their ranks shrunken. None of them complained. Everyone understood that this was a war that had to be won, whatever the cost. Each day the men looked death in the eye and took on the challenge. The more exhausted and dispirited they were, the more heroic they became, thought Talbot.

As he walked back into his headquarters, his sergeant handed him an envelope. Glancing at it, he saw it was from Sarah. He smiled and took it into his office to savor it in private. It was the first letter he'd gotten from her in over two weeks and he'd been worried. The Nazi V-2 rockets had hit London badly. They were fast and undetectable, hitting without warning.

"My dearest Bill," she wrote. "This is a hard letter for me to write. I don't know how to begin, and I don't know how to soften the blow, so I'll tell you plainly and hope you will read this letter to the end and not tear it up before you finish it . . ."

He took a deep breath and continued to read. "Several weeks ago, the International Red Cross contacted me to tell me that Scott was in a German prisoner of war camp. From what I can gather, when his position was over-run, he was too badly hit to continue to fight. He threw away his identification discs before he became unconscious. He didn't want the Germans to know they'd captured a brigadier. He told them he was a regular army sergeant, and they sent him to Germany with the other prisoners. A few months ago, he tried to escape from the prisoner of war camp with some other men. The guards spotted them and opened fire, wounding Scott badly and killing several of the others. That was when he told them his real name, rank and serial number so he'd receive better medical attention. He was transferred to another prison hospital, and that's where the Red Cross found him several weeks later. Now that I know Scott is alive, it means I am a married woman, not a widow." Bill stopped reading and just looked out the window. He felt numb. Without Sarah, what was the point of all this? It was a few minutes before he was able to continue reading. "I shall be honest, Bill. When I got word that Scott was still alive, I was very confused, which is the reason I haven't written sooner. I want you to understand me when I tell you I have thought things over very carefully, and I have made up my mind. You are the only man in the world for me. I received a letter from Scott through the Red Cross, and it made me realize that Scott is still the same selfish egotist he was when I married him. So, my darling, if you still want me, and can wait for me until after the war ends and I can decently tell Scott what has happened and get a divorce, I am yours. If your sense of morality makes this impossible for you, then please destroy this letter and don't bother to explain or write. I'll understand. Know I shall love you always, Sarah."

Bill's anxiety dissipated, and his gloom disappeared with Sarah's last sentences. He took out a piece of paper and began writing. "Sarah, darling, I just received your last letter. As soon as you can leave your husband I want to marry you."

"Mail truck going out in a few minutes, sir," came the sergeant's voice through the closed door.

Bill finished the letter quickly and sealed it. "Come on in, Sergeant Kelly. My mail's ready."

∞

Colonel Enders, who was in charge of the headquarters' staff knocked on Talbot's door loudly. "Something important?" asked Talbot.

"Possibly, sir. One of our mail trucks hit a mine and got blown to hell. Not much left, I'm afraid."

Talbot nodded. He knew mail was important to the men.

"My problem is this, sir: should we advise the men what's happened, which will really destroy their morale, or should we keep it quiet, and let them think their letters just got lost along the way somehow?"

Talbot shook his head. "They'll find out what happened, anyway, no matter what. So, we should advise them. I think a lot of the boys have already started to write Christmas letters to their families in the States. If we can notify them in time they can re-write their letters. Send in Sergeant Kelly. I'll draft the communique and send it out to all company commanders and everybody else involved."

"Yes, sir. Thank you, sir."

General Talbot dictated his memo to Kelly; he hoped the men wouldn't be too upset. It never occurred to him any of his letters might have been on that truck.

Talbot had picked a rather comfortable hotel not far behind the lines to be his division headquarters. In the suite he used as his office and sleeping quarters, he had pinned a large map of the entire front from the North Sea to the Swiss border. Every morning, he studied the intelligence reports and the recapitulations of the actions of the day before.

In the north, the U.S. First and Ninth Armies were being held at a virtual standstill by the German resistance, especially in the vicious Hurtgen Forest fighting, also at Aachen and the Roer River. The British and Canadians were not doing any better. But the Third Army was making progress. It had been slow and nasty work. Patton had given orders to close on the Saar River in Lorrain, cross the Saar at Saarlautern, and enter Germany itself. The 20th was ordered to hold the southern shoulder, while other divisions kicked a breach in the Siegfried Line.

After going over the details of their orders and giving the necessary instructions to his infantry regiments, artillery, and other units, Bill turned his attention to the overall situation.

The First and Ninth Armies were attacking in the Roer River

area. The Third was across the Saar, and the Sixth Army Group, comprised of the U.S. Seventh Army and the French First, had come up from the Mediterranean and was now linked up with the Third Army and fighting to the south of it. They had captured Strasbourg and were closing on the Rhine. With the port of Antwerp operational, the supply situation was greatly alleviated. In the spring, the American and British armies would drive into Germany and win the war once and for all. As Talbot gazed at his maps and reports, he analyzed the situation. If this were a chess game, he thought, Hitler would concede. We've got him. The Russians are closing in from the east and we from the west. It's over. So, what's he trying to do? Hold his positions at the Siegfried Line and Roer? Fall back to the Rhine? Maybe. The Rhine was the most formidable defensive barrier in Europe. What else could Hitler do? Talbot shook his head. Nothing.

In the middle of the night of December 8th, Talbot woke suddenly and sat up in his bed. Yes, there was something else the Germans could do. They could pick a weak spot in our line and concentrate their forces for a counterattack. Maybe try to barrel through to Paris. Or Antwerp? Without Antwerp, we'd be in desperate shape.

General Talbot didn't sleep much that night and at dawn was studying his map. He had already satisfied himself that the enemy would not attack the Third Army. First, there was no place that was suitable and, second, the Germans had much too healthy a respect for Patton to try anything like that in his sector. That would be courting a disaster. So, where? Talbot continued studying. Finally, he nodded his head. His expression was somber as he picked up his phone to call for an appointment with General Patton.

☙

"You're crazy," said Patton. "Where in hell would they get enough men and tanks to mount an offensive like that?" But Talbot observed an inkling of doubt behind the general's words.

"When we broke out of Normandy," said Talbot, "everybody thought the German army was finished, remember? A bunch of disorganized bits and pieces. So, why are we still fighting a strong German army and getting no place? Where did they get the men and guns and tanks to fight us effectively all the way from the North Sea to the Alps?"

"Okay, Bill. Tell me what you think they're up to."

"Look—here in the First Army area. What do you see that sticks out like a sore thumb? I'll tell you. The Ardennes. It's thinly held by two green divisions who've never seen combat and by two veteran divisions that were so shot up in the Hurtgen Forest, they're in the Ardennes for rest and recuperation. They're reorganizing."

"Yeah, but they're two of the best. The 28th and the Fourth. The Krauts know better than to try anything with those guys. Besides, the area's forest. It's a natural barrier."

"Sir, where did the Germans attack in 1914 and 1940?" asked Talbot.

"In the Ardennes," replied Patton slowly. "You may be right. The Jerries have pulled at least thirteen divisions out of the line, including six panzer and SS panzer divisions, and they're bringing three more divisions down from Scandinavia. For what it's worth, my intelligence people agree with you. Let's see what somebody else thinks about this." He picked up his phone. "Get me Colonel Dickson, First Army Intelligence."

In a few moments, Patton heard Colonel Dickson's voice on the other end of the wire. Patton got right to the point. "Anything unusual going on up there, Monk?"

There was a pause. "I think so. I think the Jerry is building up for one hell of a counteroffensive. Everything that comes in confirms it. German prisoners corroborate it. But, General, nobody believes me, so maybe I'm wrong."

"If you're not wrong, Monk, where do you expect it'll come?" asked Patton.

Dickson practically whispered, "In the Ardennes."

A day later, General Patton poured over plans with his staff. "Yes. We can do it," he said slowly after they had studied the maps. "If this German offensive comes off—and none of the top brass believes it will—we can start moving north within a couple of days."

Talbot agreed. "Right now, the Third Army's attacking westward beyond the Saar. So what you're saying is that you can break off your Saar offensive and throw the Third Army into the attack northward in two days. Change direction by 90 degrees. If you pull it off, sir, you'll be a military genius, officially."

Patton's brow furrowed. "How soon do you think they'll come?" he asked. "I've got to work out some sort of schedule on this thing. It won't be easy.

"We'll have to pull out four to six divisions and move them north, then have them attack to cut off the Germans. It'll be tricky. How much time, Billy?"

"I think they'll attack just as soon as the weather closes down and our planes can't fly air support. They'll move into position under cloud and fog cover and attack while our planes are grounded."

"When?" repeated Patton. There was a trace of irritation in his voice.

"The weather people tell me it'll be pretty nasty by the middle of the month. Say, the 15th, 16th, 17th. Somewhere around then."

"You know," said Patton. "I sure as hell hope those stupid sons-of-bitches do try to attack through the Ardennes. Let them come. We'll cut them off and chop them up, then eat them for breakfast."

∞

At Edwina's house in London one late afternoon, there was a knock at the door. "Come on in, Jocko," she called down from her bedroom. D'Arcy entered.

"Make myself a scotch?"

"Certainly. Make me one, too. Make it stiffish. We're both going to need it."

Coming down the stairs, Edwina looked lovely, as usual. Jocko thought how beautifully her dark hair contrasted with her white face and red lips. She was truly stunning. Thin and sensuous, she enhanced the clothes she wore.

After a perfunctory kiss, Edwina said slowly, "He didn't respond. No letter from Bill Talbot. Do you think he wants to get out of marrying our Sarah?"

D'Arcy shook his head slowly. "No. He's not that kind of man. And Sarah getting a divorce from Hayward wouldn't bother him a bit.

"I think Sarah's putting too much faith in the United States Army's mail system. Remember that mix-up about Bill going back to marry some floozie in the States?"

Edwina nodded. She and Jocko sat silently for a minute.

"Sarah's very broken up about this," said Edwina finally. "I left her in tears this afternoon."

"Let's go by her flat and cheer her up," said D'Arcy. "Then, I'll see what I can arrange to contact Bill and find out what's *really* going on."

Before dawn on December 16, 1944, young Sergeant Jack Reynolds of the 28th Infantry Division sat peacefully in his outpost dugout. For some reason, he hadn't been able to sleep, so he'd gotten up, checked to make sure the blanket over the opening of the dugout was securely closed, lit a couple of candles, and wrote a few Christmas cards and letters. He started to write his mother that he was in a quiet sector of the Ardennes Forest in Belgium, but he realized the censor would cut that out, so he'd have to find another way to let her know he was now fairly safe. Reynolds was nineteen years old. He stood six feet tall and was handsome and red-cheeked. He'd been near the top of his class and captain of the football team in high school. A week ago, he'd still been a private. Three weeks ago, he'd come into the outfit as a green, untried infantry replacement. Most of the other replacements who had come in with him were already casualties. In fact, he reflected, all of them were. He was lucky. There was a saying in the outfit that if a replacement survived the first day in the line, he might just make it . . . to the second day. But if he made it through the first week, he'd be a veteran and at least have a fighting chance.

As soon as he finished the card to his mother, he'd write a real long love letter to his girl. But first, he blew out the candles, opened the blanket flap, and went to look at what was going on outside. There were a few snowflakes, and the sky was very dark. Jack Reynolds looked at his watch. German artillery usually threw in a couple of rounds about this time to keep everybody awake and on their toes. "Anything happening?" he called to the two men who manned the outpost with him.

He could barely see, but one man turned and shook his head. The other said, "No. I don't see nothing, sarge."

You just came into the line yesterday, Reynolds thought. You wouldn't know anything was happening if a German walked up to you and said, "Boo!"

He grinned as he fastened the blanket across the opening and lit the candles again. He sealed the envelope addressed to his mother and pulled a piece of paper from his field jacket pocket. He looked at his watch again. 5:30 a.m. "My darling Alice . . ." he wrote.

He never finished the greeting. At that precise moment, the world exploded around Jack Reynolds. For an instant, he heard the shriek of the German shells. Then the crescendo of the explosions as the earth shook and jarred under his feet. There had been no warning. No gradual buildup. Just this sudden, unexpected rain of steel and high explosives that was blowing everything to pieces.

Reynolds threw himself flat on the bottom of the dugout. He lay there a second, heart pounding, then started crawling forward to see what was happening. A shell hit the outpost like a thunderclap! A flash! A roar! Suffocating smoke and wood splinters flying in all directions. Reynolds was lifted up and flung backwards so hard he hit the rear of the dugout in a sitting position knocking the wind out of his lungs.

As his head cleared, he heard machine-gun fire. Heavy machine-gun fire. He wondered how long he'd been knocked out. He was still sitting on the ground protected on three sides by the walls of earth, but the front of the dugout had been blown away by the shell's explosion. Sergeant Jack Reynolds's glazed eyes stared unbelievingly at his shattered, shredded left arm. It looked awful. But it didn't hurt. His two companions lay sprawled on the ground outside. Neither one moved. There was blood all over the snow.

The shelling had stopped. There were no more explosions on the American positions, and Reynolds realized this meant the German infantry was already closing in. He saw a lot more snow-flakes now. Through the blown-out openings of the dugout, he thought he had never seen so many Germans in his whole life. And panzers. Where the hell had they all come from? Only a few shots came from the American lines, and they didn't even make the Germans pause.

In a purely reflexive movement, Reynolds reached out his good arm and picked up the field telephone. To his surprise, it still worked. By some strange chance, the exploding shells had not cut the wires. When he spoke into the apparatus his voice came in short gasps. He was having trouble breathing. "Jerries attacking," he gasped. "In strength . . . panzers. Lots of panzers . . . infantry . . ." He had to stop. He was afraid he'd pass out. It was snowing hard now.

He tried to breathe deeply, but it hurt him. The field telephone dropped from his hand, and he didn't bother to pick it up. The last thing he saw on this earth were three German soldiers with their rifles pointing at him from the entrance of the dugout. The last thing he felt was the impact of their bullets ripping into his body.

∞

Three days later, the German offensive in the Ardennes had already driven a bulge into the American lines. High command knew they had a battle on their hands. General Patton had already sent his Tenth Armored Division north. It had been in reserve and was available. The 101st Airborne had begun arriving in Bastogne the day before. The Seventh Armored had moved down to defend St. Vith. The American 99th and Second Divisions, along with the battered 28th and understrength Fourth, were fighting valiantly, delaying the Germans and playing hell with their timetables.

On December 19th, the top generals met to discuss strategy. General Eisenhower was the first to speak.

"The present situation is to be regarded as one of opportunity for us and not of disaster. There will only be cheerful faces at this table," he said, setting the tone of the proceedings.

The simple strategy the generals adopted was not unexpected. General Patton was to counterattack the enemy's southern flank, fifty miles north of his present positions, relieve Bastogne and cut off the Germans' retreat. It was a difficult and bold move.

"How soon will you be able to attack?" Eisenhower asked Patton.

"In forty-eight hours," came his quick reply.

The other generals gasped.

Patton smiled at them and lit a cigar. "This time," he said, "the Kraut has stuck his head in a meat grinder. And this time I've got hold of the handle."

☙

Talbot was excited. He had made all his plans, lined up his transportation, briefed his regiments.

"George, I'm ready," he told Patton over the phone.

"Good, Billy. Good," said Patton.

Talbot knew that tone of voice, and it disturbed him. He could imagine Patton smiling slyly. "I'll be right over," he said and hung up the receiver.

A worried General Talbot walked slowly into Patton's headquarters, wondering what was afoot. Something was not quite right, he was sure. As soon as he entered the building, he became instantly aware that he was the only person walking slowly. Everybody else was rushing around frantically. The Third Army was in the middle of an intricate and vital movement. Talbot stiffened and began to walk briskly towards Patton's office. The sergeant ushered him straight in.

As he closed the door behind him, Talbot saw that Patton was talking on the phone.

"They're already on the road, Brad. And I'll have four more right behind them. I'll keep you posted. Bye." Patton hung up and looked at Talbot.

"Bill. Glad you came. We're cutting your orders right now." Patton smiled, and Talbot knew he'd been right. The old fox was up to something.

"Would you care to fill me in, sir?" he asked in his most deferential tone of voice. "Give me an idea of my objectives, my route of march . . ."

"Sit down, Billy. Sit down."

Patton cleared his throat, obviously relishing the moment. "We can't leave Sandy Patch's Seventh Army bare, you know. Seventh Army's already on the Rhine in several places. They've had to extend their front to cover our pull-out to the north. Patch has asked for some of our divisions to add to his very thin, spread-out forces." Patton paused. "I've decided the 20th will be a perfect addition to the Seventh Army."

"Sir!" Talbot was on his feet. His face was red.

"I'm afraid you'll miss the headlines, Bill, but then that's war," Patton drawled.

"Sir. I'm all set to go north. My men are ready. We're in top shape to attack . . ."

Patton made an impatient gesture. "No, you're not. You're hurting for replacements. Seventh Army's taking over our southern sectors. That's where the 20th is, so it's natural for you to transfer over to Patch's Seventh Army. I understand Patch wants to move you into the northeast salient. You'll be holding a thirty mile front . . ."

"Sir! Thirty miles? Not possible. It's too hot a corner, anyway."

Patton paused for a moment then smiled as he continued in his high-pitched Virginia accent. "I've been meaning to mention it before, Billy, but I kept putting it off. I didn't like it one bit the way you played up those correspondents during our drive across France. And I don't want to see the same thing happen again. This is my show, Billy, and I'm not taking any chances on your stealing my thunder."

"Fine, sir," Talbot said bitingly. "But for the record, I did not 'play up' to the newspaper men."

"Good, Billy. Good," said Patton. "I'm going to miss you."

Talbot was furious. Just who the hell was it who made it possible for Patton to make this move north so quickly? If I hadn't studied the situation and figured out what the damned Jerries were up to, Patton would still be trying to pull things together, Talbot thought angrily, as he drove back to his headquarters.

∞

In Versailles a high-level meeting was about to turn into World War III. Winston Churchill, invited by General Charles De Gaulle to attend the luncheon session with General Eisenhower, had arrived late due to rough weather above the English Channel. Since the discussions had already begun, he decided to sit and listen. It seemed De Gaulle and Eisenhower were the only ones doing any talking, while their staffs sat as spectators. Churchill lit a cigar and sat back in his large armchair.

"I have told General Eisenhower that we shall never abandon Strasbourg," said De Gaulle.

Churchill merely nodded.

"The Germans are attacking our Sixth Army Group," said Eisenhower, addressing Churchill. "The U.S. Seventh Army is part of that group, along with the French First, and they're spread too thin to hold their present line. Our only alternative is to pull back to the Vosges Mountains and shorten our lines to prevent the enemy from trapping the Seventh Army between the attacking Germans and those in the Colmar pocket. This means we'll have to abandon Strasbourg . . ."

"We shall defend Strasbourg," declared De Gaulle. "We don't care what you do. I am prepared to withdraw French forces from your command and fight to the last man for Strasbourg if necessary."

"You do that, and I'll see that the French army doesn't get one more bullet, nor one more gallon of gasoline, nor one more shell." Eisenhower was uncharacteristically angry.

"Bon," said De Gaulle. "And I shall see that the French government denies the American army the use of our railroads. Supply your forces the best way you can."

There was a silence in the chamber. Scowling, without a word, Eisenhower walked over to the large map that had been hung over a mirror on one side of the room. He studied it carefully for several long, silent minutes. When he turned around to face the others he wore his customary smile. "I didn't realize you felt so strongly about Strasbourg."

De Gaulle slapped his forehead.

"All right," continued Eisenhower. "Suppose we do this: I'll instruct Sixth Army Group under General Devers to shorten his lines and fall back to the Moder River. We shall hold the Alsace. I'll redraw the boundaries and give the responsibility for defending Strasbourg to the French First Army . . ."

After a beaming, triumphant but grateful General Charles De Gaulle departed with his entourage, Eisenhower turned to Winston Churchill and said, "Before the meeting, I talked the situation over with the generals of the Sixth Army Group and Seventh Army. They both agreed that pulling back was premature. The German NORDWIND offensive has been a heavy blow, but they think they can contain it. Besides, we can't let anything threaten our lines of communication across France . . ."

Churchill spoke for the first time that afternoon. "I think you've done the wise and proper thing," he said.

⟨⟨⟨

Talbot's 20th Infantry Division had been transferred to General Patch's U.S. Seventh Army. It was a cold January day, and Talbot shivered through his wool uniform as he sat down to read his instructions. Instead of pulling back to the Vosges Mountains, the Seventh Army was to stay and defend the Alsace. His forehead creased with worry. The great divisions of the Seventh Army were going to stand and fight, and Talbot's 20th was ordered to join them at the Moder River immediately. "Don't waste a moment," the instructions said.

Talbot would, of course, comply and move to the Moder. Due to the urgency and severity of the situation, Talbot's corps commander had not had the time to properly brief his new division's general. Nevertheless, Talbot, as a trained soldier, should have obeyed his orders unquestioningly and to the letter. Instead, he modified them to suit what he thought the situation required. He decided to wait until he was prepared, then march out under the cloak of night, during the darkest hours, which were just before dawn. Under ordinary circumstances, it would have been a sound decision.

It was an honest mistake—but a very serious one.

One of the worst things that can happen to a military commander is to be strongly attacked by the enemy while his own troops are strung out on a road march. And that is precisely what happened to Talbot on the morning of January 6th. He suffered a disaster. The last man to leave his headquarters, General Talbot departed in a communications truck with several of his staff, mostly from his signals section.

The scene of Talbot's debacle looked like chaos in Hades. There were wrecked trucks and jeeps all along the road, some burning in the ditches. Artillery pieces sat, knocked out and useless, their barrels pointed at the sky, some on the road, some in the adjoining fields where they had been set up to fire. The dead and wounded were everywhere. Equipment was strewn over the landscape, standing out against the white of the snow-laden fields. Smoke rose into the sky like huge black ostrich plumes. But Talbot's practiced eye discerned that it was not chaos.

His experienced commanders had formed their veteran troops into defensive lines. And they were moving their perimeters forward. There was no panic. Just hard fighting. He saw a group of

German soldiers attacking. He saw his men cut them down. He saw the enemy mortar shells falling onto his men's hastily dug shallow depressions in the hard ground.

"Can you get me General O'Hara?" Talbot asked Captain Minelli of his communications section. He wanted to contact as many of his commanders as possible and find out their situation so he could make sensible decisions.

"I'll try."

The radio man was exceptionally capable and practiced. He reached General O'Hara in a little over a minute.

"They caught us on the march. I lost half my guns. I'm using the other half as antitank guns. We have their tigers under direct fire." That was as much as Talbot could hear before O'Hara's voice was drowned out.

The din of firing all around them was particularly ear-shattering.

"All right," he shouted. "Keep trying to get our commanders, Minelli," said Talbot as their truck sped off to the head of his columns.

It drove forward through the winter landscape. The blackened skeletons of trees looked like sinister witches against the snow. Beyond the fields was a pine forest, with evergreens standing like an honor guard for Talbot's tattered troops, who moved slowly. Except for the drivers and the shotgun riders, everybody was on foot.

"Geez. Look at that," Talbot heard the driver say to his shotgun. Talbot couldn't resist looking over the side of the truck. He quickly wished he hadn't. There were clumps of dead G.I.s in the snow, their contorted bodies the quintessence of death. From the looks of them, they had been killed during the initial enemy onslaught.

∞

By noon, Talbot realized he could withdraw no further. Superior enemy forces blocked his line of retreat. He formed an egg-shaped perimeter into which he moved the two communications trucks, plus several other vehicles that had survived the march. Within this rough circle formed by the 483rd, 484th, and 485th regiments he determined to hold out until he could break out. In a farmhouse, he spread a map on a kitchen table. Colonel Enders, who had been with the other radio unit, saw to it that what was left of the headquarters staff was functioning again. The three regiments, joined together, now were surrounded by the enemy. They were held together by small towns and farmhouses that had been converted into strong points. Their position was the equivalent of "circling the wagons" against an Indian attack in the Old West, but on a much larger scale.

"Sir," called the radio man, who had set up his equipment in the farmhouse on Captain Minelli's instructions, "it's corps again."

Talbot had advised his corps commander of his situation. He hadn't asked for help. He hadn't requested instructions. And, for his part, the corps commander had simply acknowledged Talbot's report without comment. Talbot figured he'd catch hell just as soon as corps realized what was happening.

"Talbot?" asked a voice on the other end of the radio transmission. It wasn't the corps commander.

"Yes, sir," responded Talbot.

"You've got yourself in a mess. This is General Patch. I don't know when I'll be able to spare any units to come rescue you. We're spread thin, and everybody's under attack."

Talbot sucked in his breath. "Don't send anybody, sir," he said slowly and deliberately. "We shall hold together until the planes can fly. Then, I want all the air support I can get. I'd like a parachute drop. Armor piercing shells for my 105s, rifle and machine-gun ammo, hand grenades, mortar rounds. And sir, we need medical supplies. Lots of morphine syretes. That's it. We'll remain defensive until the weather clears."

"How did you get caught like that?" asked Patch. Clearly he was not pleased, yet there was no accusation implied by the question.

Talbot paused before answering, then said, "An error in judgement on my part, sir. I didn't know how imminent the German attack was, and I delayed my withdrawal in order to avoid any confusion in the move and take advantage of the darkness, as I advised corps at the time." He paused, reminding himself that out of everything bad that happens, something good has to result.

"Sir," he said loudly enough for everybody in his own headquarters to hear, "Look at our situation from this point of view: the 20th Division is fighting at least half a German panzer division, several German infantry divisions, and assorted SS and paratroops.

We are keeping them engaged and off the backs of other units in your command. And, sir, they can't bypass us. They know who we are, and they don't want us in their rear. Do you understand, sir?" Talbot knew he would. General Alexander Patch was a realist.

There was silence at the other end except for the radio static. Talbot thought they might have been cut off. Then, Patch's voice came back, "How long can you hold?" The words were simple.

"We're in the same position as a paratroop unit, sir. We can hold as long as we have ammunition, and I figure that will depend on the strength of the enemy and the frequency of his attacks." Then, he had an inspiration. "As soon as I can get air support, I plan to mount an attack against the enemy."

"In which direction? He's got you surrounded."

"To our original objective," said Talbot, hoping General Patch would realize he was telling him he planned to pull back to the Moder as ordered. He only hoped that was possible.

"Understood," came the reply. "Good luck."

"Don't forget the air support."

"You'll get it. But don't hold your breath. The weather doesn't look good."

∞

"Don't you think you ought to visit the wounded, General?" asked Colonel Franks after reporting his situation. "Have you been out of your command post since you got here? Have you seen your troops? The men who are still alive are bleeding. They're freezing and exhausted. Go out and get your feet frozen off with them."

With that, Colonel Franks turned and left, the only commander to tell General Talbot what he really thought of him, even though the difference in their ranks required him to do so obliquely.

∞

To his credit, Bill took the advice. He began to visit the barns full of wounded. He gave them encouraging words of hope and sympathy. They felt better for his visit. The next morning, his riflemen and machine gunners were glad to see a general, their general, on the line with his troops. Their morale was good, despite the frightfulness of their situation. Even Pat O'Hara didn't complain. He'd used all of his small supply of armor-piercing 105 ammunition but had discovered that a direct hit with a high explosive shell would cause a tiger to turn and run. And, if he was lucky, he could even knock the tiger out or shoot off its tread and immobilize it.

As he trudged through the snow from one forward position to another, Talbot realized he might have to break through without air support, and he wasn't sure he could. He'd sent out patrols. One sergeant brought his patrol back with some news. "We discovered something you'll like, sir. The Krauts're just as beat up and shot up as we are. They didn't even try to stop us. We went past one Jerry outfit that was sound asleep in the snow. They never even heard us go by."

The German attacks that morning were weak, but, by now, the American infantry was running out of ammunition. The artillery pieces were silent, medical supplies used up, food rations exhausted. Talbot knew they were finished, but he also knew he had to hold them together any way he could until the planes could fly. The weather had to clear. In the meantime, he would visit the troops on the line, and try his best to restore their morale.

It was a grey morning. Several members of his staff accompanied him as he walked through the fields. A divisional commander could not just go wandering around a battlefield by himself. He could disappear, get killed, captured, lost, and nobody would know where, how, or when.

Talbot walked slowly. He was bone tired. A German shell sang in and crashed behind him, close enough to spatter him with snow. He heard the stutter of a machine gun. How anybody could see well enough to shoot at anything in this weather was beyond him.

As he made his way from one battalion command post to another, he came to a small clearing in the pines. Through the fog he saw a man kneeling in prayer. Talbot approached him quietly. It was a young G.I., just a boy.

As he mumbled the words of a half-remembered prayer, the boy fingered an old key that hung on his dogtag chain.

"What's the key for?" Talbot asked gently.

The boy looked up. "I'm pretending it's a cross," he said. "It's all I have."

Without a word, Talbot took off his helmet and crunched it heavily into the snow, as he fell to his knees beside the boy. Talbot still felt guilty, even though his decision to prepare properly and move at night had been sound. Locking his fingers together, he raised his hands in front of him, and bowed his bare head as he prayed silently, "Oh, Lord God, I confess in the presence of this brave young soldier and all the valiant dead that lie around us in this dreadful place in this terrible war, that I have committed the sin of arrogance."

The officers with him gazed in disbelief at their commander's bowed head, as he continued to pray silently to himself. "I was going to pray for Your help. Now I pray only for Your mercy on my men. God, take from me anything you will. Take my rank, my position, my worldly goods. But spare my men, and everything I have is Yours."

"Sir! Sir!" The cry brought Talbot out of his meditations. It was Minelli.

Talbot turned towards him. It was then that he saw it. The sunlight was glistening in the pines. The snow no longer looked grey. It was shining white. Talbot jumped up. The roar of the planes above him drowned out his words, "Thank you, God. I don't deserve it, but thank you, God."

That morning, Talbot returned rejuvenated to his farmhouse headquarters, contacted his units and started them moving. After the air corps had broken the back of the Panzers, the 20th Infantry Division doughboys were ready to go. Ecstatic, even manic, Bill Talbot arrived at the jump-off point. Len Franks was preparing to go with all three of his battalions. The riflemen had already fixed their long knives onto the ends of their rifles and were eager to attack. Most had less than a clip of ammunition left. Some had none. It was going to be like the flashing bayonets of the gallant 20th some twenty-six years ago in the Argonne.

The 20th received the airdrops it had requested and made its famous fighting move to the Moder River with all three regiments abreast, nothing in reserve. There it held against several more vicious German attacks. After a week on the Moder, the 20th counterattacked. They broke through all enemy resistance and ended the last German offensive in the west.

After his victorious attack from the Moder River line, Talbot sat down and wrote the letter he had determined he would send in as soon as it was feasible. He based its contents on the fact he knew he had failed as a general. He did not deserve high command. He was a failure. He knew it. In his heart, he knew he had no alternative but to take this step. Only by this means could he bear to live with himself. He wrote out a request to be relieved of command of his beloved 20th Infantry Division, to be reduced in rank, and to be assigned a staff job. He wanted to add "in England" but decided that would denigrate his deed of contrition. As he signed the request, a feeling of great peace came over him.

"What the hell is this letter all about?" General Patch's voice at the other end of the field telephone was indignant.

"It means what it says, sir," answered Talbot. "I made a bad mistake. I want to be reduced in rank. I'll even command a line company in any division that needs me."

"I need you to command the 20th Infantry Division," barked Patch. "I'm tearing up your damned letter. You will continue to command the 20th until I tell you not to. Got that? That's an order."

"But, sir, . . ." began Talbot.

"But, sir, what?" asked Patch. "Lost your nerve? Is that it?"

"No, sir. I made a terrible mistake. What happened to the 20th under my command should never have happened."

"Nuts," snapped General Patch. "The 20th held off three and a half German divisions, then attacked and beat their ass." There was a pause. "Talbot, everybody makes a mistake once in a while. That's the only way we learn not to make them again. Besides, the way you handled a tough situation and the way you regrouped and deployed your troops under the most adverse conditions are what count with me. You did a superb job, Talbot. You won a battle you should, by all rights, have lost, so if you think I'm going to let you go, you're out of your mind. I need more generals like you, Talbot. So, that's that."

After his conversation with General Patch, Talbot's faith in himself slowly returned.

After the crisis in the Alsace was over, it was inevitable that the 20th Division would pull out of the line to receive new equipment and infantry replacements. Officially in army reserve, their days of rest and re-equipping would be few. Talbot began to function as his old buoyant self. Fighting the terrible winter war had taken all his brains and energy. Now his mind turned from soldiering under the most adverse conditions to more pleasant subjects. He wrote to Sarah every day, sometimes twice a day. He wondered if she'd written. The confusion caused by the German offensive had snarled up all the mail. He knew that. His thoughts were interrupted by a sergeant, who had entered his office and quietly laid an envelope on Talbot's desk.

Idly returning the sergeant's salute, Talbot glanced at the envelope. The handwriting was his. The address was Sarah's. Stamped on the envelope was "UNDELIVERABLE AT THIS ADDRESS." Beside it someone had written in pen: "Addressee deceased."

"No!" Talbot screamed. "No! Not Sarah . . ."

Talbot stumbled from his desk to the army cot in the corner of his bare office and fell into it. And that was where Red Parks found him when he came in to confer with his commanding general, hours later.

Parks knocked at the open door, then, getting no response, he walked in slowly. He saw Bill Talbot lying on the cot, his face to the wall. "Are you all right, sir? Are you hurt?" His voice betrayed his alarm.

Talbot rolled over to face Parks. "Here," he said, putting his hand over the left side of his chest.

"Heart attack," breathed Parks. "I'll get a doctor . . ."

"No," said Talbot. "I've had a bad blow. Just leave me alone. I'll be all right." But Red was already gone.

The doctor found nothing physically wrong with General Talbot, of course, except extremely high blood pressure.

"Look, Doctor, before you go putting me in as a combat exhaustion case, I'd like to tell you what really happened." He walked to his desk and showed his returned envelope to the doctor, then explained that Lady Sarah, his fiancee, was dead.

The doctor nodded. "I'll give you a sedative. Get some rest. The whole thing might be a big mistake, General. There's no reason to assume that she's dead. It's more likely that her place was bombed and some nitwit in the postal service made the mistake of thinking she was there when it happened."

Bill simply nodded and lay down on his cot. Before his mind went blank again, he almost sobbed, God, when I said you could take anything I have in exchange for sparing my men and bringing them through, I didn't mean Sarah, dammit! That never even entered my mind! That night Talbot slept soundly, thanks to the doctor's sedative.

He was still groggy when he awoke the next morning. Mechanically, he brushed his teeth and shaved. What was it the doctor had said yesterday? He tried to focus. There was something that ought to be followed up. He snapped his fingers. Right. The doctor said that the whole thing could be a mistake. That was it.

But that same morning another letter arrived on his desk, stamped "undeliverable." This time he decided to use his rank and connections to get information from London. After a few telephone calls he was finally connected to the right office. When they called him back, it was confirmed. There were reports, he was told, that a German V-2 had exploded directly onto Sarah Hayward's apartment building early one morning. Several bodies had been found amid the rubble, all unrecognizable. One of the dead was a WREN, her uniform tattered by the blast. Lady Sarah was the only WREN living in that building.

Talbot hung up the phone. So this was it. She was gone. Stunned, he returned to his office.

He closed the door behind him and pulled his .45 from its holster. He checked it, removed the clip, which was full, and slid the receiver back and forth a couple of times, then replaced the clip, pulled back the receiver, and let it return, loading a .45 bullet into the chamber of the piece. He clicked the safety off. As he looked down the barrel of the gun, the words of an old prep school coach in a far-away gym came back to him. "Never take the cowardly way out, Bill. You have to face your battles head on. Run towards them, not away from them . . ." Bill put the gun down. Yes, that was the answer. To go bravely.

There was a knock on the door.

"Can I come in?" It was Parks.

"Sure, the door is open," Talbot called, clicking the safety on and putting the pistol back in its holster.

"You had a call from General Devers, commanding Sixth Army Group, asking if we were combat-ready enough to move in to help the French and a couple other Seventh Army divisions clean out the Colmar pocket."

"We're ready."

"What do you know about the situation at Colmar?" Parks asked.

"The generals want it eliminated at all costs . . . the Germans have been there long enough to be well dug in, and they're good units. That's why the Jerries are still there. Nobody's been able to dislodge the bastards."

"It's going to be tough, isn't it, sir?" Parks said.

"Yes, it'll be the worst yet," Talbot answered.

Parks could have sworn his commander seemed pleased by the thought.

⊗

The 20th Infantry Division had moved into the line facing the Colmar in good order. Many fresh replacements had filled the gaps in the ranks, but the division was still at about half strength in its rifle companies when it returned to the front. In that respect, it was like every other infantry division that had been in combat for any length of time.

The First and Second Battalions of the 484th Infantry were to spearhead the first main attack. Reggie deWitt was on hand to see them off. He was still discussing the pending attack with his battalion commanders when General Talbot arrived. He jumped out and strode over to the officers, motioning to them to continue their conference.

"Which is your lead company?" he asked when they were finished.

"A Company," replied deWitt.

Talbot nodded his approval.

⊗

"Sir, we're taking off in five minutes," said the startled captain commanding A Company. "You'd better go to the rear. No offense, sir, but the way you're dressed, you'll draw enemy fire like a magnet draws nails." In contrast to the other officers and men who all wore olive drab field jackets, Talbot had on a light-colored officer's top coat. His two stars glistened on the front of his helmet.

"Sir, you're bound to attract the attention of every German gunner in the area."

"Nonsense," said Talbot. "I'm going with you on this one."

The captain appeared shocked. "Sir, I don't believe you should do that. It's going to be a bitch. Why don't you just stay here in my C.P. until—"

"I intend to lead the attack," Talbot interrupted. "Now, let me address the men. It's almost time to go."

With his back to the enemy, but obscured from them by the fog, Talbot stood in front of the A Company foxholes.

"Our objective today is a tough one, and I have no intention of sending good men to do something I wouldn't do."

He clicked a bayonet into the end of the M-1 rifle he was carrying, a dramatic gesture that was not lost on his now wide-eyed soldiers. He looked at his wristwatch. "It's H-Hour. You have your orders. Good luck, and God bless. Now, follow me."

Talbot turned and began to trot towards the enemy positions. With Sarah dead he had nothing to lose. At least he would die nobly. In the mist, the enemy did not see the Americans start forward.

Unlike their allies, who always shouted insults or screamed obscenities to frighten the enemy, the American infantry always advanced silently. Talbot went forward calmly with his rifle at high port arms. Then, as the American shells screamed overhead, landing on the Germans with muffled explosions, enemy machine guns and artillery began to answer them in spades. Some of the men, inspired by having a major general lead them into battle, were passing Talbot. He saw a few of them cut down by enemy fire.

With his heart in his throat, he sprinted to the safety of a hole and jumped into it as machine gun bullets kicked up a line of mud splashes only inches from his body, spattering slush and earth all over him. He rose to his feet, his once light-colored coat now caked with grime and as discolored as any G.I.'s, the stars on his helmet obscured by mud.

He gritted his teeth and trotted towards the enemy, determined not to go to ground again. This time he would stay on his feet until they cut him down. A machine-gun's chatter almost broke his eardrum. He was practically on top of a German position. He detached a hand grenade from his belt, pulled the pin, let the lever flip, counted to five, tossed the grenade in the direction of the machine gun, then ducked. As soon as he heard the explosion, he jumped up and ran to the gun. Pointing his rifle into the sandbagged hole he emptied his clip into the Germans, not knowing if they were already dead from the grenade's fragments.

As he stood there, slightly dazed, he saw the Germans retreating. It had started to rain.

"Are you all right, General?" A lieutenant beside him asked.

Talbot nodded. "I think your men did magnificently, Lieutenant. I also think you and your fellow officers can handle things here very well from now on ..."

"Oh, yes, sir!" said the lieutenant, handing Talbot back his helmet which had toppled off during his last dash forward.

Talbot smiled at him. "I don't think the damned Germans can kill me but if I keep this up, a heart attack might. So long, Lieutenant."

Talbot turned and began to walk back slowly towards the rear. Once again he had looked death in the face, asking to be taken. And once again death had rejected him. As he made his way across the frost-bitten field, the full meaning of what his coach had tried to tell him all those years ago came to him. As a boy he had wanted to be brave, wanted it so terribly. But, when he was faced with despair, he'd turned to self-destruction. Now, finally, he was being given a chance at true valor. To face life without Sarah—that was bravery. To carry on, to live, to endure suffering, not to run away from it. That was what his coach had been talking about those many years ago. Now, his mind was clear. He could hold his head up to anybody in the world.

That the 20th Division had been the only unit to take its as-
signed objectives was credited to the fact that General Talbot
had personally led the attack, thus inspiring his men and bringing
them through victoriously. By the time the French and Americans
had wiped out the last German pocket of resistance, Talbot was
already known as "the tiger of the Colmar."

But his own officers were dismayed by his actions. What he'd
done was sheer madness. Talbot was summoned to General Alexander Patch's headquarters. Anticipating a reprimand, Talbot nervously entered the office of the commanding general of the U.S.
Seventh Army. Patch was alone and greeted Talbot cordially, but
with a hint of disapproval. After they sat down, General Patch
wasted no time with small talk.

"I don't know what you were trying to do, but I think you're
a fool and a silly ass to boot. If you ever try anything like that
again, I'll have you court-martialled."

"Yes, sir."

Patch surveyed Bill Talbot. He saw nothing but misery on

his face. In a kinder tone of voice, General Patch said, "Bill, I'm relieving you of command of the 20th Division."

Talbot jumped out of his chair as if he'd been jabbed with a bayonet.

"Sir!"

General Patch smiled and motioned to Talbot to sit down. "You see," he said, "your action at the Moder didn't go unnoticed. It was a brilliant military feat. Besides that, our French allies were terribly impressed by the 20th Division's attacks in the Colmar Pocket and, of course, it was that crazy charge you led that really got things going in the sector."

"That's no reason to relieve me."

"Besides the French decorations you're going to receive, you were recommended for the Congressional Medal of Honor. It's been approved. General Eisenhower was to have made the presentation, but now President Roosevelt wants to award it himself, as he did for General Jimmy Doolittle after his daring air-raid on Tokyo in 1942. I'm relieving you so you can go home to be decorated by the President of the United States for valor above and beyond the call of duty."

Talbot sat absolutely amazed.

Sandy Patch held out his hand. "Congratulations, General Talbot. You're a damned good soldier."

∞

The plan was for General Talbot to proceed to Paris, then to London for a few days before taking the long flight from London to the United States, made even longer by the necessary fueling stops.

He said farewell to his officers with whom he had shared so many triumphs and miseries. Before departing, he sat alone in his headquarters, his responsibilities fulfilled, his duties done. On the wall was a large replica of the 20th Division patch, the red bayonets. He looked at it a moment, and said quietly, "Yes, we had quite a ride, didn't we." But now he was leaving the 20th and was going home. To what? To absolutely nothing. He'd have his moment of glory at the White House, then an existence without purpose, without any reason to live . . .

"I'm glad you're still here, sir," said Sergeant Kelly deferentially. "I thought you'd left."

Talbot was surprised to see him. They'd said their goodbyes almost an hour ago. Kelly handed him a card. Glancing at it, Talbot read, "Major General Sir Godfrey Giacomo Cecil D'Arcy, M.C., D.S.O." He jumped up.

"Send General D'Arcy in," he was saying as the door opened and Jocko walked through it.

"D'Arcy! I thought you were in London. Gosh, it's good to see you," said Talbot as the two men embraced warmly.

"Just wanted to meet the local celebrity," said Jocko. "You're quite a hero now, according to the newspapers, anyway."

"Don't believe what you read in the papers. They'll print anything. What can I offer you, Jocko?"

"Nothing." D'Arcy shook his head.

"Well, I'm damned glad to see you. I'm on my way back to the States. Going to Paris for a day, then to London for a few, so I would have missed you."

"Everyone hoped you'd come back one day to stay," said D'Arcy.

"I'm afraid London is the last place on earth that I want to spend any time now," Talbot said quietly. He stood up and walked to the window, trying to compose himself. D'Arcy looked at him strangely.

"I'm sure it's none of my business, Talbot, but it does seem that you've taken the news about Sarah badly."

"Well, what the hell did you expect?" Talbot said brusquely.

"She told me that was the way you'd react."

"What difference does it make now?" Bill said sadly.

D'Arcy looked shocked. "For what it's worth, Sarah wanted you more than anything in the world." D'Arcy rose to leave. "She told me you never answered her letter about Scotty being found alive, even though she told you she was still crazy about you and would divorce Scott and marry you. By not writing, you signified you wanted out. Frankly, I'm surprised. So was she."

"You're crazy ... Oh, my God, the mail truck!"

Jocko looked at Bill as if he were not quite right in the head.

Bill's face reflected his agony. He said, "Right after I wrote to Sarah telling her I loved her and was looking forward to marrying her as soon as she could decently divorce Hayward, our mail truck was blown up, and I was so concerned with the problem of my men's mail, I completely forgot about my letter to Sarah. It was on the same truck. I'm desolated," he said slowly. "She died without knowing ... I feel dreadful."

Jocko seemed perplexed, a fact unnoticed by Talbot. "Are you all right, Bill? I think perhaps a good psychiatrist, a nice quiet retreat in the country . . ."

"Don't talk rot, Jocko. What's gotten into you, anyway?"

"Because of Scotty showing up, you consider Sarah dead?" D'Arcy gave a queer little smile. "You didn't bother to write her after that?"

"Of course I did," said Bill testily, as he fished into his breast pocket for the envelope he'd kept ever since he received it. It was a poignant reminder that his heart was broken and his life was over. He threw it onto the table at D'Arcy.

Jocko picked it up and read the legend "UNDELIVERABLE AT THIS ADDRESS" and the penned "Addressee presumed deceased." He looked up at Bill Talbot with understanding. Neither man spoke.

D'Arcy nodded. "The buzz bomb," he said slowly. "It destroyed the flat completely."

"I know that," snapped Talbot. "I checked with our London people. Where Sarah's flat was, there's nothing but a hole in the ground."

"And you checked with the Admiralty, of course?"

Talbot felt a little bit sheepish. "No. I forgot to do that."

Bill studied Jocko's face and caught the hint of a smile. He asked, simply, "Is she alive?" Then he realized his heart had stopped beating and wouldn't start again until he had the answer.

Jocko nodded. Bill slumped down in his chair, his ecstacy so profound he was temporarily in shock, too moved to speak. Then, he jumped up and threw his arms around Jocko D'Arcy and hugged him.

"No kissing, old man," said Jocko. "No offense, of course, but I'd just rather not."

D'Arcy was still smiling. It was pleasant to be able to give good news to a friend and to rectify a transgression for which he'd felt guilty for far too long. He said, "I decided to take things into my own hands. I had to make sure you wanted to break up with Sarah."

"Thank God you found out I don't," said Talbot.

Now D'Arcy was shaking his head. "I'm damned if I can see how such a mix-up could happen."

Bill pointed to the returned letter, which Jocko had put back on the table.

"Oh, yes, of course." Jocko shook his head. "Damnedest coincidence," he said, rummaging in his pocket. "This was returned to Sarah. She doesn't know why, but supposes it was because you were cut off during the Bulge. Anyway, it's the only one they returned to her. She never heard from you again, of course."

D'Arcy handed Bill an envelope, addressed to him in Sarah's handwriting. On the envelope was the rubber-stamped legend "UNDELIVERABLE." That was all. Bill turned it over. Nothing else, no reason, no explanation. Nothing.

"Can I read it now?" asked Bill. "Here. Take this. It's today's *Stars and Stripes*." Jocko nodded, took the American army newspaper, and sat down comfortably while Talbot read. "Bill, darling, This is written in haste. My flat was bombed. Buzz-bombed to the ground. I was not there, thank God. I was at Buckland trying to settle things a bit. I've moved in with Edwina Beauchamp, whom you'll remember from dinner. Her address is the one on the envelope. (Mine no longer exists.) Edwina has been Jocko's girl ever since last summer. As you know, she and I are old friends and we talk a lot, so I won't have a chance to write much more. The things you left with me, your medals, your citations, your father's gold watch, were all lost with the flat, of course. Please write if you have any questions about any of this. Edwina and I shall keep each other company. I'm terribly upset about the flat, but I wanted to let you know I'm all right. I'll write more later. I love you, Sarah." Talbot looked at the date Sarah had scribbled at the bottom of the letter. He cursed the delay. It had almost gotten him killed, and had certainly made him want to die.

Facing D'Arcy, he said, "You know what's in this letter from Sarah? It's about her flat getting bombed."

"Damned buzz-bombs," said Jocko.

"To hell with them. Tell me about Sarah."

"She's fine. But I'll tell you one thing, Bill, she was shaken badly when she got the news Scotty was alive, then absolutely crushed when you failed to write. I've been told she cried for three days after the realization sank in that you weren't going to answer her letter."

"Of course she was devastated. I would have been too if it were the other way around."

D'Arcy nodded. "Yes, I can understand that. You see, I'm sort of engaged, myself."

Bill cocked his head, much in the manner of Sarah Hayward.

Jocko smiled. "Edwina Beauchamp. I've, uh, known her a long time, as you are aware. In fact, we've always been dear friends. Ever since Sarah told me *you* were her man and I had no chance, I started taking Edwina out, and, do you know what? I discovered it was Edwina I really loved, not Sarah. I absolutely adore her, and I'm going to marry her as soon as I get back."

"That's great! Congratulations, Jocko." The two men shook hands.

"I have some more news, old man," said D'Arcy. "Scotty Hayward died of his gunshot wounds in that German prison camp about the same time you started neglecting his poor widow."

Bill stood still. Then he said, "I'd like to wring your neck, Jocko. Why didn't you tell me that first?"

D'Arcy shrugged. "I didn't know whether or not you'd be interested."

"I *am* going to wring your neck!"

"No, you're not. I'll tell Sarah and keep you in the doghouse forever."

Talbot smiled and walked back and forth a couple of times, digesting the new circumstances. D'Arcy had given them to him awfully fast, but, in essence, Sarah was alive and Hayward was dead instead of the other way around. Bill was happy for the first time since he'd received Sarah's returned letter. In the back of his mind, ever since his conversation with General Omar Bradley, he'd worried about the application of the Enoch Arden law to Sarah. Now, he could forget about it. She was a widow, certified and beyond any doubt. Finally, he turned to D'Arcy. "Look, my dear friend, I need a favor. I'm not ever going to leave Sarah again. Not as long as I live. Life without her is unbearable. So, here's my problem: I have to go to Washington. They're going to give me a medal . . ."

"I rather thought they would, Tiger." D'Arcy smiled.

"I'm taking Sarah with me."

D'Arcy raised his eyebrows.

"And the only way I can do that is to marry her before we leave."

D'Arcy was nodding.

"Can you arrange it? I don't know what formalities you have to go through in England. I know I have to get permission from my commanding officer, who is now Ike, and he'll give it. A registry office is fine by me. We can have the church wedding sometime later. But Major General and Lady Sarah Talbot are going to Washington together—or else I don't go."

D'Arcy was silent for a minute. He cleared his throat. "Uh, Bill," he said. "When I left 'Merry Old,' Sarah was not exactly pleased with the way she thought you were treating her. As they used to say, she was 'taking umbrage' and pretty bitterly too."

Bill scratched his head. "Maybe you'll help me heal the wounds?"

D'Arcy laughed. "Only if you'll tell me about the Colmar, Tiger."

"If I'd gotten Sarah's buzz-bomb letter, there wouldn't be any 'Tiger of the Colmar.' From what you tell me, though, I think we'll have to hatch something pretty spectacular in the way of a plot for me to win Sarah back gracefully and marry her on my way to Washington. Do you think you can swing it?"

"Tiger, as far as cutting through the formalities and arranging weddings go, in church or out, I am very well connected. I am also the craftiest plotter you'll ever meet. Leave things in my hands, old man, and you'll be kissing your carefree bachelor days goodbye before you know what's happening. When do you arrive in London?"

Edwina Beauchamp was in an upstairs robing room of the church getting dressed for her wedding to Major General Sir Godfrey Giacomo Cecil D'Arcy. Lady Sarah Hayward, who was in the process of changing her name back to Lady Sarah Fitz-William, was already dressed as the matron of honor and was helping her friend arrange her skirt. They wore identical long pink gowns. "I refuse to wear white to my second wedding," said Edwina. "It's not right. After all, I'm no virgin."

Sarah giggled. "I didn't think you ever were," she said archly.

"Here," said Edwina. "Let me straighten your halo." She adjusted Sarah's hat.

Sarah laughed. "Your marrying Jocko has made me as lightheaded and as giddy as a schoolgirl. I'm so happy for you!"

"It's good to hear you laugh, Sarah."

"I'm happy, too, because there's no man in my life anymore, and there never will be again."

Edwina raised her eyebrows. Then, she smiled. "That's nice, my dear."

"I'm much better off. I know that now."

Edwina saw Sarah's lower lip tremble, but she said only, "Yes, darling."

Now they were set. Sarah gave Edwina a last reassuring inspection and seemed pleased with what she saw. "Ready?" she asked. "I'll go tell the organist, if you are."

"I'm almost ready," said Edwina. "But first, I was asked to deliver this to you." She held out an envelope. It was a heavy stiff envelope, the kind that usually contained an informal card.

Sarah looked at her friend questioningly but got no response. She opened the envelope slowly, obviously curious. She read:

> My dearest Sarah,
>
> I don't have time to explain everything that's happened in the last few months. It was a tragedy of errors. After receiving your letter about Hayward being alive, I wrote you to tell you that I still love you with all my heart and that I always will. You never received my letter because the mail truck got blown up, so I shall tell you again, my darling Sarah, I adore you, and I am asking you if you will do me the very great honor of becoming my wife . . .

Sarah stopped reading and, as the tears rolled down her cheeks, said, "Oh, I will! I will! Oh, Edwina, he loves me. I knew there had to be a good reason for not writing. I knew it! Oh, Edwina . . ."

"Why don't you finish reading his note, sweet girl?" asked Edwina.

Sarah nodded and turned her tear-streaked eyes to the page at the place where she had stopped reading: "If you will marry me, my darling, everything's arranged. I'm waiting for you at the altar with Jocko as my best man . . ."

She didn't finish. In that instant, Lady Sarah Fitz-William went flying out the door and down the steps to the altar. When she saw Bill Talbot standing there smiling, she sailed into his open arms. Her feet never touched the ground—and she never looked back.